BURDEN
of
LOVE
MYA

WWW.BLACKODYSSEY.NET

Published by
BLACK ODYSSEY MEDIA

www.blackodyssey.net
Email: info@blackodyssey.net

Library of Congress Control Number: 2024916881

First Trade Paperback Printing: March 2025
ISBN: 978-1-957950-68-6
ISBN: 978-1-957950-69-3 (e-book)

Cover Design by Navi' Robins
To the extent that the image or images on the cover of this book depict a person or persons, such person or persons are merely models and are not intended to portray any character in the book.

10 9 8 7 6 5 4 3 2 1

Manufactured in the United States of America

Distributed by Kensington Publishing Corp.

Dear Reader,

I want to thank you immensely for supporting Black Odyssey Media and our ongoing efforts to spotlight the diverse narratives of blossoming and seasoned storytellers. With every manuscript we acquire, we believe that it took talent, discipline, and remarkable courage to construct that story, flesh out those characters, and prepare it for the world. Debut or seasoned, our authors are the real heroes and heroines in *OUR* story. For them, we are eternally grateful.

Whether you are new to Mya or Black Odyssey Media, we hope that you are here to stay. So please be sure to check out more of Mya's array of stories over at our sister and fellow publishing mate B. Love Publications. Our goal is to make a lasting impact in the publishing landscape, one step at a time and one book at a time. We also welcome your feedback and kindly ask that you leave a review. For upcoming releases, announcements, submission guidelines, etc., please be sure to visit our website at www.blackodyssey.net or scan the QR code below. And remember, no matter where you are in your journey, the best of both worlds begins now!

Joyfully,

Shawanda Williams

Shawanda "N'Tyse" Williams
Founder & CEO, Black Odyssey Media

TRIGGER WARNING

This book contains topics that may be triggers to some people. If police corruption, crime, sexual situations, and explicit language are triggers for you, please proceed with caution.

*To my boys, you motivated me to find
my lane and thrive in it. Mommy loves y'all.*

*To my man, you trusted the process and
gave me the tools to create my best content. I love you.*

*To my mom, you're my guardian angel. You always gave me the
strength to follow my dreams . . . and I did. I miss you dearly.
I know you know how much I love you.*

This one is for y'all.

AUTHOR'S NOTE

A few things to note before you begin reading. In the first five chapters, the main characters are referred to as an alias in each other's POV.

Leah is Talia.

Matt is Maddox.

You'll understand as you continue to progress through the story.

Also, as you read, I would like you to do so with an open mind and heart. What may seem unrealistic to some can be someone else's reality. Regardless, this is a work of fiction and should be treated as such.

I hope you enjoy it!
Mya

PROLOGUE

Red and blue lights mixed to create a purple hue around the neighborhood. The flashing lights illuminated the darkness with an eerie glow, capturing the attention of families within the houses on the usually quiet and reserved street. Sirens blared as the police cars sped down the gravel-covered road coated with refilled potholes in a quiet suburb in Houston, Texas. Nosy neighbors peeked through the blinds or stepped onto their porches to see what was happening. The police unit was dispatched by the 9-1-1 operator with an aggravated robbery in progress. The caller indicated one lone suspect waving a firearm. The woman stated the assailant had demanded her neighbors fill his backpack with their jewelry, money, and other valuables. The neighbor had become aware of the situation after she heard gunshots and saw the scene unfold from her kitchen window while she washed dishes after dinner.

Decorated Officer David Mitchell was the first on the scene with his partner, Officer Reynolds, and another squad car with Isaacs and Franklin close behind. When he emerged from his vehicle, he witnessed a young Black male sprinting from the home. The young male brandished a firearm and a backpack as he took off down the alley. All Officer Mitchell could see was the back of his head, his clothes, and the unmistakable designer shoes on his feet.

"Isaacs and Franklin, the two of y'all check the perimeter. Reynolds, you check the house. I've got the suspect!" Officer

Mitchell shouted through the communication system before he pulled out his standard police-issued Glock 22 from the holster and chased after the suspect.

Officer Mitchell was an older biracial man with skin the color of the sand on the beach. He was in his early forties and had been on the force for two and a half decades. With twenty-five years as a police officer in the Houston Police Department, he was a veteran amongst his peers. He'd seen his fair share of crazy crime scenes. He'd apprehended his fair share of suspects throughout his career. A night like tonight should have been a walk in the park for him . . . or so he thought.

Around nine p.m., Officer Mitchell turned the corner to see a split in the alleyway. One way led into a sub-neighborhood with a cul-de-sac, and the other led to the parking lot of a shopping center with several stores and a gas station. Officer Mitchell froze and took a deep breath. *Dammit!* He swore under his breath as he paused. A split-second decision could be the difference between losing the suspect and catching him.

He pressed the radio and gave a general description of the suspect. "This is Officer Mitchell. I am in pursuit of a young Black male, about six feet tall, wearing dark jeans and a dark hoodie. The suspect was last seen fleeing the scene on the 1600 block of—"

The radio went silent as he spotted a young man wearing a hoodie coming out of a gas station. He pressed his radio again. "I am in pursuit of the suspect on the corner of Main Street. Send backup!" He pumped his arms and used all the power in his legs to approach the young man.

"Freeze! Let me see your hands!" Officer Mitchell shouted as he pointed his gun in the direction of who he assumed was the suspect.

Upon further examination of the young man, Officer Mitchell saw that this man had the same height and build as the suspect in question. The young man was also wearing dark jeans and a dark hoodie but did not have on the designer shoes from before. This young man's shoes were worn down, with dirt and scuff marks covering the fabric.

He could have tossed the shoes and the backpack in the few moments I lost him. He could have made a quick switch in the gas station. Officer Mitchell's thoughts were going haywire as he tried to make sense of something that was far from black and white. The area was as gray as it could get.

The young man froze with a look of fear in his brown orbs. He turned around to see the officer with his gun pointed directly at him. Donovan Duncan was a seemingly good kid. He grew up in a two-parent household with a younger sister and brother. He made good grades in school and graduated high school in the top 10 percent of his class. He'd spent two semesters in a community college and then went to a university only a short drive from his parents' home. At twenty years old, he never would have imagined being in a predicament like this.

Donovan's friend, Jeremy Charles, discreetly pulled out his phone and opened the social app. He hit *Go Live* as they awaited the officer's next instructions. It was hard to remain calm with the pounding of their hearts ringing in their ears, but the young men did their best to stay as calm and compliant as possible. The officer didn't say anything for a moment before he closed the distance between him and Donovan and snatched the youth by the arm. Then Officer Mitchell pushed Donovan onto the ground and pressed his knee into the young man's back.

As he placed his gun in the holster and pulled out the metal handcuffs, Officer Mitchell recited the Miranda rights. "You're under arrest."

"What did he do?" Jeremy asked. His voice cracked with fear as he watched his best friend get handcuffed by the officer. "We were in the store getting snacks, bro. You've got the wrong guy."

"You have the right to remain silent. Anything you say can and will be used against you in a court of law. You have the right to an attorney. If you cannot afford one, one may be appointed to you by the court," Officer Mitchell continued.

"What did I do?" Donovan cried out. He wanted to resist, but he knew better than to give the officer a reason to use more force. He'd seen enough news articles and videos to know what his fate would be if he didn't comply . . . or if he did comply with too much *aggression.* "Please," Donovan begged, "what did I do?"

"Shut up!" Officer Mitchell shouted at the young man.

"What did he do?" Jeremy asked again. "Bro, you've got the wrong guy. Please, whoever you think he is, he's not." Jeremy knew going against authority could be the difference between living to see tomorrow and becoming the next viral hashtag. He didn't want his friend or himself to become the next trending topic.

Officer Mitchell's eyes snapped up to look at Jeremy. His eyes were wild with shock. He'd been so focused on the man in the hoodie that he hadn't noticed the other young man who stood only a few feet away. *I messed up.* Officer Mitchell's thought caused a sinking feeling to enter his stomach.

One of the first rules as an officer is to evaluate the entire scene before making a move. Unfortunately, that wasn't the case tonight. He had made several hasty decisions that could possibly blow up in his face.

"Put your phone away!" Officer Mitchell ordered as he pulled his gun out again. This time, the Glock 22 was pointed at Jeremy. At the same moment, two squad cars pulled up, and the three officers emerged from their vehicles.

"You're going to shoot me on camera?" Jeremy's trembling voice created a pause for Officer Mitchell. "Do y'all see this?" Jeremy asked the people on his live. "I'm trying to protect my best friend, and this *pig* has his gun pointed at me because he racially profiled an unarmed Black man coming out of a gas station. Tag the news networks!"

This isn't how this was supposed to go down, Officer Mitchell thought. He shook his head and put the gun back into his holster as his eyes locked with the confused officers awaiting his orders.

"Reynolds, this one has been read his Miranda rights. He's good to go into the car." Officer Mitchell removed his knee from Donovan's back and stood up. Then he pulled Donovan onto his feet and handed him off to Reynolds, who escorted him into the back of the police car.

Next, Officer Mitchell turned to the other police officers and gave them their next set of instructions. "Isaacs and Franklin, can you take the friend home? Get his statement and make sure he makes it home safely."

Officer Mitchell's voice was calmer than before. He knew his job would be on the line if he didn't gain control of the situation.

"No. You've got the wrong guy! Me and Don were in the gas station getting snacks. How many times do we have to tell you this? You don't have to take him away! You can check the security camera!" Jeremy's eyes burned with large streams of tears. He didn't want to leave his friend or go with the officers. He wanted to stick beside Donovan until he was sure his friend was safe.

Donovan looked over at his distraught friend. "It's okay, Jerm! Call my mom. She'll know what to do."

News had broken out about Donovan Duncan's arrest and had spread like wildfire before they'd even made it back to the precinct for questioning. Charles's video caught the eyes of several influencers, and all of the local stations flooded the police station to get the first scoop on the incident. Officer Mitchell swore under his breath as the squad car rolled up to the front of the building.

Officer Reynolds shook his head. "Vultures."

Camera flashes immediately swarmed the police car when the reporters spotted Officer Mitchell emerge from the vehicle. They bombarded the white Charger like a herd of lions who circled their prey. Like vultures, they shot rapid-fire questions with microphones, cell phones, and recorders pointed at the three men as Donovan was escorted through the crowd.

"Keep your head down, and don't say a word," Officer Mitchell ordered in a volume only Donovan could hear.

"No!" Donovan shouted. "I am innocent! This idiot arrested the wrong man! *Free* me!"

"Officer Mitchell, how confident are you that you've made the right arrest?" one reporter asked.

"Donovan, will your family enlist the help of Tate and Associates?" another reporter asked.

"No comment," Officer Reynolds muttered as he walked Donovan up the stairs into the building.

"Ladies and Gentlemen, please step away from the suspect. We will do our due diligence to make sure justice is served." Coming out to appease the growing crowd, Detective Reed stepped out onto the stairs as Officers Mitchell and Reynolds escorted Donovan into the station.

This would be the start of a long battle between law enforcement, the community, and a family of lawyers.

CHAPTER ONE

Talia

Three months before the Donovan Duncan Incident . . .

"**I**t is with great pride and joy that I announce the newest associate lawyer for Tate & Associates. Ladies and Gentlemen, give a warm welcome to my heart in human form, Talia Tate!"

Cheers erupted throughout the large conference room. The introduction from my father warmed my heart and face at the same time. My cheeks burned a bright rouge against my deep, brown skin. My skin reminded me of coffee with the perfect amount of cream and sugar and just a slight orange undertone. The hue of my skin hid most of the blush whenever I felt embarrassed. I hated being the center of attention, especially in a cutthroat business such as law, but I would hold my head up and attack the new position with everything I had.

"Thank y'all for the warm welcome. I've worked my ass off to secure this position. I went to an Ivy League school and learned from some of the best professors in the world, so I know for a fact I'm going to be a great asset to the T&A team."

My credibility was extensive, and I wanted to dismiss all claims of being given the position *just* because my father owned the company. I spent seven years of school securing my law degree. Four years of undergrad at an HBCU, and then three *gruesome* years at an Ivy League to finalize the degree. In those seven years, I shadowed my father on many cases, obviously, not the real high-profile cases, but the smaller ones were where I learned the most.

"I'm so proud of you, baby girl," Daddy stated as he hugged me tightly after my speech.

I smiled and hugged him back while I reveled in the love he bestowed upon me. I have wanted to make my daddy proud since I was a little girl. He was my hero, best friend, and confidant. There were countless college nights when I'd call him at eleven o'clock to help me with a test or essay I struggled with.

Once we stepped away, I replied, "Thank you for believing in me, Daddy. I love you so much, and I know I'm going to live up to and exceed all of the expectations you have of me."

"I do not doubt you will do exactly that. You should work the room. Network. Mingle. Most importantly, I want you to get to know the people of the company as their peer and not an intern. This will one day be your firm, so the sooner you gain respect, the better."

"Yes, sir."

My grandfather, Julius Tate, created Tate & Associates. When he got sick, Daddy took over and has run the business for several decades. My time would come when the torch would be passed down to me. The anticipation was exciting, so I couldn't wait. Tate and Associates was a family legacy.

My eyes perused the room at all of the painted smiley faces. Everyone moved around the large conference room as they talked to one another. Although they were here to welcome me, I also knew they enjoyed the few hours away from the caseloads they worked on. The paralegals would handle the firm while all associates and partners briefly partied.

"Welcome to the team," Janice, a fourth-year associate, greeted me with a warm smile and hug.

Janice was a dark-skinned woman with a pixie cut. She wore glasses and sported a nice skirt suit to flaunt off the curves God blessed her with. She was the first person to introduce herself to me after my speech. She was one of the few associates who always had a grin when I visited the firm during my internship. She was stunning with a beautiful soul to match. I strongly felt she would become a great work friend once I settled into the daily routine at the firm. She had many wins under her belt, so a connection with her could be beneficial.

"Thank you so much, Jan. I'm excited to be an official member now." I held my hands behind my back and swayed from side to side.

I didn't like to show the fidget in my fingers when I talked. There were a few tells I had that blatantly displayed my anxiety and nerves that I fought hard to suppress most of the time.

"Girl, you've *been* an official member," Janice reminded. "And don't you worry about the haters. Once they see you winning cases, they'll shut up."

"You've heard them gossiping too, huh?" I asked. "Even if they hate me, they should know my father well enough to know he wouldn't have *anybody* unworthy of the job taking up space in his firm. This business is his pride and joy, so I know for a fact he wouldn't have me here if he weren't completely certain I was ready to take on the position."

"Oh, trust me, I know," Janice agreed.

There were only three things Stephen Tate cared about in this world. At the top of the list was my mother, Emilia. She was his soul mate and the reason he woke up every morning. Number two on the list were his children. Stephen Jr., SJ, and I were the apples of our parents' eyes. SJ was a thirty-six-year-old surgeon and father of three. He was married to Kiara. She was beautiful with her golden-brown skin. What I loved most about her was that she owned a day care. She cared for my nieces and nephew while caring for a dozen other kids five days a week. I didn't see them often, but when we all were together, it was nothing but fun times and lots of laughs.

Number three on my father's list was Tate & Associates. T&A dated back in the family for over fifty years. In a way, it was our way to honor my grandfather. Daddy took the responsibility to heart and did all he could to uphold the family business. Thousands of lives were saved because of the hard work my patriarch put into building a legacy I would one day take the reins of and run.

Glasses of champagne were passed around as we toasted in celebration of my new role in the firm. People wouldn't understand, but my passion was in the criminal justice system. The system was unfair to people who looked like me. Black skin was *bad* skin in the eyes of many people in and around the system. Racism was prevalent to this day, even if people wanted to pretend it wasn't. It was my job to change the narrative that Black people were criminals—especially since we were disproportionately targeted and arrested. Most of the prison population was stacked with African Americans and other minorities because law enforcement targeted areas where minorities were the majority. I spent years learning about the intricacies and biases of the criminal justice system. I wasn't a lawyer because of how good the pay was. I was a lawyer because my duty was to be a voice for the voiceless. I wasn't here to play games. This wasn't a get-rich-quick scheme.

As the champagne settled in my bloodstream, the nerves disappeared. My anxiety took leave as I worked the room like a professional orator. I talked to nearly everyone. The first- and second-year associates were the easiest to talk to because we all had some things in common. Then I made my way through the third- and fourth-year associates.

A sly smirk stretched across my face when I spotted Dylan and Paul. Fueled with the bubbly liquor in my system, I called out to them. "Dylan! Paul! I'm glad to see you two enjoying yourselves." I closed the distance between us and offered them a closed-mouth smile. My eyes twinkled from mischievous intent. "Remember when y'all used to pick on me during my internship days? I used to get your coffees and do all of the research for your cases. Now, we're equals . . . Ain't that something?"

Dylan Richards was a lanky white man with blond hair and blue eyes. He had the type of face I'd see in magazines. He was a brilliant lawyer who worked his ass off to provide the best service for all his clients. Paul Westwood was a legacy. His entire family consisted of lawyers, including prosecutors, family law, business law, and criminal law. He knew the Bill of Rights and the Amendments before he was in kindergarten. Paul was a Black man a few inches short of six feet. His lack of height didn't matter much because his personality drew women in, and *apparently*, his sex game kept them coming back for more.

Dylan rubbed the back of his neck while he scrutinized the floor. Paul mimicked his motions. My smile stretched as wide as it could as I marveled over their guilty mannerisms.

"Oh? Cat got your tongues?" I continued.

"We only teased you because that's just how things go around here. All interns are subjected to those types of things during their time here," Dylan explained.

"In all honesty, I didn't think you would choose your father's firm to go through your first year. I assumed you'd start in a smaller firm to get the hands-on experience most first-years need," Paul added.

My lips stretched into a big grin as I patted them both on the shoulders. "Why are y'all sweating bricks right now? I'm just teasing you back. It's not like I could get y'all fired or anything."

They shared a look before they turned to me with deep frowns. My father ran a strict business; everyone knew how he felt about hazing and taking advantage of interns and lower-level associates. However, the older associates still got their hands dirty now and then.

The look on their faces made me laugh even harder. "I promise." I lifted my pinky fingers for them to loop theirs with mine. "I didn't take the teasing to heart. I know all about the hierarchy of the firm. You two are great lawyers and shouldn't worry about losing your jobs at all. You both are too valuable for that."

Dylan relaxed immediately. "Cool." He looped his pinky with mine, and Paul followed suit.

"*But* I want you both to know that now I'm on an equal playing field . . . so you need to expect me to get my lick back with both of you." I winked before sashaying away.

The party was great. It felt good to mingle with my new colleagues, current partners, and senior associates. I couldn't wait to celebrate with my real family: Mama, Daddy, SJ with his little family, and my best friend, Monique. They would throw a more heartfelt celebration of my latest accomplishment.

Stepping into my apartment, I was greeted with silence. I'd been on my own since I graduated from high school. My parents got me a cozy two-bedroom apartment in downtown Houston. I had a stunning skyline view, a large balcony, a medium-sized kitchen with granite counters and black and silver appliances, and a beautiful bathroom with a walk-in shower and a large garden tub.

My bedroom was my sanctuary. The walls were decorated with beautiful paintings of Black women. There was a walk-in closet that mainly housed my wide collection of suits, slacks, and blouses. Most of my loungewear consisted of leggings and oversized T-shirts folded in my mahogany-colored dresser. My favorite feature in the bedroom was the bathroom. Peace was present at all times in my bathroom. A hot bubble bath after a long day of studying, researching, or running errands was the perfect recipe for relaxation—which was exactly what I was doing as I sank into the bubbles and tapped Mama's icon on my phone.

"Well, if it isn't Associate Lawyer Talia Tate," Mama greeted me with a giggle.

"Hey, Mama." My smile was so broad that my cheeks ached.

"How was your first day on the job?" she questioned.

"Well, it wasn't really a workday. I networked and mingled with folks, but I haven't received a case yet. Everyone welcomed me with open arms, and I was so relieved. I know some people think I will get special treatment, but I earned my spot in Daddy's firm—fair and square."

"Damn right. You worked your butt off to get through law school. You put in the effort to learn and not just memorize to pass your tests. This is in your blood." She cleared her throat. "Plus, why wouldn't your *father* put you in a high position if you are qualified to do the job? We don't believe in making our children struggle to reach the top."

Emilia Tate was my biggest fan. She spoke life into me even when I didn't do so for myself. She always told me no matter what, I could do whatever my heart desired. She wanted nothing but the best for her kids and did her best to make it happen.

"I can't wait to officially start on Monday," I announced. "I'm going to see what cases are hot and what I can do to help. I want to hit the ground running. I don't want to fall into the shadows. I'm trying to be just as influential and legendary as Daddy."

"You got this, Tally."

"Thank you, Mama." A yawn escaped from my lips. "I'm going to call you tomorrow. I want to relax in the tub before I go to bed."

"Okay, honey. I'll talk to you tomorrow. Sweet dreams."

"Good night."

After I hung up the phone with my mother, I sank into the tub and turned on the jets. The lavender-scented bubble bath almost lulled me to sleep, so I took this as a sign to get out and finish my bed preparation.

After I poured a glass of wine, I tucked myself into bed and turned on the TV. I wasn't sure what was on the screen because my eyes were focused on the sea of men on my phone. My life was hectic during the day, but when night greeted me, I was reminded of the loneliness I felt. My career took precedence in my life, so I rarely had time to date. The only time I got companionship was after matching on a discreet dating app and getting a few moments of pleasure to hold me over until the next time I got the urge.

This particular app was my go-to because of its discretion. One of my favorite features of the app was that it required all participants to upload documents showing current test results, with moderators who approved or denied them based on the credibility of the documents. Before anyone can make a match, the document has to be dated within the last fifteen days. The promotion of safe sex was always a bonus for me—especially in a society that makes going to the doctor for a full workup seem like a bad thing.

Personally, I downloaded the app because I wanted casual hookups during college and law school to get me through long nights with nothing to do. I made sure to regularly get checkups to make sure I didn't contract any STDs or STIs, but I was definitely a girl who enjoyed the company of a man. I wasn't looking to settle down just yet, but I did make sure to get my sexual gratification when I needed it.

After over ten minutes of declining potential matches, I stumbled across the profile of a man who used the alias Captain Matt. I giggled at the name but tapped his profile to see the full-size pictures he uploaded. The first one was a selfie.

Examination of his appearance was vital. His mocha-complected skin reminded me of fallen acorns in autumn. His skin was smooth and blemish-free. There was a slight five o'clock shadow, but otherwise, his face was bare of facial hair. His eyes were the color of new pennies. His dark pink lips fit his face beautifully. They were the perfect amount of plump and juicy. My mind played with the idea of how those luscious lips would feel against mine if given the chance.

The most attractive feature had to be the tattoos I saw on his arms and the chest piece peeking from the deep collar of his T-shirt. His hair was cut into a nice fade. He had the type of face that would make any woman want to sit on it.

After liking his profile, I kept scrolling through his pictures. I paused at the full-body picture of him clad in a pair of gray sweatpants and . . .

You have a match!

The notification startled me as I clicked to see if we had matched each other. A soft smile tugged on my lips as I read his initial message.

Captain Matt: Hey, beautiful.

Me: Hey, Cap'n.

The eye roll was vicious as I immediately regretted my greeting. *How corny is that? He probably won't reply now.* I agreed with my pessimistic thoughts because if I were him, I damn sure wouldn't have replied.

Captain Matt: Lol, you're a little corny, but I like it. What are you doing up this late, beautiful?

Me: You must be an old man because it's not late at all. It's only 11:00 p.m. Don't tell me you're an old fart who can't stay up 'til midnight.

Captain Matt: Ain't nothing about me old, baby.

My heart beat a little faster. As I tapped the keyboard to reply, a second message popped up.

Captain Matt: Do you mind if I call you baby, or do you prefer Leah?

I was confused about who Leah was for a brief moment until I remembered my alias on the app was Lady Leah. I wasn't very creative with names, so I took the "Lia" of my first name and spelled it generically. Reading Matt's text made me smile. Most men skipped the cordial talk and went straight to "Let's meet up and have sex." Those dudes rarely got a reply back out of me. Even though I didn't mind casual hookups, I needed to know *something* about the men I was going to let enter my fortress.

Me: Let's start with Leah and work our way to baby.

Captain Matt: I can respect that.

Matt and I texted each other well into the wee hours of the morning. Somewhere during our conversation, we exchanged numbers. We made plans to see each other for brunch tomorrow morning because he said he wasn't comfortable with me driving to meet up with him so late at night. Plus, he said it gave me time to really figure out if I wanted to meet him in person. He said all the right things all night, and I eagerly awaited meeting him—especially with the promise of breakfast and some good loving on the side.

CHAPTER TWO

Maddox

Staring at my reflection in the hotel room's mirror, I gave myself a brief pep talk as I awaited the arrival of Leah. From the moment I laid my eyes on her profile, I'd been intrigued by her beauty and personality. Leah's profile caught my attention while I sat at the bar last night. The stench of stale beer and old peanuts filled the air of Olympia's Pub—the late-night spot for all law enforcement to decompress after a long, trying shift.

Working as one of the lead detectives for a city as active and widespread as Houston, most shifts were long, tiring, and draining. We worked four consecutive days on and four consecutive days off, although I also needed to be on call for major situations. Friday was the fourth day of my shift schedule, so today, I could enjoy Leah's company without the threat of being called into work.

I was on my third shot of tequila when I matched with Lady Leah on a discreet dating app I discovered one lonely night. The goal was to find a woman to satisfy my sexual hunger for the night, but instead, I found myself engaged in a conversation too good to ruin with sexual innuendos and horny conversation. I couldn't recall the last time I engaged in playful banter with a woman, so texting Leah had been a breath of fresh air. I felt like a true captain when she agreed to meet for brunch. I wanted everything perfect for our first encounter, so I booked a full day at a hotel that would give us discretion, comfort, and peace of mind.

The hotel was located in Downtown Houston. We would spend the morning at the Grand Marquis Marriott in the Cosmopolitan Suite. The suite was decked out with a king-sized bed, sofa bed, and a pool view, and it was a corner room. The hotel had a large lazy river in the shape of Texas. It was the most prominent tourist attraction for the hotel, and we'd have a wonderful time enjoying mimosas, the view, and each other. The bathroom had a separate tub in front of the window of the Houston skyline with a walk-in shower and detachable showerhead. If things progressed, we'd have such a *beautiful* time together.

I brushed my waves down with the palms of my hands and splashed some water on my face. There was a gentle tap against the door as I walked out of the room. I took a peek through the peephole and fought the urge to smile at the sight of Leah standing patiently on the other side of the door. With a deep breath, I unlocked the door and greeted the beautiful woman with a wide grin.

"Hey," I spoke first.

"Hi," she replied.

Damn. Her voice was as gentle as a feather and as smooth as silk. It was on the deeper end with an unmistakable southern drawl. From the simple greeting, I could tell she was born and raised in Houston. As I took in her appearance, I realized those pictures didn't do her justice. Her skin was a rich cocoa complexion, free of blemishes. Her lips were covered in a clear gloss, making her natural skin-colored lips even more kissable. Her hair was dark burgundy, with springy curls styled neatly into a ponytail. The sundress she wore sculpted her body perfectly. She wasn't wearing a bra because the strapless material held her round, perky breasts securely. The dress stopped just above her ankles, and her feet were on full display in the sandals she wore with pretty white nail polish.

Suddenly, I felt underdressed in my gray sweatpants and black tee. I had a single gold chain hanging around my neck, and my feet were comfortable in a pair of black and white Nikes. Should I have worn something flashier? Would she assume I wanted to get right into the action? I was out of my comfort zone as I ogled the beauty before me.

"Um . . . Are you going to invite me in? Or will we stand in the doorway the whole time staring at each other?"

The sound of her voice broke me out of the trance her appearance had me in. I cleared my throat and let out a nervous chuckle. I bit down on my bottom lip and scratched my neck before pulling the door wider for her to step in.

"Come in." I moved out of the way as she entered the hotel room. Her scent raided my nostrils as she walked by with the most pleasant greeting.

Leah's scent was fresh, floral, and uniquely hers. The fumes were intoxicatingly delicious. I wanted to bury my nose in the crook of her neck and get lost in the fragrance, but I refrained from letting those primal needs escape my thoughts and find their way into reality.

"This is a nice room," Leah commented as she scoped out the place.

"Thank you. I figured I'd make our meeting as special as possible."

"This is definitely something special. I've never been here before, but from the valet to the ambiance of the décor, I'm quite pleased."

My chest swelled with pride and accomplishment. I hoped the duration of our time together would be a constant pleasure for both of us. I wanted to make a lasting impression.

"I wasn't sure what you'd want to drink or eat, so I haven't ordered anything."

She placed her purse on the counter and sat on the leather chair near the window. She stared out at the view with a soft smile on her kissable lips. "I'm cool with whatever."

"They've got a wide variety of mimosa flavors. I was thinking for breakfast, we do pancakes to keep us from getting too drunk with a side of fruit. Most places don't cook their breakfast meat how I like it, so I rarely order it."

She turned to face me and nodded. "Dude, I *never* order bacon or sausage from restaurants because it's never how I make it at home. I don't know why it doesn't taste good, but I always avoid the disappointment."

We shared a laugh. "Glad we're on the same page. I'm going to call in to room service now. Do you have any other requests?"

"Nope. What you're ordering is perfect for me."

I nodded my head before picking up the phone and dialing room service. The whole time I spoke with room service, my eyes watched Leah like a hawk. Her beauty radiated a light so bright she would command the attention of everyone in the room. After placing our order, I hung up the phone and walked over to her to admire the view—not outside the window, but the view beside me.

"You probably hear this a lot, but you are so damn beautiful," I commented. "I can't keep my eyes off you. I bet you've got men jumping over hurdles to be with you."

She turned away from me and fiddled with her fingers to distract her from my words. Using my thumb, I tilted her head back in my direction and offered a gentle smile. "Don't act shy now. Where's my Lady Leah with the exquisite conversation?"

"She's right here," she answered. "I'm usually not this nervous, but you've got my anxiety up."

"Why?"

"Because you're even more attractive in person than in pictures, and you smell *so* good."

She took a step back and cleared her throat. I stepped forward and placed my hand on the small of her back, just above the curve of her ass. "Oh yeah? Baby, your fragrance had me intoxicated as soon as you walked into the room. Not to mention, your pictures didn't do you justice at all. You're beautiful in your photos but breathtaking in person."

Her cheeks tinted a hue of rouge as she smiled up at me. Our height difference was just right. I stood six foot and five on a regular day, and from the way she stopped at my shoulder, I estimated she was about five foot eight. The best part was that she was thick in all the right places. The sundress left the perfect mystery for my imagination to run wild. The reveal would be the icing on the cake.

"Room service." The knock on the door broke us both out of a trance.

I rubbed the back of my neck and put space between us. "You can have a seat at the table. I'll get our stuff and bring it over."

She nodded.

It took about eight minutes for us to get seated at the table with the mimosas and breakfast arranged for our consumption. It surprised me when she bowed her head to say a quick prayer before she lifted her glass and smelled the strawberry mimosa. Her eyes briefly closed as she allowed the sparkling fumes to saturate the air around her. She brought the glass up to her lips and tilted it upward slightly. Then she took a sip and placed the glass back on the table.

"Mmm," she moaned. "The champagne isn't too strong, and the strawberries were the perfect touch of sweetness."

How could a woman make the simple act of drinking look so damn sexy? At the moment, I was too far gone. I couldn't leave here without getting a taste or two.

"What are your favorite drinks?" I asked to start up a conversation.

"Alcoholic or nonalcoholic?" she countered.

"Both."

"Lemonade is my favorite nonalcoholic drink, other than water. I like how versatile and refreshing it is. Lemonade could literally go with anything," she explained. "Now, for alcohol . . . I'm a cheap wine kinda girl. A good bottle of Taylor Port or Stella Rose will do it for me every time. If it's not wine, I wouldn't mind tequila shots or a strong daiquiri."

I nodded. "Those drinks definitely fit you."

"How about you?" she asked. Leah cut into her pancake and dipped it into her small syrup container before wrapping her lips around the fork and sliding the breakfast treat into her mouth.

Visions of her wrapping those same plump, juicy lips around my member infiltrated my mind. A few rapid blinks pushed them to the back of my mind as I quickly pulled out the answer to her question. "I don't mind a few beers after a long day of work or a few shots of tequila. I like red wines too."

"Beer?" she repeated. Her nose turned up in disgust as she frowned her lips. "Beer is absolutely disgusting. All it does is give people gas and bloated stomachs."

The laughter followed. "Some would say your taste buds just weren't mature enough for the power of a good quality beer."

"Oh, brother." Leah rolled her eyes playfully. "I have *elite* taste buds, sir!"

"We'll see about that on the next date."

She paused. "The next date?"

I rubbed the back of my neck and licked my lips. "Well, I figured if we both enjoyed today, there would be more to come."

Her cheeks tinted again as she nodded. "I would like that."

"Can I be honest with you?" I asked while I slid my plate to the side. I grabbed a napkin and dabbed at the corners of my mouth.

"Yeah."

"When I matched with you, I was on some heavy horny energy. Then we started talking, and I suddenly wanted *more*."

She smiled. "Same. When I opened the app, I was just looking for someone to tickle my insides for a bit, and then you made me smile and laugh, and I didn't want to ruin the conversation by telling you to pull up and ravish me."

My eyebrows lifted toward the sky. "Oh yeah?"

"Sir, I wasn't on the app by mistake. I'm fresh out of college and barely settling into my big-girl job. I enjoy casual hookups every now and then to make the lonely nights a little more tolerable."

I licked my lips. The app was made specifically for high-profile individuals who enjoyed discretion with their hookups. One of the rules was not to disclose personal information unless both parties agreed. I wasn't as willing to tell people I was a detective because of the implications of my job. With all of the negativity police officers get in the world, the last thing I wanted was a woman to lecture me about my position in law enforcement.

As a child, I dreamed about being a local hero. I saw how they saved lives on TV shows and wanted to do that in my own city. Even after a traumatic experience with some cops when I was a teenager, I still applied to the academy to be the change I wanted to see. However, years of witnessing death, years of apprehending criminals, and years of working with crooked cops tainted me. It was no longer about being a light in the dark but more so being what I had to be to care for my family.

"Matt?"

The sound of my alias coming from her lips brought me back to reality. I smiled to assure her I was all right. "I'm good. I just got lost in my thoughts."

"I apologize if I said something wrong," she stated.

"You didn't," I replied. "I will admit I was slightly caught off guard by how similar our reasons for being on the app are. I work long, stressful hours, which makes dating hard. Many women don't understand or underestimate how much of my time is spent in the field. When I do get a break, instead of gambling my chances to release my pent-up frustrations, I go to the app to guarantee the woman I hook up with is on the same type of time as I am."

"I'm glad we matched," Leah confessed.

"Me too," I agreed. "I don't want to ruin the flow of things, but I've wanted to kiss you since you stepped into the room."

She shifted in her seat. Her hands folded in her lap as she slid her tongue across her bottom lip. The temperature in the room rose. "Kiss me."

"C'mere," I instructed.

I slid my chair back and angled it outward, away from the table. I adjusted my sweatpants and lifted my hands up for her to close the distance between us. She timidly stood from her seat and made her way over to me. She fit perfectly between my legs as I gently placed my hands on her waist. Our eyes locked, and time seemed to slow down. At this moment, the two of us together were the only people on earth.

"Kiss me," I demanded. My voice dropped several octaves, resulting in goose bumps on Leah's beautiful cocoa-complected skin. Her eyes traveled from my eyes to my lips as she wet her lips with her tongue. My grip on her waist tightened slightly. "I said, kiss me."

"O-okay," she stuttered.

With a dip of her head, our lips connected. Leah's bow-shaped lips were the softest things I'd ever felt. Her warm breath blew against my face as she let out a whisper of a moan.

"Matt ..."

"How far do you want to go?" I asked. My eyes gazed into her brown orbs. The chocolate irises held an unmistakable fire.

"I want to see stars," she answered.

My hardening erection thumped with excitement at her decree. "Where do you want it? On the bed, right here, against the window? Let me know."

She rubbed her fingers against the nape of my neck. "Press me up against the window, please."

The way she spoke sent signals through my body and straight to my heating core. If I didn't calm down, I'd be a two-pump chump from the built-up arousal begging for release. I rubbed my hands on the curve of her ass and raised an eyebrow. "Are you wearing panties?"

"Come find out."

She stepped away from me and walked over to the floor-to-ceiling windows. The view was immaculate as the sun beamed over the city. However, my eyes were locked on the beautiful woman who swayed her body from side to side, enticing me to take a bite of the round ass jiggling like Jell-O.

As much as I wanted to fill her with raw, unfiltered dick, I knew better than to test my luck like that. I stood up and grabbed a condom from the counter. It took all of two seconds to open the package, slide it on, and close the distance between us.

"Pull this dress down," I commanded through gritted teeth.

With urgency, she slid the fabric down her body in one quick motion. My assumptions were correct. There were no panties. My journey inside her fortress would be void of any obstacles. My body pressed against hers, trapping her between my chest and the glass. Her hands pressed against the window as I snaked my hand between her legs. The heat . . . The heat radiating between her thighs was like the door to the oven opening to reveal a freshly baked cake.

"Mmm," she moaned softly. Her voice was gentle as she ground her hips against my fingers as they explored her warmth. I stretched her, prepping her hole for my length.

"You're so wet," I admired.

"I need you," she panted. "I'm ready. *Please*, fill me."

"*Shit*!" I hissed. The way she begged for me sent shivers down my spine and heat to my core. The desperation and *want* in her tone were music to my ringing ears. "Bend over. Touch your toes."

She obliged. Her dripping warmth greeted me with throbbing kisses. I rubbed my tip against her entrance as I planted my feet for the plunge. Slowly, I slid into her, inch by inch, until her fortress completely engulfed me. Her walls hugged me like we were old friends rekindling at a class reunion.

Leah was . . . special. Everything she did evoked powerful responses from my body. Her moans caused my body's temperature to rise to burning degrees. Her whimpers of pleasure caused my toes to curl. Her body . . . Man, her body was my kryptonite. I was quickly becoming undone with each stroke into her.

"Mmm . . . Matt, this feels so good," she moaned blissfully. "I'm close."

I gripped her neck with one hand while I rubbed her bead with the other as I pumped quicker. Her head tilted back as her eyes rolled into the back of her head, and she reached her peak. Her juices flowed down onto me as her walls suctioned me tightly. The grip of her orgasm pushed mine over the edge. I buried my face in the crook of her neck and groaned as I shot my load into the condom. We used each other for support until we both regained control of our limbs.

She turned in my arms and wrapped hers around my neck. She pulled me down into a kiss. The kiss said more than her words ever could. The kiss explained how much she enjoyed the first round and how excited she was for the next.

"The shower has a detachable showerhead. Let me clean you up."

"Oh, you're nasty. I like that . . . I like that *a lot*."

If someone had told me I'd spend five hours finding new ways to make this woman come, I wouldn't have believed it. However, the reality was Leah unlocked an insatiable beast within me. I'd milked her off her juices twice in the shower and once more on the bed. After the fourth round, we both passed out. Then we woke an hour later just to fit in two more rounds. The final round was in the same position as the first, against the window, but this time, the setting sun created a simmering spotlight on our lovemaking.

"Today was..." Leah searched for the appropriate description of the day, "surreal."

"I agree. I can confidently say no other woman has ever given me this level of pleasure ... ever. You unlocked something I didn't even know I possessed."

She grinned. "I can't lie ... I didn't expect this at all, either. I'm almost tempted to go another round."

I laughed straight from the belly. "You're something else. I honestly didn't expect to spend the entire day with you, but damn, am I glad I paid for the full night."

"Me too. I will have a busy day tomorrow running errands because you stole my whole day with that hypnotizing wand in your pants."

I smirked. "You can have it any time you want if my schedule permits."

She licked her lips. "I'd like that."

"Don't do that."

"Do what?" she asked innocently as she pressed her body against mine.

"Leah ..." I warned, already feeling the arousal try to creep back into my body.

Her grin was mischievous as she rubbed my arms, massaging my muscles with the tips of her fingers. "I won't get you started so late into the night, but I do want to make one thing clear ..."

"What's that?"

"This . . ." She stroked my length, "is mine now. I don't want you giving it to anybody else."

"Yes, ma'am," I replied. "As long as you do the same for me."

"Deal."

We sealed the arrangement with a kiss. As our lips touched, I felt an electric current pass through our bodies. Had this agreement been signed by our souls? Had a day of pleasure turned into a soul tie between the two of us? No woman could compare to Leah. No woman could say she'd ever gotten this level of passion from me. If our first sexual encounter was this strong, I couldn't imagine the magnitude of our passion when we thoroughly learned each other's bodies.

◆

After the fantastic day I had with Leah, I strolled into the squad room the next morning. I was initially off, but I took the shift to help with the paperwork backlog. Because of Leah, I felt like a productive man. My team sat at their desks, chatting about their weekend festivities. When I placed my jacket on the back of my chair and sat down, all eyes trained in on me.

"Look at this smiling Kool-Aid Man," Detective Elena Chavez teased. Chavez transferred to the HPD crime unit five years ago and was an amazing asset.

She was a feisty five-foot-four firecracker and played no games. Detective Chavez could bring down a perp three times her size.

In addition to Chavez were Detectives Lisa Barnett and Kenneth Parsons. Barnett was the daughter of the captain. She was decent people, but we kept her at arm's distance because we didn't need her sharing our personal lives with the captain during family dinners. Barnett was a mocha-complected woman with honey-brown hair. She stood at five foot eight and was the newest addition to the squad. She had transferred from special victims. Barnett was strong as hell to have been there for as long as she was. Even the strongest detectives couldn't fathom the type of crimes those units handled.

Detective Parsons was a younger dude. He'd moved up the ranks fast as hell. He was six foot two and had the whole *Miami Vice* look going on. He was tan and had sun-kissed blond hair. His eyes were a wild green, making him the perfect interrogator for the women. They'd gaze into his eyes and start spilling their guts to him.

"I don't know what you're talking about," I replied to Chavez.

Everybody tossed their hands up with incredulous laughs.

"Oh, brother," Barnett chuckled. "You look like you've hit the lottery."

"I know your cheeks hurt from smiling so hard," Detective Brent Carruthers commented as he leaned against my desk. Brent was my partner. Every case we worked, we had each other's back. The day I came into the squad room and was assigned as his partner, we clicked instantly. I would take a bullet for him, and he'd do the same to me. He was the brother I never had. He'd saved my ass more times than I could count.

I rubbed my hands together and smirked. "I'm usually not one to kiss and tell, but I had the *best* time last night with my new lady friend."

"Here we go!" Chavez yelled. "We're about to hear him talk about this lady like she's some whore!"

"Nah," I disagreed. "I actually like the woman. She's got me intrigued. I wouldn't call her out her name."

Barnett's eyebrows rose up to her widow's peak in shock. "Really?"

"Is that so hard to believe?" I questioned.

"Absolutely," everybody stated in unison.

"You were a menace to these women not even three weeks ago, so this new perspective is hard to believe coming from you," Parsons added.

"Everybody is capable of changing when they find the one worth evolving for," Carruthers added.

"Talk to them!" I shouted with a clap of my hands. "Who I was in the past does not define who I am today."

"Damn, she must be an extraordinary lady," Chavez commented.

I nodded. "I think she is."

Saying it out loud to other people was the eye-opener I didn't know I needed. After just one day with the beauty, I was in very deep. I was ready to tell everyone who would listen how good she made me feel.

Leah is a dangerous woman.

CHAPTER THREE

Talia

"To Talia!"

The sound of the champagne bottles filled the air. The grin on my face was unwavering as I took in the feel of my parents, brother, sister-in-law, nieces, and nephew celebrating my achievements.

Sunday was supposed to be my day to catch up on errands, but I woke up to instructions to meet my family for brunch at my favorite spot. It was the only time in everyone's schedule when we could get together and celebrate. My mother arranged the whole event within a few hours, and everyone had no choice but to drop their plans to celebrate.

I was on a natural high after my mind-blowing day with Matt. I'd have to mellow out before my giddiness tipped off my family about my wild night with a stranger.

"Thank y'all so much for taking the time to celebrate me," I commented. "Law school was lonely, but the reward was worth it. It's such an honor to live in this moment with my best friend." I lifted my hands to create a heart with my fingers and aimed it at Daddy.

"You've always been talented and goal-oriented. You're going to do great things." Daddy smiled.

"Can I have some?" Kellan asked.

SJ raised an eyebrow at the six-year-old. "You've got juice."

"I want the sparkly drink," he replied.

"We'll order you some apple cider," Kiara proposed.

She was an extraordinary mother to her three. Kellan was the oldest. Then there was Kyari, who was three, and Stephanie, who was two. Stephie was the "*we couldn't wait six weeks*" baby. She was the drama I loved so much. She ran their home, and I encouraged it by spoiling her rotten and sending her back home.

I admired Kiara. She was an excellent mother. SJ had a busy schedule, yet Kiara made sure she did what needed to be done to keep a happy home for her and my brother. Sometimes, I wondered what type of mother I'd be, but the idea of putting my career on hold to make it happen was never something I could commit to. I'd only *just* gotten my position at the firm. The last thing I wanted to do was put my hard work in jeopardy by starting a family prematurely . . . even if after the night I had with Matt clouded my judgment.

"Your first day is tomorrow," SJ addressed me. "Are you ready to dive into the *real* stuff? I know you did internships and stuff, but you're about to be on your own."

I licked my lips. "If we're being honest, it doesn't seem real. I wanted it so badly. Reality hasn't set in that I actually made it. I have my outfit picked out, ironed, and waiting for Monday morning. My alarms are set, and my briefcase is prepped."

"Like the first day of school," SJ teased. "You know you got this, right?"

"I know. Even if it gets overwhelming, Daddy's there. You're a call away. Mama always checks up on me too." My tribe was solidified. No matter what happened once I dove into the major leagues, I'd have my family and Monique to help me through the hard times.

"When your dad first started as a lawyer, several cases tested him in every way possible. Grandpa Jay warned him, but everybody reacts to trauma and pain differently. Please do not bottle things up. Get a therapist if you want professional help, or come to one of us," Mama advised.

I was lucky. I grew up in a two-parent household with a caring mother and an emotionally balanced father. Of course, my brother and I bickered, but he was also eight years older than me, so he wasn't as annoying as most older brothers were. He was my protector, just as my father was. With my tribe by my side, I'd be just fine.

The smell of coffee permeated the air. The coffee machine worked overtime to prepare my special blend as I stood near the creamer and sugar. After my wild weekend, I woke up with a permanent smile as I headed to work. My joy derived from the abundance of pleasure I'd experienced in the hotel room with Matt and the pure love from my family on Sunday.

Captain Matt—a captain he was while commanding my body to do unspeakable things. No man in my history of sexual intercourse had ever made me cum so many times in one night. To have him milk me completely dry, replenish my thirst, and do it all over again was new. I hadn't expected to want to see him again, but I did . . . *really bad.*

When I arrived at work, I spoke pleasantly to everyone as I dropped my bag and purse at my desk and made my way to the coffeemaker. As I stood waiting for my first cup of fresh brew, my mind couldn't ignore the images of the time I had with Matt. Several times, I'd blinked away visions of us pressed against the hotel windows with his hands exploring my body.

The ring of my phone brought me away from my flashbacks. I pulled out the rectangular device and swiped the screen once I'd seen my best friend's name on full display.

"Hey, Mo!" I sang in a cheery tone once the call connected.

"Good morning, Lee," she replied. "What's got you in such a good mood?"

My cheeks ached from the smile plastered on my face. "Girl . . ." I chewed on my bottom lip and looked around the break room. No one was in view, but the walls were thin, so I lowered my voice. I didn't need the whole firm in my personal business.

"Ah, shoot. What have you gotten yourself into?"

"When I tell you I had the *best* time this weekend . . ."

"Give me *all* the details," she giggled.

Monique Isaacs was also an associate lawyer but for a different firm. She worked in a subdivision of a highly accredited company with nationwide locations. My girl was one of the best family court lawyers in the North Side of Houston. She always prioritized a child's best interest, no matter which parent was her client. She didn't cut corners. She ensured she did what needed to be done to ensure a child's well-being was upheld.

We met during our freshmen year of undergrad. She was my roommate, and we bonded over our majors together. Monique and I had seen each other at our worst during college and stuck through the hard times and were now so happy to see each other prospering in our careers.

"So, I met this guy on that app we used to use back in college, and, girl . . ." I chewed on my lip to contain the squeal inching up my throat. "He had me seeing *stars*. I mean, I had never experienced anything so *powerful*."

"I know that's right! Did you block him like you usually do?" she asked with amusement.

"No," I answered quickly. "I was going to, but then I woke up to a 'good morning' text and decided to let him stick around. Not only that but also after the night we shared, we kind of promised each other to do it exclusively. I never had done anything like this before, but I'm going to see where it goes."

"What?" Monique dragged. "Little Miss Hump 'em and Dump 'em is holding on to a one-night stand! Is the world ending?" she teased.

She had a point. Before Matt, every man I'd met on the app would get their one encounter with me. Then I'd block them to avoid another link. My theory was I couldn't find a real man worth settling down with on a hookup app, so there was no point in allowing communication after the deed was done.

"Right," I agreed. "I had every intention of blocking him, but, girl, . . . after what he'd done to me . . ." I trailed off as images flooded my mind once again. Finally, I bit down on my lip and cleared my throat before responding. "Yeah, I'm going to keep that line of communication open for more."

Monique cackled. "Let me find out you've met your match."

"I honestly don't know. It's too soon to say much of anything about the seriousness of whatever the hell we have building between us. This could all be powerful lust at play, and in a few weeks, we'll ghost each other and forget the sex was even a thing, for real."

"All I can say is, enjoy it while it lasts. Do you know how hard it is to find a man who can adequately please a woman in this generation? The dating pool got boo-boo in it. These men and women do not want to find a real relationship. They just want internet likes and cute videos for validation."

"Come on, Pastor Mo," I joked. "You ain't lying, though. I'm cautious because the last thing I want to do is misunderstand what Matt and I are doing. Anyway, what did you do over the weekend? I thought you'd want to link Sunday with my family, but you were MIA."

My family treated Monique like an additional daughter. Since they met her, they welcomed her with open arms. My father even wrote her a letter of recommendation for law school and to get the position at her current firm. She calls my mom weekly as well. Friends like Monique were hard to find. I was so grateful God put her in my life.

Monique chuckled. "I was also exploring the body of a man."

"Oop! I know that's right. How was it?"

"Horrible."

My smile instantly flipped into a frown. "What happened?"

"Girl, he gave me the best dick of my life without kissing me a single time. You know I'm a sucker for a good, delicious lip-lock, and he gave me *nada*."

I poked out my bottom lip as I felt her present frustration. "These men think kissing is too intimate, even though they're stuffing us with their little weenies."

Monique and I cracked up. I poured my hot coffee into my mug, then added my creamer, sugar, and a splash of oat milk. I took a sip, tasting my ingredients. Once I was satisfied, I walked cautiously over to my desk.

"We're going to get our 'happily ever after' soon enough," I finally spoke again after downing 80 percent of the coffee in my mug.

"Damn right," Monique agreed. "My boss just walked in with a stack of new cases. I'm about to try to snatch all the good ones. Talk to you later, Lee."

"Bye, Mo."

The call ended. After placing my phone facedown on my desk, I took a deep breath. Monday morning, my official first day at the job. I was ecstatic to get my first assignment as an associate lawyer. Would it be a high-stakes criminal case or a low-level misdemeanor? Either way, whoever my first client was would get 100 percent of my hard work and dedication to ensure their freedom from the justice system.

"Good morning," Janice greeted me.

My head lifted to see her setting her things down on her desk. All associates were given desks to work in cubicle design while the partners had their own offices on the third floor. Paralegals and interns were housed on the ground floor, where they conducted most of their research. My father's office and the conference rooms were on the top floor. We also had a staged court to conduct mock trials as needed.

"Good morning," I replied in a singsong manner. "How are you?"

"I'm good. I'm excited to see what cases we'll be handed this week. Do you think your dad will let you be the first chair on your first case? Or will you be the second chair for a few cases just to get your feet wet?" Janice queried.

My shoulders lifted into a slight shrug. "I'm not sure. Either way, I'm excited to see what today brings."

My eyes traveled to Dylan and Paul, who had strolled in with Gabriel, Connor, and Kyle. Dylan and Paul made eye contact with me, and I nodded in their direction.

"We can work together if you'd like. I help you, you help me, and we be each other's second chair."

My heart beamed. "I would love that."

"Great."

Kelly waltzed into the room, wheeling the case cart. All chatter ceased as she cleared her throat. Kelly Mathews was one of the firm's partners. She handled most of the business with the associates while the other partners focused on the business aspect of the firm or would do one-on-one mentor sessions. My father rarely dealt with associates as a whole. He'd pick his mentees for the month and have them shadow and learn from him through the cases he'd take on.

"Good morning, Associates. We've gotten quite a few cases over the weekend. We have four homicide cases that I have reserved for fourth-year associates—each case was handpicked for a specific associate. There are a few robberies, aggravated assaults, and minor felonies. Those are all first come, first served. Once I've placed them all out, it'll be up to y'all to decide who gets what. May the odds be in your favor," she snickered devilishly.

My chest tightened as I realized my distance from the table could be a setback for getting the first pick on cases. I chewed on my lip and darted my eyes throughout the room, mapping out the perfect route to the files.

"You'll be my second chair on the homicide case I'm assigned," Janice reminded me as she looked at me in panic.

I relaxed. "You're right. But I do want an easy case to get my feet wet. Part of me wished I'd have gotten special treatment from my father, but I knew better than to think he'd spoil me with high-profile, black-and-white cases to defend."

"And go!" Kelly shouted.

I sprang to my feet and dodged bodies as I approached the table. Folders were snatched quickly, but I grabbed one and reclaimed my seat. I opened the manila folder and skimmed the pages briefly.

Smith, Devon (34)

M

African American

Domestic Assault

I let out a frustrated sigh. *Great.* I would have to defend a man accused of assaulting his wife. Domestic violence trials were harsh for the victim. I prayed I could speak with the wife and have the case dismissed or have her team offer a plea deal that works for us before going to trial. Unlike most first-year associates, I didn't want to take any and every case to trial. That's not the type of lawyer I wanted to be. I had to pick and choose my battles appropriately.

Domestic cases were a slippery slope and hardly ever were in favor of the male. Once I'd done my complete research and background check on Mr. Smith, I'd better understand the situation and know what to do.

Walking into my dark, silent home, I switched on the light and welcomed the cool, crisp air as I tossed my things onto the floor near the door and toed off my heels. My feet were *begging* for a rubdown, but the best I could do was soak them in the bath. And so, I did. After eating a chicken pot pie, I poured a glass of wine and drew a hot bubble bath. Then I sank into the water and allowed my eyes to flutter shut. The warmth of the water soothed my aches.

Now that I'd gotten to the luxury of my career, I craved something new. I'd been content with hookups and lonely nights for years because I couldn't afford a distraction or detour from completing law school and getting the associate title behind my name.

I wasn't sure when the shift came, but something in my core wanted more. After a long day at the office, I wanted to go home to a significant other to massage my feet, rub my shoulders, and share stories of our day. I wanted companionship, romance, and comfort.

I know I wasn't ready for a whole family—children who looked like the perfect blend of me and their father—but I was prepared for a boyfriend or, at the very least, a male companion. What was the point of having a big-girl job if I didn't have anyone to share my nights with?

It was as if God was sending me a sign as my phone pinged from the edge of the tub. I gently shifted through the water to grab the phone and smiled at the sight of Matt's name on the text thread. Since he entered my life, my views on dating have shifted quickly. Before Matt, the thought of slowing down and focusing on anything other than my career had never crossed my mind. However, after just a weekend with the man, I'd started thinking about . . . more.

Matt: Hey, beautiful. You were on my mind. How are you? How was your day?

Me: Hey! I'm exhausted but blessed. Today was my first day at my big-girl job, so I'm on a natural high. My day was thrilling yet exhausting at the same time. What about you? How are you? How was your day?

Matt: ·Aw, shit! Did you celebrate your first official day? You should be turning up. I'm glad you had a good day, though.

My day was stressful. My job had me ripping and running through the city all damn day. Other than the aches and pains, I'm good.

Me: The closest I got to turning up was taking a bath and drinking a glass of wine. lol

I'm sorry you had such a draining day. I hope tomorrow is better for you!

I contemplated sending a few kissy-face emojis but refrained. I didn't want to overdo my role and give off too much to a simple conversation. He hearted my message, and the three dots popped up as he typed a response. As I waited, I pulled the plug on the tub to drain the water and rinsed my body in the shower. Once I'd wrapped my towel around my body, I stepped out of the shower and grabbed my phone.

Matt: Aww, that's boring, Leah. Do you have some liquor? Let's take a shot to celebrate your accomplishments.

Me: I have a bottle of tequila sitting on my bar. What if I pretend to take a shot? I hate drinking by myself.

Matt: Nope. Are you decent? Can we FaceTime?

My heart thumped against my chest. FaceTime calls weren't a big deal, but for some reason, my palms began to sweat as my face rose in temperature.

Me: Please hold.

I dropped my towel and slid on an oversized T-shirt and some panties. Then I pulled my hair into a lazy ponytail and applied lotion to my skin. I slid my feet into my house shoes and went into the kitchen to grab the bottle of tequila. After that, I texted Matt that he could call me. A few seconds later, the FaceTime ringtone sounded throughout the kitchen. I swiped my finger to answer and smiled as Matt's handsome face appeared.

His chocolate orbs were darker than usual, but his smile shone bright. I propped the phone up against the paper towel rack and shyly waved.

"Hey."

"Damn, you're so beautiful," he complimented.

"Thanks."

"You got your shot ready?" he asked.

I nodded and lifted the bottle of tequila. He smirked and rubbed his hands together as he held out a bottle of Cognac. He licked his lips and twisted the top off the bottle. Then he looked into the camera, but I felt like his eyes pierced my soul.

"To Leah completing her first day on her big-girl job! May every day forward be smooth sailing." Matt lifted his bottle and tossed his head back, allowing the liquor to flow through the open top down his throat. I mimicked his motions and placed my bottle on the counter as my face contorted from the bitterness of the alcohol.

"Yuck." I turned and opened the refrigerator, quickly grabbed a water bottle, and gulped the contents down.

When I turned back to the camera, Matt was staring at me. I tugged at the bottom of my shirt, suddenly feeling naked under his gaze. "What?" I finally asked.

His tongue slid across his juicy lips. "Don't take this the wrong way, but when you turned around, I got a flashback of Saturday. My mind replayed those moments I had you pressed against the window while I filled you with this dick."

The tone in his voice was drenched in arousal. I bit down on my lip and shifted to clamp my legs shut as heat saturated my panties with a thick wetness.

"Matt," I whined.

"Our night together has been plaguing your mind too, huh?"

I nodded as I tucked my bottom lip between my teeth. I'd been catapulted back to the night in the hotel a few times. My breathing would falter as I felt phantom touches of Matt's hands on my body. I was addicted—and didn't mind overdosing on his ecstasy. The pearl between my legs thumped. She let me know she would need another fix of the intoxicating sex.

"It's late, and I'm sure we both have early mornings ahead, but . . ." He trailed off as he rubbed his hands together. "Can I see you play with her for me? Can I see how you pleasure yourself while I talk you through your orgasm?"

A soft gasp flew from my parted lips. "I . . . I've never done that before, but I'm not against trying."

"Prop that leg up for me, baby." The deep baritone sent a chill down my spine.

"Do you want me to take off my panties?"

"Nah, keep them on."

"Okay . . ."

I stared at the fire in his eyes as I propped up my leg. I slid my hand inside my panties and tentatively rubbed circles on my throbbing bead. Never in a million years would I have imagined standing in the middle of my kitchen with my leg propped against the counter, putting on a show for a man I'd only known for five days.

CHAPTER FOUR

Maddox

"Mmm," Leah moaned.

The sight of this beautiful, cocoa-skinned woman playing with herself on camera for me had me harder than a college statistics class. I hadn't expected our celebratory shots to turn into something so *naughty*.

I'd had my phone in one hand and my erection in the other as I watched Leah please herself to my deep, arousal-laced voice. I wanted to talk her through her orgasm. I wanted to watch her fingers erratically move against her wetness while her hips slightly rocked and her eyes lulled shut.

"You're so wet, Leah," I cooed. "I wish I was there to replace those beautiful fingers with this thick, hard dick." I shuddered as I beat off. I wanted Leah more than I wanted to breathe. She was my life source. She had the fountain of youth between her legs, and I was ready to dive in headfirst. I didn't understand why my feelings for her were so intense or how long they would last, but I didn't shy away from them. I embraced them.

"I'm so close," she warned in a voice so small I almost didn't hear her.

"Cum for me, beautiful. Let me see your dam burst."

She gasped as her sexy-ass lips parted, and quiet whimpers escaped as she rode out her orgasm. With a deep grunt, I released into my hand. Then I grabbed some Kleenex and wiped myself off. Leah looked at me with hazy eyes as she moved away from the camera. Moments later, the sound of a faucet filled the silence. She let out a soft yawn once we were both cleaned up and in bed.

"Wow," she murmured. "That was . . . something."

I chuckled. "Right. You looked so beautiful."

"Please, shut up," she begged. "My face is already hot as hell from doing that in the first place."

"Why? I've been inside you, I've had my mouth on you, and I've seen you cum more times than I could count on two hands."

"Sir!" she giggled. "We've only known each other for like . . . five days. This is all so wild to me."

"Five days or five years, you can't deny the attraction between us."

"You're right. I can't. That fact alone is so terrifying. This doesn't seem realistic. How could you already have such a hold on my body?" she asked in a whiny whisper.

"I have a question," I prompted.

"Hmm?"

"Did you think we'd talk after what we did Saturday?" I quizzed.

She was silent for a moment before replying, "Honestly, no. When I usually met up with men from the app, I'd block them as soon as we parted ways. I'll admit, I thought about blocking you but decided not to. I kind of wanted to see if we'd take those last-minute promises seriously."

I laughed. "Same here. I rarely doubled back to a woman I hooked up with. But I'm drawn to you. You satisfy me and make me insatiable at the same time."

"What do we do now?" she asked. "Is it lust or something stronger? Is it temporary or potentially forever?"

Forever.

The word made me bite my lip to avoid saying the wrong thing. Between my job, side hustles, and family issues, I never imagined spending a solid month with a woman, let alone forever.

"Beautiful, I don't know. I don't want to lie to you and make promises I know I can't keep. All I can tell you is that what I feel is *new* and, oddly, invigorating."

She shifted in bed. "I feel similar. I will admit, I wasn't expecting more than sex, but I also can't ignore the fire in my soul when we're together."

"I think the best way to decipher these feelings is for me to take you out on a date. We can share our *real* names and see if the vibe is there without the sex," I proposed.

It was weird to feel such strong feelings for a woman who I didn't even know her real name. We used aliases for a reason, and I was sure when we found out about each other's field of work, our feelings would change things drastically. Something deep in the pit of my stomach said we were treading on a tightrope—a single gust of wind could knock us off our journey.

"I'd like that, but can I make a request?" she inquired.

"What's up?"

"Can we go somewhere out of the city? I have too many clients around the area, and there's no telling who could see us out and about. I don't like people to be in my business before I'm ready to share."

"Yeah. I got you. We could take a weekend trip to Dallas if you're cool with that."

"I'd like that a lot."

"It's a date. I'm off Thursday through Sunday, so I can pick you up Friday morning, and we can have a little fun out of town."

She yawned. "Perfect."

I could see in her eyes and hear it in her voice that sleep crept around her. Sleep had already knocked on my door, but I was trying to fight it. The need to hear Leah was more important than a good night's rest.

"Do you have to work in the morning?" she asked.

I nodded. "Yup. Bright and early."

"Same. I should probably go to sleep soon."

"Me too."

Silence washed over us. Neither one of us wanted to be the one to end the conversation. Luckily, we didn't have to. Within a few quiet moments, Leah's gentle breaths filled the air. I smiled and adjusted my body so my head was buried deep into my pillow. Sleep welcomed me with open arms since I no longer fought the feeling.

One final thought ran through my mind as my eyes drifted shut: *I will go on my first date in almost a decade this weekend. How the hell did I get here?*

⋅•———••◆••⋅•———•⊙

The petulant ring of my cell phone woke me up before my alarm did. The last thing I remembered before welcoming sleep was the melodic sounds of Leah's soft snores. My eyes remained closed as I contemplated whether turning over to answer the phone would be a wise choice in the matter. When the room finally fell silent, I relaxed into the plush pillow again. As I dozed back off into the land of slumber . . . The phone rang again.

Snatching the phone up from the nightstand behind me, I looked to see my sister's name on full display. I rubbed the last bit of sleep out of my eyes and answered.

"What's up, Britt?" I asked.

"Mama's been rushed back to the hospital. Her blood sugar was high as hell," Brittney explained. "I have to drop Brielle off at school and go to work. Can you meet her at the hospital?"

"I have to work today as well."

"Call in," she spat.

I put the phone on the table and rubbed my hands down my face. Bailey Reed was the matriarch of my family. She raised two kids on her own because my father had passed away while she was pregnant with Brittney. She worked her ass off to provide for me and my sister, but sadly, genetics wasn't too kind to her. Not only was my mother a diabetic, but she also had high blood pressure, high cholesterol, and was a double amputee due to the severity of her condition.

"Last time I checked, *I'm* the one who pays for every hospital visit, every medication, every doctor's appointment, and every home nurse to care for her. I can't afford to call out when there are so many bills to pay."

Sleep was no longer an option. The last hour before my alarm went off was gone for good. After standing up from the bed, I headed to the restroom. Irritation boiled my blood. I was usually a kind person to my sister, but when I was awaken prematurely from my sleep, I tended to be more irritable than usual.

"So? You might pay all the bills, but me and Brielle take care of Mama. She stays with *me*."

"We know why she stays with you. You don't work an irregular shift schedule like I do. You're not on call at any moment. You clock in at nine a.m., and you're off at four. Please don't act like you're just overextending yourself."

Brittney was three years younger than me. As the only man in the house, I had a lot on my shoulders. I was tasked with being the breadwinner for my family because of my mother's health issues.

"She needs one of us there with her, Maddox," Brittney stated. "Can you take off work for our mother?"

"Tell Uncle Maddy I said, 'Hey!'" Brielle's voice demanded from the background.

"Girl, finish getting dressed for school," Brittney instructed.

Brittney worked at a call center, and Brielle was in the fifth grade. Brittney had Brielle at the young age of twenty. She'd gone off to college, and one of them fraternity dudes talked her out of her drawers. Rontre wasn't the ideal partner for my sister, but he's a damn good father to my niece. He isn't on child support because he voluntarily provides for Brielle and ensures Brittney is taken care of. He and my sister swap out every two weeks, giving them enough time to live their lives. I know Brittney never gets a break because of her responsibilities to care for my mother.

"Hey, Bri," I called out before muting the microphone so I could empty my bladder.

"See? My uncle loves me," Brielle giggled.

After flushing and washing my hands at the sink, I turned on the shower. The phone remained muted until I found the response I needed to appease Brittney.

"Look," I began, "I'll go up there once they have given you a call with an update on her. I'm not about to go up there and sit in the ER for hours with no clue about what is happening. That's a waste of my time."

"I can agree to that. Keep your phone near you."

"Always." I grabbed a dry-off towel and washcloth for my shower. "You know you must watch how you talk to me this early in the morning. I was sleeping well, and you woke me up with *demands*. You lucky I even answered the phone."

"As my big brother, you would answer regardless, especially since I care for our mother *and* your niece!"

"Yeah, yeah." I waved her off. "I'm finna take a shower. I'll be waiting for your call."

"Sounds good."

The call ended after a brief goodbye. I made a mental note to spend time together with them this week. I hadn't taken time out to check on them in a few weeks. Between working my ass off to make enough money to pay for my mother's medical expenses and wanting some time to relax, I hardly visited my family. Before my date with Leah, I'd go see the three generations of Reed women.

———— ••••• ————

"Maddox."

The light twinkled in Mama's eyes as she took in my presence. She was hooked up to three IV bags with an oxygen mask hooked up to her nose. She had her stumps covered in her favorite quilted blanket as her soap operas played on the television mounted on the wall.

Bailey Reed was still as beautiful in her sixties as in her youth. Despite all the pain she suffered daily, she always made sure she looked her best with her gray hair brushed into a sleek ponytail and her nails painted a vibrant color. Today, her nails were a bright pink, and her skin was as moisturized as possible. She kept a small bottle of lotion tucked in her purse for easy access. Her hands could get dry and give her cracked skin if she didn't moisturize them often—dry skin being a symptom of her diabetes.

"Bailey Elaine Reed." The distance was erased as I claimed the seat beside her bed. My eyes pointed toward her after I leaned over to kiss her cheek. "Why was your blood sugar in the four hundreds?" I asked. "Do you know how dangerous that is? You could've suffered horrible consequences."

She waved me off. "That's not important right now."

"Yes, it is. I had to leave work early to sit with you until Brittney gets off work."

"That's what we should be focusing on. How have you been, Bear?"

"Mama," I sighed, "can you answer my question first? Have you been taking your medication like you're supposed to?"

"Yes," she answered defensively. Her arms were crossed, and a frown tugged at her lips.

"So why wasn't your blood sugar under control?" I quizzed.

"I may or may not have eaten some cheesecake late last night."

"You know you can't have sweets like that, Mama."

"I know, but I wanted it. I didn't think it would affect me like this."

I held her small, fragile hand as I softened my tone. "You gotta get diabetic-friendly sweets."

"Please. Sugar-free is nasty."

We shared a laugh. "You have to do right. You know how hard it was for us when you went through the surgeries. We can't afford something more severe."

My mother's diabetes had gotten so bad a few years back that she lost blood flow in both of her legs. It took nearly two years for her to completely heal and learn how to navigate life in a wheelchair. Luckily, I'd gotten enough money to afford a live-in nurse to give her the professional help she needed to get through the recovery process. My mother's health was my main concern. I did a lot of questionable things in order to afford the medical funds needed to keep her alive.

"I know. I'm sorry, Bear."

"It's not okay, so I hope you take this seriously. Has your sugar dropped?" I asked.

She nodded. "I'm down to the two hundreds now. They said they won't discharge me until it's at a manageable number."

"I can stay a few hours."

She smiled again. "Good, I haven't seen my Bear in *months*. How are you? How's work?"

"It hasn't been that long," I commented. "I'm all right. I get worked like a dog every day, but I'm doing the best I can. I met this girl, and I'm taking her on a date this weekend."

"Oh?" The wide-eyed look on her face enhanced the surprise in her voice. "I didn't know you were dating."

"I wasn't until about six days ago," I replied.

"Who is the lucky girl?" she asked. "Where'd you meet her? When do I get to meet her?"

"Ma'am . . ." I chuckled, "I ain't ready to tell you any of that until I know if I really like the girl."

"Is she pretty?" she asked.

"First of all, I don't date ugly women." I placed a hand on my chest. "I'm offended you even asked that. But, yeah. She's beautiful. I couldn't take my eyes off her when I first saw her. Not to mention, she always smells *heavenly*. It's like God himself makes her perfume."

"Do you have a picture?" she questioned.

I nodded as I pulled out my phone. I scrolled for a second before I found the selfie she sent me the other day for her contact picture. Mama took the phone, tilted her head down, and examined Leah's face on the screen. When she finished, she returned my phone to me and smiled.

"She's beautiful."

"Very."

She hummed. "It's about time you started putting your love life higher on your list of priorities. I was worried I'd be dead and gone before you decided to find your soul mate."

I shook my head. "Don't talk like that."

"It's true. My health isn't in the best condition. I'm on so much medication, and I have to get help going to the restroom. It's not—"

"Let's just focus on the present. What's been happening on your show?"

I didn't know much about my father. My mother was all I knew. She was the only parent I had. Caring for her was a lot of work, but I was glad she was alive and with a working mind. I had to cut corners to make ends meet, but I was okay with that.

"Baby! So, supposedly, he's had a secret baby this whole time."

I gasped. "What? No way!"

"Yes! And you'll never guess where the child has been."

"Where?"

"Working for him *at his company*."

"Despicable."

As I listened to her tell me about the current plots in her never-ending soap operas, my mind drifted to my childhood. I could vividly remember when things shifted for the worse. When I was fourteen, I noticed my mother's health decline rapidly. She was working two jobs, barely getting rest, and stressing to keep the bills paid and food in the house. I got into a bit of trouble with my best friend. We would do odd jobs for the drug dealers around the area to earn money. My money would go toward helping out my mother. Having that drive as a teenager shaped the man I am today.

Between the long hours and bad eating habits, it was only a matter of time before all of the fast food, snacks, and sugary drinks caught up to Mama. She had transitioned from prediabetic to full-blown type 2 diabetes, which was very aggressive to her body, especially her kidneys.

Bearing the financial responsibilities for my family was stressful, but I did what I had to do to make ends meet for us. When my back was against the wall, I was left with one option. I was okay with it because I was content knowing my mother was well cared for, even if I had to sell my soul to the devil to make it happen. There were too many skeletons in my closet. I could sponsor a nation of anatomy classes.

"Granny!" Brielle sang as she burst through the hospital room and sprinted to Mama. "How are you?"

"I'm all right, baby." Mama placed her hand on Brielle's cheek and smiled gently.

Brittney walked in with a box of Popeyes chicken.

"And *this* is why her health is so bad now. Why did you bring this?" I asked. The attitude in my tone made everybody pause and look at me, but I didn't care.

"Man, a three-piece wing and mashed potato ain't gon' kill her." Brittney waved me off.

"It might since her sugar ain't dropped down to a manageable number yet."

Brittney was an enabler. She meant well, but she was easily one of the reasons our mother was on such a rocky health plan. She constantly snuck her food outside of the recommended guidelines. Frustration was prevalent every time I witnessed them break the diets the doctor set for her.

"If you're going to be a party pooper, you should go. You need to get back to work anyway, right?" Brittney asked with an attitude.

I stood up. Mama placed her hand on my arm. I looked down into her pleading eyes. She spared her daughter because I was seconds away from putting Brittney in her place.

"I love you, Mama. Please don't eat all those mashed potatoes. Drink plenty of water and avoid sweets until you can guarantee a snack won't result in you staying here longer or returning to the hospital, okay?"

"Okay," she smiled.

I leaned down and pressed a kiss to her forehead. Then I hugged Brielle and pushed Brittney in the head as I left the hospital room. It was only six o'clock, but I was ready to call it a night.

CHAPTER FIVE

Talia

"Ready?" Matt asked after placing my suitcase in his trunk.

I nodded. "Yes."

He opened the passenger door to his dark blue Ford Mustang and held my hand as I sat inside. We met in the parking garage of the hotel, where we'd first had introductions. It was the safest way to meet up because neither of us was comfortable giving each other our addresses. I assumed he was also in a career field where he saw firsthand what could happen when the wrong person got ahold of someone's place of residence.

After we were both settled in the car, he put in the address to the hotel in Dallas where we'd be staying for the weekend. This was my first time going on a date out of the city with a man. I was not only traveling more than four hours away from my home, but I was also doing so without my family knowing. The only person with whom I'd shared my location was Monique. I told her I'd send a codeword if things went left, but something in my gut told me this would be a weekend I'd never forget.

"How do you do road trips?" I asked while he pulled out onto the main road.

"What do you mean?" he questioned as he merged onto I-45 North toward Dallas.

"Do you stop at Buc-ee's? There are two from here to Dallas. They are one of the few gas stations I trust to do restroom breaks," I explained.

"Stopping at Buc-ee's is a given. They got everything."

I smiled. "Perfect. Do you like to talk or listen to music? I try to be a good passenger and not fall asleep, but this is one of the most boring drives ever. There's *nothing* but grass, trees, and cows for *miles*. The only way to guarantee I stay up is if we have some interesting conversations. I don't mean we have to discuss the meaning of life, but I would like to get to know you."

Matt chuckled. "Yeah, I don't make this drive often, but when I do, it's a struggle staying awake."

"I believe you."

"But to answer your question, I listen to music mostly since I'm used to making the drive by myself. I'm down to have music playing and talk to you. A little soundtrack to our road trip while I learn more about you."

I smiled at his response. "I'd like that."

"What music do you like?" he asked. "You can open up my music app and queue some songs or hit one of my playlists."

My eyebrows rose to my hairline.

Open his music app . . . Oh, he has nothing to hide. I like that.

Most men and women were very territorial about people being on their phones. To know he trusted me enough to navigate his phone said a lot about the man he was—a man who didn't do sneaky things on his cellular device.

"I like a little of everything. I love R&B the most, but I like rap, pop, and a little country," I explained cheerfully.

"Country?" he repeated in shock.

"Not too much . . ." I warned. "Let 'Tennessee Whiskey' by Chris Stapleton come on shuffle . . . and I'm singing every word like I'm going through it in the bar."

He laughed. "You got me there. 'Tennessee Whiskey' is a banger. I think every Black person likes that song."

As I scrolled through a few of his playlists, I decided to share one of my playlists with him instead and pressed *shuffle*. "I'm going to put you on to a few of my favorites."

I nodded. "I'm open to it."

I shifted in the passenger seat, cuffing one of my legs under my butt so that I could get a better view of him. Matt looked so good in his plain black T-shirt, sweatpants, and slides. He dressed comfortably, as did I because the drive was *long*. The last thing either of us needed was to be in apparel unsuitable for a road trip.

The way his hand held the steering wheel as his free hand perched on the armrest drew me in. His muscles were so defined against the material of his shirt I wanted to *taste* him. I wanted to slide my tongue along each dip and curve of his broad, firm, smooth body.

After he moved through traffic to get into the fast lane, we were going at least ninety. We were about an hour from the first Buc-ee's location in Madisonville, Texas. Madisonville was small but popular because of its enormous tourist attraction, known for its brisket and beef jerky.

"I think now is a great time to share our names," I commented.

"Yeah?" He glanced at me and smirked. "You want to go first?"

I shrugged. "I can."

Though I had a calm exterior, internally, I was shaking like a saltshaker. Many thoughts evaded my mind as my tongue slid across my bottom lip to moisten the dry surface. How would he react to hearing my government name for the first time?

"My name is Talia."

"Talia," he repeated. "I like it."

"Thanks." I cleared my throat. "I chose Lady Leah as my alias after taking the 'Lia' in my name and spelling it the most common way."

"Creative," he smirked. "Talia."

"Your turn."

"My name is Maddox. I picked Captain Matt as my alias because when my niece was younger, she'd pronounce the *D*s as *T*s."

"Maddox," I repeated. "Maddox. I've never met anyone with that name before. You're unique."

He chuckled. "Thousands of people are out there in the world with my name."

"Hmm. I want to think you're the only one, so don't ruin my fantasy."

"Yes, ma'am," he chuckled. "So, Miss Talia, tell me about you—not your career or job field—but you as a person."

I chewed on my lip. "Oh, we're getting deep today."

He nodded. "I love intellectual conversation. Yes, I could talk you through an orgasm, but outside of the bedroom, I also like to see what kind of mind a woman has."

"Well . . ." I trailed off.

Who was I outside of my career? I'd spent almost a decade to become an associate lawyer. It was damn near all I knew. "Is it bad that I don't really know who I am outside of what I do for a living? I spent eight years working my ass off to get to this point in my life to have the title I have . . ."

"That ain't bad. You're still young. Some people spend their whole lives never having an identity."

"What's your identity?" I asked.

He licked his lips, rubbed his chin with his free hand, and glanced at me briefly. "I'm just a man trying to make a way."

"Mysterious," I teased. "Make a way for what?"

"My family. My mama has a lot of health issues, my sister takes care of her, plus my niece, and I'm left with all of the medical debt. Insurance ain't much help when the copays are still thousands of dollars."

"I'm sorry to hear that," I commented. "I'm sure you're doing the best you can."

"It's all I can do. I work double shifts sometimes to make sure we're okay. This is the first time in years that I've taken my full four days off. I'll take one or two, but the full four hasn't happened since my early years on the job. Those overtime shifts help a lot."

I was glad he hadn't shared his career field. Too many reveals in one day would stress me out. We'd leave that for the second or third date . . . maybe. It was interesting to know he was also devoted to his job. We had that in common.

"It shows how much you value family, which is admirable. It's beautiful. I pray your mother's health improves to relieve some stress. I pray all your hardships disappear and you can stand a little straighter with the weight lifted from your shoulders. I know what kind of sacrifices men must make for their families because I watched my father and grandfather bust their behinds to make a way for our family."

I stretched my hand out to gently rub his arm. He switched steering hands so that his left hand gripped the wheel and locked our fingers together. In a swift movement, he brought the back of my hand up to his lips and kissed the skin gently before placing our hands against his leg.

My heart melted. Such an innocent gesture swelled my heart with many emotions. My love organ pounded in my chest in powerful thrums, pressed against my rib cage. While my heart drummed, my stomach welcomed a family of butterflies. The flutters of their wings tickled the lining of my belly. I didn't know whether to clutch my chest or rub my stomach. Either way, I was stuck in a blissful state as I felt the ghost of his lips still lingering on my hand. His fingers were firmly intertwined with my own.

"But on a serious note, I've made some decisions I'm not proud of. I try my hardest to counter the bad I do with as much good in my community as possible. Many people have a bad view of me from my mistakes, but I'm trying my best to be a better man than I have been."

I resonated with him. Some decisions I've made were not in my best interest. Seeing a man admit to having done wrong in his life was nice. The more I talked to Maddox, the more I connected with him.

"I feel that," I sighed. "I've been in someone's shadow most of my life. Because of whom I'm associated with, people have a preconceived notion of who they think I am, but I like to prove those people wrong by working my ass off to make a name for myself. I'm new right now, but give me a few months, and the city, if not the entire state, will know who I am. I want to be more than so-and-so's daughter. I want to be more than a 'nepo baby.'"

Maddox laughed deep from his gut. "Nepo baby?" he repeated.

I nodded. "Yup. Some think I have an easy life because of who my people are, but I worked my ass off. I got the grades, passed the tests, and put in the energy to achieve my goals."

"That's what I'm talking 'bout," he cheered.

Soon, our conversation shifted to more lighthearted topics. Maddox was hilarious, or maybe I really liked him and just found amusement in everything he said. Regardless, the hour to Buc-ee's went by in a blur as he pulled into the crowded parking lot. We didn't need gas yet, so we would only empty our bladders and stock up on snacks for the last two hours of the trip.

I got Hot Cheetos, a large cup of ice, a bottle of *good* water, a fruit cup, and sunflower seeds. Maddox got a brisket sandwich, an energy drink, a cup of ice water, and a cheese cup. When we got to the checkout, he slid my items over with his and waved me off when I told him I'd pay for my stuff.

"As long as you're with me, you don't have to pay anything. I got us."

"But—"

"—Save your money," he interrupted my protest.

I shut my mouth and fought back the smile as I grabbed the bags and followed him to the car. Yes, I was an independent woman, but I wouldn't allow my independence to stop a man from paying for my things. Many women couldn't allow themselves to be pampered and spoiled by a man to preserve their independent woman status. Personally, I like to be spoiled and would love to be with a man who enjoys spoiling a woman. Many internet debates wouldn't exist if everybody were open and honest about what they wanted their partners to do without forcing them to be something they weren't.

Maddox opened the passenger door and helped me enter the car before rounding the front and hopping into the driver's seat. He brought the engine to life, and I settled comfortably as we arranged our drinks and snacks for the rest of the ride.

"I would like to point out that eating a brisket sandwich at ten o'clock in the morning is kind of wild. This is still breakfast time."

Maddox glanced at me as he unwrapped the foil to his sandwich.

He took a huge bite, and I almost thought he had eaten the whole thing in one chomp. After he chewed the contents in his mouth for what seemed like a solid two minutes, he cleared his throat. "Breakfast can be anything I want it to be," he clarified.

"Eh, that's debatable."

"The same way people eat breakfast food for dinner, I can eat dinner food for breakfast."

"Well—" I abruptly stopped talking. I contemplated his words and ultimately nodded. "You've got a solid point."

"Of course I do. I'm not new to this, Talia. I'm true to this, baby."

Baby?

The butterflies were back. I wasn't sure how long I'd last before I was *begging* Maddox to wrap his arms around me and give me everything I needed.

"Oh, wow," I mused. "This is so fancy."

Maddox had reserved a rooftop dinner at RH Rooftop in Dallas. The view was beautiful. A large fountain was in the center, and the food smelled delicious. We were swiftly seated and handed our menus to peruse.

"Have you been here before?" I asked, scanning my dinner options for the evening.

He shook his head as his eyes met mine before returning to the menu. "I've never been here. I googled places to eat out here, and this one was worth a try. I love a good steak and fry combination, and that's what most of the reviews raved about."

A giggle slid from my mouth as I tilted my head to look at him. "So, we're trying something for the first time together. Cute."

He smacked his lips. "I guess you could put it that way."

"Good evening," our waitress greeted. "What can I start you off with?"

"Let us get a bottle of your finest wine," Maddox explained. "I'll also take a glass of ice water on the side."

"I'll also take water on the side," I chimed in.

"Are y'all ready to order your entrées?" the waitress asked.

Maddox looked at me, and I nodded to confirm I was. He ordered the rib eye steak with golden potatoes. I'd changed my mind immediately after hearing how good his meal sounded. The waitress smiled and jotted down our orders before walking away from the table to retrieve our drinks.

"Was the steak your original order?" Maddox inquired with a raised brow.

"Not at all," I admitted. "Your order sounded too good not to try."

Maddox smirked. "I would've given you a bite if you wanted to try it. You could have gotten your . . ." He hummed as he guessed my original order. "Salmon and broccolini?"

"Nope. It was the *half chicken* and broccolini," I corrected.

"I was close," he replied.

"Here's your red wine," the waitress said with two wineglasses and the bottle. After she filled our wineglasses, she went back to get the water. Once the water was placed on the table, she informed us that our food would be ready within ten minutes. We thanked her and fell into a comfortable conversation.

"What part of Houston are you from?" I asked out of the blue.

"South Side," he answered easily. "You?"

"My grandparents had a family home right off 1960. My parents moved to Katy when I was in middle school, though. I guess I'll claim Katy since that's where I'd spent the pivotal moments of my life," I explained.

He chuckled. "Really?"

"I don't give Katy vibes?" I asked.

"Not at all."

"Good."

We shared a laugh, something I'd done more in the few days I'd spent with Maddox than in the past several months combined. Maddox brought out the giddiness in my character. He made me comfortable enough to laugh out loud without worrying about who was around to hear my giggles and hoots of amusement.

I had to admit, this was the first time I'd ever been romanced by a man to this degree. It was new and exhilarating to have a man in this capacity. In college, the most I got from a man was dinner at a cafe or Whataburger after drunk sex in the backseat of his car. This was grown and uncharted territory.

The entire night with Maddox was something I had dreamed about for years. He kept me elated from the rooftop to the hotel.

Though we both agreed this weekend was supposed to be sex free for us to sift through what was *likeness* or lust, temptation slowly entered the conversation after the two glasses of wine, soft R&B music, and a seemingly innocent foot massage.

"We set ourselves up for failure—or success, depending on how you want to chop it up—but this wine has me feeling very *sexy*." I practically purred like a cat in heat.

"I didn't think the wine would have such an effect on you," he commented. "But I'm enjoying the experience nonetheless."

"It's your fault for rubbing my feet so perfectly."

"I strive to put forth my best at everything I do." His voice dropped several octaves as he rubbed my inner thigh.

We sat on the couch, gazing into each other's eyes and discussing trivial things. I learned he is the oldest of two kids and has a niece who runs his pockets whenever she sees him. I learned about how he took on the role of the man of the house after his mother grew ill. His father had passed when he was young, so he didn't have many memories of him.

It touched my heart to have a man open to me so willingly. I was used to the closed-off, reserved men from college, but Maddox was utterly different. He was sensitive, sweet, and passionate. He was kind, gentle, and funny. He was everything I dreamed my soul mate would be—*not saying I thought he was my soul mate*—but he made me feel all the right feelings.

I shared things about my childhood as well. Like how my older brother set the bar high when he got into medical school, but I followed up with my own achievements. I almost slipped up and told him I was a lawyer, but as my mouth opened, his lips were on mine like white on rice.

It was amazing to have this weekend to be pampered, spoiled, and pleasured by a man who wanted to get to know *me*. My career was put on the back burner while my body was lifted into the forefront of ecstasy.

Our bodies had become one from the moment we met, and slowly, our hearts would connect too. I was excited and terrified to see how this whirlwind romance played out. I prayed it was for the better, but something in my gut didn't fully accept the idea of jumping into a relationship with Maddox after such a short time.

Was it love at first sight, or were we in for a tragic demise?

CHAPTER SIX

Maddox

After a weekend of bliss with Talia, reality hit me like a ton of bricks Monday morning. The back-and-forth drive to and from Dallas took an unexpected toll on my body, so I rested Sunday evening. After eating a cup of noodles, I lay in bed and slept through the night into the early morning. My phone rang two hours before my alarm was set to go off, so in the dreary dawn of morning, I emerged from my police-issued vehicle before the sun appeared in the sky.

Stepping onto the crime scene with Detective Carruthers by my side, I assessed the situation as I'd been trained to do. The crime scene investigators had already marked most of the scene. "What's the situation, Karmen," I asked the short Hispanic woman as we approached the body covered in a thin, white sheet. Blood had already begun to seep through the material.

"Looks like a domestic dispute gone awry," she explained, "even though my job is to assess a scene, while yours is to draw assumptions."

Carruthers chuckled. "Details on the victims?"

"Female victim: Ashlyn O'Neil. ID says she's twenty-eight and resides in the condo on the twelfth floor. Male victim: Terrance Davis. ID says he's thirty and does not live in the condo. However, he fell from the twelfth floor as well."

"Where's the other body?" I asked.

"Due to the severity of the injuries, we had to prioritize removing him from the scene. He was marked with markers twenty-three through forty-six," Karmen explained.

I winced. "Heard you. We'll canvas the area, get a few witness statements, and look for anything in the condo that could provide some insight into what happened."

"We'll be in touch," Carruthers called out to Karmen.

The two of us made our way through the building lobby and took the elevator to the twelfth floor. The front door of O'Neil's home was taped off, with an officer standing guard. We greeted the man with a nod before ducking into the home. There were clear signs of a struggle: glass was shattered in the kitchen, a hole in the wall, and furniture was in disarray.

"They must've been dating and had a little lover's spat," Carruthers commented.

I hummed in response, pondering the probability. When my phone rang, and I looked at the caller ID, I knew then that this wasn't the case I wanted it to be. I swiped *answer* on the phone and looked over at Carruthers. "I'm going to take this outside really quick."

"Okay."

I walked out of the room and spoke. "Hello?" I opened the door to the staircase and leaned against the adjacent wall.

"You were called onto the case on San Felipe?" the voice questioned.

"Yeah."

"Good. I need you to do what you do and ensure nothing ties back to me and mine."

"Okay."

The call ended without another word. I pocketed my phone and rubbed my hands down my face. Devon "Diablo" Kingston was one of the most powerful kingpins in the state. He pushed more illegal contraband through the state than some criminals pushed across the country. He had many people in high positions cleaning up his messes, including me.

I'd crossed paths with Diablo as a rookie cop doing an undercover investigation. I fit the description of the type of dudes he liked to have in his crew, and it didn't take long for me to infiltrate the organization. I wormed my way through the ranks to get to Diablo. I remembered the interaction as if it were yesterday.

⋅—⋅—⋅◆⋅—⋅—⋅

My heart beat rapidly against my rib cage. Beads of sweat accumulated on my forehead as I entered the office of the man everyone feared. Diablo.

"When we get in here, please, let me talk. Diablo doesn't do well with outsiders," Isaac, one of the runners I'd befriended, explained.

I nodded. Sitting at the mahogany desk was a dark-skinned man with a deep scar stretching across his face in a jagged line. He had dark brown eyes that almost looked black. He wore a black suit with a white button-down and red tie. I could tell the suit cost more than some people's rent because of how the material fit his body. His hair was long with freshly twisted dreadlocks.

Three other men were in the room, two manning the door with shotguns and one standing firmly behind Diablo with a large automatic machine gun ready to go on command.

"Hey, Diablo," Isaac greeted the man with a bright smile tugging at his face. "I brought Martin with me."

Isaac referred to my alias at the time—Martin Morris, a petty thief looking to score big on the next shipment coming to Diablo's warehouse.

Diablo looked up from his paperwork and eyed me for six seconds before he shook his head.

"You brought a pig into my establishment." The statement had barely registered before the man standing behind Diablo aimed and

shot Isaac between the eyes. Blood splattered on me as I watched Isaac's lifeless body fall to the floor. My hands went up in surrender as fear settled in the depths of my gut. I was going to die.

"I knew you were a pig from the moment Isaac scooped you under his wing. The stench of shit surrounds you," Diablo explained as his eyes bore into my wide orbs.

"I-I . . ." I didn't know what to say.

"The only reason you aren't lying next to your buddy is because I can benefit from using you." Diablo's lips turned upward into the scariest smirk I'd ever seen.

◆

That day, he made an offer I'd be foolish not to accept. He'd pay me triple my salary if I could guarantee to keep the cops away from his organization. I'd contaminate evidence, frame someone else, or other things of that nature. I could pay off my mother's medical debt in under two years. I could provide the best insurance to keep her healthy with the best medical team available. I might have sold my soul to the devil, but it was worth it to be able to take care of my family.

I rejoined Carruthers on the crime scene, and we spent the next three hours gathering evidence, with me discreetly sabotaging some of the samples. By the time the scene was completed, I was exhausted but knew I had a lot of work ahead to keep Diablo's men away from the radar of Houston's best detectives.

As I stood in the break room, pouring a hot cup of coffee, my thoughts consumed me. *Can Talia love a man who has done as much wrong as I have?* That thought made me pause as I felt a strange tug against my heart. The damned organ had gone through so much this weekend I wasn't sure it could react to anything else. Over the weekend, Talia had allowed me to open up more than I'd ever been able to around another woman. She tore down the chains of my heart, and I was left vulnerable. Talia was the type of spirit that felt like home. The date weekend in Dallas showed me what we were feeling went beyond sex. Our souls had tied with the world's strongest thread.

"Hey," Carruthers called out as he entered the break room. He walked over to the coffee machine and grabbed a cup to fill with the fresh brew.

"What's up?"

"Are you all right?" he questioned as he opened the refrigerator and grabbed the cinnamon toast-flavored creamer with his name written in a red permanent marker.

I raised a curious brow. "Yeah? Why do you ask?"

"You've been standing in the same spot, staring into space for ten minutes. It seems like something is weighing heavy on your mind," he commented. He tossed in some sugar and stirred his spoon before bringing the steaming brew to his lips to taste his blend.

"There's a lot on my mind, but I'm okay."

"You know we don't talk outside of work much, but I am here. You're my partner, and if you ever need someone to talk to, I'm here," Carruthers explained.

I nodded and lifted my hand to pat him on the shoulder. "I know, Brent. I appreciate you always having my back, even when I don't deserve it."

Carruthers snorted. "You have a point. Speaking of . . ." His eyes darted around the room and toward the door before his voice fell a few octaves. "You need to be careful with your dealings with the bad guys."

My eyebrows knitted together. "What do you mean—"

"Don't give me that bullshit. You know what I'm talking about. I know who that was on the phone earlier. I've known for a while, and I always make sure to double back to save your ass if you get sloppy."

Nausea settled into the pit of my stomach. "What?"

"You thought you were on some double agent shit all these years on your own?" Carruthers chuckled. "Man, I've had your back since you returned from that undercover job. I know a man in trouble when I see one."

"Brent—"

"Don't sweat it, brother. Just know that what's done in the dark will always come to light. Does what you're doing align with the main reason you decided to become an officer in the first place?" Carruthers asked as he gave me a final glance and walked out of the break room.

Left with the question, I felt the stinging behind my eyes as I remembered my purpose of attending the academy straight out of high school. The fateful night I lost my best friend changed my life forever.

———◆———

The sun had begun to set as my best friend, Kahlil Washington, and I exited the gas station with lemonade, bags of Hot Fries, and Now and Laters. We headed back to his house to play the new game he'd gotten on his PlayStation.

"Bro," Kahlil called out as he tossed a Now and Later into his mouth.

"What?" I asked while opening my drink and taking a swig.

"Did you hear about Chelsea's sweet sixteen bash?" he asked.

I shook my head. "Nah."

"She said she's inviting the whole football team. I can't wait to turn up with her," he explained.

Kahlil had the biggest crush on Chelsea. The crush dated back to middle school when they had a computer class together. He swore they would get married one day, yet he was never man enough to ask her out.

"Man, you know you ain't 'bout that life! Every time you're around that girl, you start stuttering like that dude from Fat Albert," I teased while cackling.

Kahlil smacked his lips. "You just mad you don't get any girls." He playfully pushed me, which initiated a round of slapboxing. We went back and forth for a while until gunshots rang through the air. We both froze and ducked down behind one of the cars on the street we were on. Several people ran in different directions around us as two cop cars sped down the road and stopped at a house on the corner of Kahlil's block.

"We should stay here . . ." I said.

"No, my house is only down the block. What they got going on has nothing to do with us." Kahlil waved me off and grabbed his snacks. After dusting off his pants, he began walking down the street. He pocketed his candy and tucked his drink under his arm. Then he pulled open his bag of chips and popped a few into his mouth before he turned to look at me.

"C'mon, Maddy!" he urged. "They are not worried about us. We'll be at my house in no time."

Reluctantly, I gathered my fallen items and cautiously followed Kahlil. As we rounded the car and headed toward his home, my stomach was in knots. Growing up in this neighborhood, we were used to the occasional gunshot or police presence, but today felt . . . off. Gun safety was drilled into us the moment we could comprehend the dangers of being a young Black boy in America. The smart thing would have been for us to stay put until the coast was clear, but Kahlil was as impatient as a hungry infant.

Pop!

Pop!

Pop!

Flinching at the rapid gunfire, I clutched my chest and picked up pace . . . only to immediately halt. Kahlil didn't make a sound as he fell to the ground. My eyes widened in shock.

"Very funny, 'Lil . . ." I eyed his still body. "Bro, stop playin' . . ."

I closed the distance between us and noticed the pool of blood spreading underneath his body. Fear and shock traveled through my blood in rapid sprints.

"Kahlil!" I cried out. The snacks in my hands fell to the ground as I dropped to my knees and turned him over. He had two gunshot wounds in his chest. The bullets pierced his heart and lung, so he was dead before his body hit the ground. I shook him in my arms, begging him to wake up.

"Help!" I shouted at the top of my lungs. "Somebody, help me, please!"

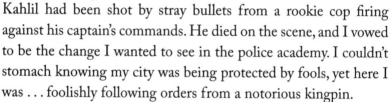

Kahlil had been shot by stray bullets from a rookie cop firing against his captain's commands. He died on the scene, and I vowed to be the change I wanted to see in the police academy. I couldn't stomach knowing my city was being protected by fools, yet here I was . . . foolishly following orders from a notorious kingpin.

When I came back to reality, my coffee was no longer hot, so I poured it down the drain and pushed thoughts of Kahlil to the back of my mind. He'd be disappointed in how I honored his name—if what I did could even be labeled as honor.

Could Talia's presence be the light I needed to climb out of the darkness? Or was I too far gone into the dark to ever see the light?

CHAPTER SEVEN

Talia

Maddox: Good morning, beautiful. I hope you have a magnificent day today. I can't wait to see you tonight.

I smiled at the message on the screen as I contemplated my reply. For the last four weeks, Maddox had been the perfect constant in my life. When we weren't working, we were together. When we couldn't be together, we would FaceTime for hours. Since our Dallas trip, we had been nearly inseparable, and I couldn't have been more thrilled.

We hadn't made things official yet, but we both agreed we were exclusive with each other. If I were being honest, I didn't want to date anyone else. I was content with the time I spent with Maddox.

Me: Good morning, handsome. Thank you for putting a smile on my face this morning. I hope you have the day you deserve. I also can't wait to see you tonight. I'm looking forward to lying in your arms.

I rolled my eyes at the last sentence. Leave it to me to be the cliché lover girl in the scenario, but it was true. I felt safe, secure, and protected in Maddox's arms. I felt invincible with him in my life. Not to mention, my confidence had tripled since we started going out on dates.

The thought that a one-night stand had turned my life upside down was amusing. I stood ten toes behind my career. It was always my main priority. I never deviated or allowed anyone to prevent me from being the best lawyer in Texas. Now, for some crazy reason, I tried to find a way to balance a career and this newfound *distraction*.

Maddox: Yeah. I'm looking forward to having you pressed against the window again.

I shook my head at the message. For the last month, we'd occupied the same hotel room as our first meeting. A part of us wanted to keep our home lives separate from the budding relationship between us. The weight of our occupations would ruin the fantasy we'd worked so hard to build over the last thirty days. Before long, I would have to disclose that I was a lawyer at Tate & Associates, and my father was one of the top-rated lawyers in the state. Until then, I would enjoy my residency in la-la land with a man who filled my stomach with butterflies.

Me: Why would you put those thoughts in my head when you know I have an important meeting today? You must hate me or something.

Maddox: I adore the very air you breathe. I adore you from head to toe. The mere thought of you brightens my day.

Me: Now you've got me blushing harder than a virgin at a strip club! I've got to go. I'll call you during my lunch break.

I swallowed hard as the butterflies swarmed my belly with a vengeance. The flutters pushed a lump up my throat, which I swallowed hard to push back down. I slid my phone into my purse and finally exited my car after sitting in the parking lot for almost twenty minutes, texting this man.

The walk to my desk was easy. I'd created a daily routine of greeting the receptionists, stopping to get coffee, and setting my things on my desk before checking in with my work friends. I'd built a nice community for myself within the ranks of the T&A staff.

Last week, I won my first case. Mr. Smith was found not guilty of his crimes and was sent home a free man, although he was greeted with divorce papers from his wife. I told him it was for the best and to find a woman who wouldn't stress him out to the point of a domestic dispute.

What a lot of people failed to realize was that love wasn't supposed to hurt. Love was supposed to feel like a warm blanket in the winter. Love was supposed to feel like flipping the pillow on the cool side during a summer night. Love was supposed to feel like drinking a bottle of water on the nightstand at three o'clock in the morning.

Love was not supposed to fill someone with dread. Love was not supposed to make someone feel anguish, heartache, or devastation. Love was not supposed to make someone *hurt* the person they so-called loved.

"Good morning," Janice sang as she sat at her desk across from mine.

"Good morning," I replied a little more enthused than I originally planned to be.

Janice raised an eyebrow. "What's got you so excited?"

I lifted my shoulders into a slight shrug. "I don't know. I think I'm still on the high of my win. I know we're going to eat the prosecution alive this week."

Janice's case was coming up. It was an honor to be her second chair, and I couldn't wait to see all of our hard work pay off when Mr. Forrest Everson was found guilty in a court of his peers.

"I know that's right. I'm so proud of how you handled yourself on your first case. You were articulate, precise, and likable. So many lawyers forget that half of the battle is being *liked* by the judge and jury. An unlikable lawyer has to work twice as hard," Janice shared.

I absorbed the advice she gave me like a sponge. "Got it. Do you have any other tips for me? I know this case is huge compared to the DV I did."

Janice listed a few more things to be cautious of and what to expect in the trial. She said these cases could drag on for months unless something drastic happened to sway the jury. I told her I was prepared to dedicate as much time and energy to protecting the client as possible.

With a tilt of my cup, I guzzled the remainder of my coffee. As I opened my laptop to view my downloaded files, my father's silhouette approached from my peripheral. Once he was a few feet from my desk, he greeted us with a wide-toothed smile.

"Good morning, ladies," he said.

"Hey, Dad—Mr. Tate," I quickly corrected.

Janice snickered. "Good morning, Mr. Tate."

"Talia, can I see you in my office?" he asked in a commanding voice.

"Yes, sir," I replied. I closed my laptop and stood to my feet. We walked the long distance to his office in a comfortable silence as he spoke and acknowledged people in passing.

When we entered his office, he closed the door and opened his arms. Instantly, I felt like a younger version of myself, excited to melt into my father's arms. I buried my face in his suit-covered chest and inhaled the woodsy scent of his cologne. His arms wrapped around me like a protective bear, and we stood there awhile.

"I'm so proud of you, baby girl," he commented. "Every day, I see you exceeding all expectations, and you are doing a damn good job."

Stepping back, I met his gaze with humility. "Thank you, Daddy."

He moved to lean against his desk while I took a seat on the couch in the corner. "What did you want to talk to me about?"

He smiled. "I wanted to see how you were doing. How are you settling in? It's been a little over a month since you were hired. I just want to gauge your experience so far."

"It's been great. I think I found my clique within the company. I enjoy Janice so much. She's taken me under her wing and drops gems all the time. Dylan and Paul aren't too bad either."

Dad smiled. "I'm glad you've found work friends. Those are always important. Building relationships with people you work with helps make coming to work a little easier on the bad days."

"Yeah," I agreed. "It's been an unforgettable experience since I got hired. I really love it here. I know I will continue to learn from the veterans and grow as a lawyer."

"That's what I love to hear. Is there anything you want to tell me? I know you've got to get back to help Janice for trial next week, but if there's anything you need to share, I'm all ears." Daddy crossed his arms over his chest.

Does he know?

No. There was *no way* my father knew what I did in my personal time outside of the office. Yeah, I didn't check in as much as I used to, but that shouldn't have sounded off any alarms to my parents . . . right? I hoped my face didn't reveal the inner turmoil I experienced at his question.

"No, sir. Everything is good," I answered as clearly as possible.

He smiled. "Good. I love you, baby girl."

"I love you too, Daddy."

I bid him goodbye before exiting the office. Once the door closed behind me, I exhaled the breath I didn't even know I was holding.

It was too soon to share my budding relationship with my parents. What I had with Maddox was too fresh and susceptible to change at any time. I couldn't introduce him to my *father* before we even knew what the hell we were doing for real.

Walking into the hotel room, I was greeted with the smell of shrimp alfredo and garlic bread. Maddox was waiting at the small dining table near the window, dressed in a comfortable pair of black sweatpants, a gray T-shirt, and some slides. The smile spread across my face before I could contain my excitement.

"Hey," I spoke gently.

"Hey." He stood up from his seat and closed the distance between us. His large, gentle hands cupped my face as he leaned down and pressed his lips against mine. "I ran you a bubble bath. I've already showered and stuff, so you can take your time. Don't worry about dinner getting cold. It can be heated in the microwave whenever you're ready to eat."

My bottom lip poked out as I touched his face and rubbed his smooth skin. "You're so sweet."

"I try," he replied, which he followed with a slight chuckle.

"I'm going to eat first and then bathe. I don't want microwaved shrimp. It'll get all chewy and nasty."

"Sounds good to me."

I placed my bag next to the bed and took off my shoes. I stopped at home to grab my bags, change out of my work clothes, and drop off my files and laptop. I didn't want to worry about anything work related tonight. As a lawyer who is exposed to a lot of gruesome images, stories, and people, I had to find a balance between my work life and personal life before the crimes I'd been exposed to ate away at my mental.

Maddox poured the wine while I uncovered the lids of the meals. The scent of the rich, thick pasta dish filled the air and hugged my senses like a thick blanket.

"The food smells delicious," I commented. "Thank you."

"You're welcome," he replied.

We dug into the food, and neither of us said a word as we shoveled it into our mouths. The alfredo sauce was thick, creamy, and seasoned perfectly.

"Damn, this is delicious," I moaned.

"It is," Maddox agreed. He wiped the corners of his mouth with his napkin before lifting his wineglass to wash the remainder of the contents down his throat. "I'm glad I picked it. The shrimp was *perfect*."

"They were. I'm so full. I'll probably fall asleep soon," I forewarned.

"Yeah, sleep is calling my name too. I'm tempted to answer the call right now."

I giggled. "Then I better get my bath done now. I can feel my eyes getting heavier by the second."

Maddox laughed. "I'll pick a movie for us to fall asleep to after you bathe."

"You're the best."

I finished my wine and stacked our dishes before I stood up to get my suitcase. I set it on the bed and unzipped the top. Then I pulled out my tie-dye gown and slippers before grabbing my towel, body wash, and exfoliant. When I entered the bathroom, my heart skipped a beat at the sight of the candles sitting on the counter and the bubble bath waiting for me.

The little things always meant the most to me. I could have easily taken a shower upon my arrival, but Maddox went the extra step to prepare a soothing bath for me. It was the sweetest thing ever. I had to return the gesture in some way tonight.

After stripping and placing my clothes into a pile on the floor, I stepped into the steaming hot water and sank deep into the tub. The water instantly released the tension in my muscles as I enjoyed the heat seeping onto my skin.

After about twenty minutes, I stood and ran the shower to wash the suds off my body. Once I was moisturized, dressed, and presentable, I walked out to see Maddox lying on the bed, drinking his wine, and scrolling on his phone.

After placing my dirty clothes into a bag, I put the bag into my suitcase and pushed it out of the way. Then I joined him on the bed and instinctively pressed my body against his. He set his phone down and draped an arm across my body, holding me firmly. His touch was always so warm and tender. It felt like I'd melted and meshed with his as our bodies lay together.

"What movie did you pick?" I questioned.

His shoulder lifted. "I clicked a random movie, I'm not even going to lie. It was the first suggested movie, so I went with it."

I shook my head as an amused smile stretched across my lips. "Works for me."

Maddox pressed *play*. We were immediately absorbed into the psychological thriller. We tried to guess the plot twists as the movie progressed, but neither of us saw the ending playing out as it did. As the credits rolled, I looked up at Maddox, and he looked down at me. We stared at each other for a long time, eyes wide with shock.

"I am . . ."

". . . speechless," I finished.

After the initial shock, we sat up and discussed all of the jaw-dropping moments throughout the movie that hinted at the big reveal and the conclusion at the end of it. Times like this were my favorite memories to make—nonsexual intimacy in vibing over our love for cinema.

"Maddox," I said in a gentle tone.

"Yeah?" he replied.

"Can I tell you something without judgment?" I asked.

He nodded. "Always."

"You're the first man ever to make me feel alive."

"Really?" he asked. "Those other dudes fumbled the best prize ever. Their loss was my gain."

"I'm so used to only being valued for my body and what I can do in the bedroom . . . I never thought I'd find a man who valued me beyond the wetness of my private parts—especially in the places I was looking," I confessed. "Well . . . as I think about it now . . . I wasn't really looking. I guess I got the treatment I was given because I wasn't looking for anything serious."

"Life is tricky like that. When we least expect to find our forever is when God throws it into our lives. I was looking for a quick hookup to fill a void I'd ignored for decades, and I found you instead. You're beautiful, you're funny, and you're a breath of fresh air. You make me want to do better in my life. You make me want to give you more than I ever thought I could provide."

My bottom lip poked out in reaction to his profession. "Aww, Maddox . . ."

He smacked his lips. "All right, let's calm down."

I giggled. "No, seriously. Do you know how commendable it is that you can adequately express your feelings to me healthily? We're a month in, and this is already the most mature and healthy experience I've ever had."

"Same here," he agreed. "If this is what a month of learning each other has produced, I wonder where we will be in a year."

"Look at you already planning your future with me," I teased. "I love it here."

"Me too." He pressed a kiss onto my forehead and then onto my lips. I smiled against the feel of his lips on mine and snuggled closer to him. His warmth was better than a fresh cup of coffee in the morning.

"I didn't do a good job of picking the movie," he announced. "We were supposed to watch the film to fall asleep. Now, we're wide awake."

"Well, when I know I should be asleep, I'll turn on a stage play and fall asleep to those. Since I was a little girl, plays have always been my least favorite form of entertainment. I fall asleep sometimes ten minutes into a play."

Maddox laughed. "Really?"

"Literally. No matter who wrote it, who is in it, or any of that, I'll be asleep before the opening scene is done," I explained in the most honest voice I could muster.

Maddox found this amusing and laughed deep from his belly. "That's an interesting fact to know. I'll cancel all dates to the theater then."

"Yes, please. Unless you want me to get some extra sleep, paying hundreds of dollars for theater tickets just for me to nap seems like a waste of money."

Maddox chuckled. "You're hilarious."

"I'm just being me."

"I like you a lot."

"I like you too."

After gazing into his eyes for a while, I finally broke the stare down to turn on a random stage play from the assortment of choices on Tubi. As the opening credits rolled in, my eyes grew heavier until I could no longer fight my sleep. The last thing I remembered was Maddox whispering a soft good night into my ear before sleep consumed me.

CHAPTER EIGHT

Maddox

The sun shone through the large floor-to-ceiling window, awakening me from my peaceful slumber. As my eyelids fluttered open, my vision cleared. When my eyes adjusted to the brightness in the room, my gaze landed on the sleeping beauty lying against my chest.

Talia was the most beautiful woman I'd ever laid eyes on. Not only was she attractive, but her heart and soul were also just as amazing as her looks. She was the sweetest, funniest, and humblest woman I'd ever had the pleasure of meeting.

The urge to do something I hadn't considered in nearly a decade coursed through my body.

Today, I will ask Talia to be my girlfriend.

There was no denying the feelings any longer. Our connection ran deeper than physical pleasure. She pleased my soul, my heart, and my mind. She was the remedy I needed to fill years of darkness. Her light was so bright I flocked to her like a moth to a flame.

Sliding out of bed, I moved like a ninja through the room—careful not to wake up my soon-to-be girlfriend. I ordered her favorite breakfast: French toast with powdered sugar sprinkled on top, cheesy scrambled eggs, sausage, and seasonal fruit, along with mimosas and water. Then I straightened up the room and ordered a dozen red tulips. The woman on the phone explained that red tulips symbolize expressing passion and affection. She dropped the L-bomb on me, and I told her I wasn't quite ready to utter the word to my lady, but it would come in due time.

I liked Talia a lot. I was infatuated with her, to say the least. Further down the line, I'd tell her how much I loved her when I was sure what I felt was love. Right now, it was a strong *like*.

While I got myself together and took care of my morning routine, I set up the breakfast and displayed the flowers. Through all of my preparations, Talia didn't stir once. I figured her day at work was more tiring than she thought. It was funny watching her drift to sleep before the actors in the play even got started good.

After setting everything up as quietly as possible, I lay back down next to Talia and rubbed her butt. I massaged both cheeks, intending to awaken her. When the booty rubs weren't enough, I peppered kisses on her lips, down her neck, and against her chest. Finally, her eyes fluttered open. Rubbing the sleep out of the corners of her eyes, she blinked until her vision was clear and our eyes locked.

"Good morning," I greeted with a joyous grin. My excitement was too strong to contain at the moment. My nerves also played a part, but I wouldn't dwell on the negatives.

"Good morning," she mumbled in a tone laced with remnants of sleep. As the sleep wore off, she stretched and pulled me into her. Her body was warm against mine as she rubbed her fingers up and down the length of my back.

"I've got breakfast and mimosas waiting for you."

Her eyebrows lifted. "You must've gotten up early."

"Nah, it didn't take long to place the order and have everything ready for you," I explained lazily. "The longest wait was the flowers."

Her eyes twinkled. "You got me flowers?"

"Yes. Now, c'mon. The food is getting cold. I want to eat soon."

"Okay."

She rolled out of bed and stood up with the most grace I'd ever seen. Though her hair was all over her head because she neglected to wear her bonnet last night, she still was the prettiest woman in the world to me.

While she went into the bathroom to take care of her hygiene needs, I stood up from the bed, walked over to the table, and poured our drinks. When she returned, her hair was brushed into a cute ponytail, and her face was shiny from her moisturizer.

"Oh, these are beautiful!" Talia beamed with joy as she leaned over the vase and sniffed the red tulips on the table. "They smell so nice. Thank you."

"You're welcome, my love," I replied. "Sit down. I got your favorites."

"French toast?"

"Yup."

She uncovered her plate and licked her lips at the breakfast arrangement. "You remember the little things, and I appreciate that more than my vocabulary can convey."

"Knowing the types of food someone likes is more than a *little thing*. It's actually important as hell to me to know what you like, what you don't like, and what you're open to trying."

"All you do is say the perfect things."

I didn't reply. I just smiled as she poured syrup on her French toast and moaned as she bit into her eggs. The sound evoked a twitch from the once-docile member between my legs. Now, he was awake and begging to replace the food with something a little creamier.

I ignored the stirring in my core and focused on the food before me. I had a simple platter of pancakes, bacon, and eggs. I wanted grits, but everybody couldn't make grits like I preferred. I liked them creamy, cheesy, and sweet. I hate salt and pepper on my grits and would even add sugar if served with shrimp. I often got side eyes from my colleagues, but I didn't care. My mama fed me grits with sugar as a child, and I never grew out of it.

After guzzling two glasses of mimosas, I sat back and allowed my body to digest the food prepared perfectly for the occasion. As I absorbed Talia's light, I watched her clean her plate and wash it all down with the mimosa. I leaned over and refilled her glass, and she thanked me before slowly sipping the contents.

"Thank you," she commented, setting her glass on the table. "Breakfast was delicious, kind of heavy, but delicious, nonetheless."

"I'm glad you liked it."

"Was there a special reason for the flowers?" she inquired.

I licked my lips. "There is." I sat up straighter and rubbed my hands together to build some confidence in my following words.

"What's the reason?" she asked with a curious tilt of her head.

"I know it's only been a month since we started this crazy journey together. I know some people take their time with this kind of stuff, but I'm the type of man who likes to dive headfirst into the deep end." I licked my lips, ran a hand down my neck, and cleared my throat. All my nervous signs were working overtime as I built up the courage to utter the question burning within my stomach. "Talia, I know we don't know everything about each other, and that's okay. I want to learn everything about you, including your last name . . . eventually . . ." I chuckled.

It just dawned on me how we'd kept most of our professional lives in the dark and only focused on the personal aspects of each other.

"We kept our occupations a secret all this time," she confirmed. "Insane, really . . . but it's been exciting not having to discuss work while I'm with you."

"Right," I agreed. "I say all of this to say I don't mind taking this as slow or fast as you like, but I'd like to do so as your boyfriend. Talia, will you be my girlfriend?"

Her eyes twinkled with unshed tears. Then she nodded excitedly. "Yes."

"Yes?" I repeated.

"Yes, I'd love to be your girlfriend," she confirmed.

"Come here," I ordered. I pushed my seat back and stood up. She mimicked my movements, and we met in the middle. I wrapped my arms around her and pulled her close. Her hands rested at the base of my neck as I dipped my head down and sealed the new relationship status with a kiss as tender as steak.

"Mmm, Maddox . . ."

Her moan against my lips infiltrated the deepest corner of my soul. I slid my hands down her body and cupped the back of her thighs. With a quick squat and lift of my arms, I hoisted her up into the air, and her legs instinctively wrapped around my waist. Hastily, we kissed while tugging at the outer layer of clothing keeping our skin from touching.

"Make love to me, please," she begged.

"That's the plan," I responded in a voice foreign to my ears.

Moving to the bed, I eased Talia out of my arms and onto the edge of the bed. I removed her panties and admired the perfect body awaiting pleasure. My throbbing erection seeped precum from the arousal pumping through my veins. I couldn't wait to dive into the warmth radiating between Talia's thick thighs.

"You're God's greatest creation," I mused as I lifted her legs and spread them to reveal the pink wetness dripping with excitement.

"Stop," she whined, lifting her hands to cover her face.

I leaned forward and pulled her hands away from her face. "Don't ever deny me the sight of this pretty face. You are worthy of every compliment, of every kiss, of every pleasure-filled stroke I'm about to bestow upon you. You deserve to feel pleasure so powerful that we shake the clouds in heaven."

"Maddox . . ." She inhaled a sharp breath.

"I love it when you say my name," I announced. I leaned down and kissed her lips. As our eyes met, I rubbed my tip against her wetness. One thing I loved about Talia was how her body reacted to mine. She was wetter than a waterpark by the time I inserted myself into her. I chomped down on my bottom lip to suppress the deep, throaty moan pushing up from the core of my body.

"Oh!" Talia threw her head back and gripped my shoulders. She tried to pull me closer to her, but not even a sheet of paper could slide between us. "Maddox, baby."

"I know, my love." I buried my head in the crook of her neck and nibbled on the skin as I stroked into her.

Talia was the type of woman who made missionary my new favorite position. I loved how expressive her face was as I dug deep into her and hit her G-spot just right. Penetrating her warm, tight walls was like opening presents on Christmas Eve and having even more gifts under the tree on Christmas morning.

"Damn, baby," I groaned. "You feel so good."

"Go deeper," she begged. "Fill me completely, *please*."

"I love how polite you are, my love."

I stood up straight and twisted her legs like a pretzel before pressing her legs against her chest and hanging her butt off the bed. From this angle, I could penetrate her with every inch of me.

Her eyes lulled shut as she arched her back and gripped my back. She pulled me as close as our bodies would allow and held my gaze as we made love. This feeling could only be described as such because I'd only ever experienced pleasure like this one other time in my life. Talia and I were making love—hard, passionate, fervent love. The feeling mimicked euphoria. The orgasm built between us as tears poured from her eyes, and her legs shook. With glossy eyes, we peaked together like a beautiful song fading into the next.

Our chests heaved and fell as I remained still, awaiting the blood to flow back into my legs, which currently felt like Jell-O.

"This was—"

"Perfect . . ." I finished.

She nodded as she leaned on her elbows and placed her feet on the floor while I stood up and stretched. My joints ached as if I'd done a full body workout—essentially, I had.

"Let me get some warm, wet towels to clean us up. Wait right there."

I walked to the bathroom, grabbed some small towels, and wet them with hot water. I cleaned myself up and tossed the towels into a pile before grabbing a few and repeating the process to clean Talia. I returned to the bed and kneeled to get a good angle of her body. I gently wiped her, making sure to clean every crease and crevice.

As I finished cleaning her up, I pressed a kiss to the swollen entrance and then sprinkled kisses on the skin of her inner thigh. She hummed a response.

"We can take a nap, baby," I offered.

She nodded before curling into a ball and welcoming sleep a second later. I grinned, scooped her into my arms, and moved us onto the pillows. After tucking us under the blanket, I welcomed sleep too.

Even my dreams were filled with Talia. I was in too deep and couldn't wait to see where life took us.

CHAPTER NINE

Talia

Two months later . . .

"**P**ersonally, I don't like the fact that I haven't seen my best friend in *months*," Mo complained on the phone.

"You know how it can be, making time for everybody when life moves so fast," I replied. "I talk to you all the time, but I haven't had time to set aside for a date with you."

"Yeah, you don't have time because you're too caught up with your new little boyfriend," she corrected.

I laughed. "Well, yeah. This experience is so new and exciting. I would live in his skin if I could," I explained. "We'll be celebrating our two-month anniversary this weekend."

"Damn, it's been two months already, and you haven't brought him to meet the family?"

I nodded. "Yeah . . ." I trailed off, searching for the explanation. "I wanted us to make it at least a few months before I proposed meeting each other's families. I like the secret of it all. Having something completely to myself without anyone or anything tainting my view of my man."

"Well, if your view can easily be swayed, is it really love?" she countered.

"I'd like to remain in ignorant bliss for the time being," I chuckled. "No, but seriously, we agreed to do family introductions at the three-month milestone. Most couples don't make it to three months, so *when* we do, we'll celebrate by adding family to the mix."

"Interesting," she hummed. "So, what are y'all doing to celebrate the two-month mark?"

"We're going out this weekend to Austin," I explained. "While we're there, we're finally going to tell each other what we do for a living."

"Girl, *what*?" Mo questioned. "You don't even know what that man does for a living, but you agreed to be his girlfriend? You don't know the man's last name or anything?"

I frowned. "So?"

Monique let out an exasperated sigh. "Girl, for a lawyer, you sure ain't making smart decisions. I understand being dumb over a man, but this is borderline *insane*."

"Mo, please. You don't understand."

"You're right. I *don't* understand how you can blindly date a man without knowing the *basics* about him. You don't know his last name, address, or occupation, but you've unquestioningly agreed to be his girlfriend. You don't know if he's secretly married, a drug dealer, or worse . . . He could be a serial killer or scammer, just waiting for the opportunity to bleed you dry . . . or end your life."

I rolled my eyes. "I appreciate the concern, but there's no way this man is faking the chemistry with me. There's no way this man can be anything other than genuine to me. I've studied criminals. Maddox doesn't fall into that category at all."

"I'm trusting your judgment, and I pray this doesn't turn around and bite you in the ass. I want this to work out for you. I want him to be your person, but, baby . . . No man in his right mind would keep his professional life a secret from the woman they want to spend forever with. No woman should want them to either."

I sighed. "This conversation is so pointless. We're telling each other our occupations this weekend. I've survived this long, so a few more days won't kill me. I expected this type of lecture from my brother. I can't believe I'm getting it from you instead."

"This isn't a lecture. All I'm saying is you're moving like a hypnotized, lovesick teenager instead of the almost thirty-year-old lawyer I know and love."

I frowned. "Okay, Mo. Thank you for the concern."

"Look, Tee, you know I love you like a sister. I would go to war for you if I needed to, but please, don't put yourself in a situation where I must ride out at dawn in your honor."

I laughed. "You're a mess. I promise I'm okay."

"I hope so."

"Anyway, how are you? How is work? I heard you got that big case with that celebrity couple and their baby."

"Girl, that case is *messy*. It'll definitely be headlining news as it unfolds. I hate it has to be this messy, but I'm fighting for that child's best interest. I don't care about the money. I care that the child is in a safe environment and well cared for."

"I know that's right."

The conversation shifted away from my life and onto hers, and I was grateful for the distraction. I didn't want to dwell on the negative *what-ifs* she kept bringing up. In my heart, Maddox was a great man. I wanted to tell her *he's a good man, Savannah*, but I knew it wasn't the time for jokes. I would have to prove her wrong in her fears of the unknown concerning my relationship.

After my conversation with Monique, I was ready to dive headfirst into a new case. I walked into work and noticed the air was a bit thicker than usual. The halls were eerily silent as everyone navigated to the conference room.

"What's going on?" I asked as I set my belongings at my desk and saw Janice grabbing her iPad and cell phone.

"You didn't hear?" she asked. Upon my confused expression, she continued. "A huge case has been presented to the firm, and your dad will pick a team to run point. I'm talking as big as Trayvon Martin, Eric Garner, and Michael Brown."

My eyes widened. "Oh my goodness." I pulled out my iPad and gulped my coffee before following the others into the large conference room. The room was filled with people ready to take notes in hopes of being on the team responsible for the case. Janice and I found seats in the middle and noticed Paul and Dylan perched up at the front of the room, eagerly awaiting the debriefing from my father.

Chatter immediately halted at the sight of my father standing at the front of the room. He was draped down in a black and grey suit. His shoes were expensive and made of leather. His hair was perfectly lined, and his facial hair was low cut and resembled salt and pepper. "Good morning, T&A."

Various responses filled the air.

"I'm sure we all have seen the viral videos surfacing in the last twenty-four hours about this arrest. Once I saw the live videos, I knew we needed to get on this case immediately," Daddy began.

He briefly described the incident as a sinking feeling entered the pit of my stomach. The more he talked, the more intense the feeling began to build. Was my intuition telling me to stay away from the case or fight to get a spot on the team? It had started to eat me alive to the point I began to feel physically ill.

"So, I am going to run point, but I'm dividing this task into teams A and B. The two teams of four will go out and do some hard work. We will investigate, research, and find any and every way to get this case dismissed before going to trial. I know we all love a controversial court case, but I want to protect this young man and his family from as much public scrutiny as possible."

I loved that my father was a compassionate man. No twenty-year-old would want to be subjected to public ridicule or for the world to be in their business. Donovan deserved discretion, privacy, and a team that would do everything possible to protect his name.

"Team A will be Rashad Brinkley, Bernadette Brooks, Calvin Lyons, and Hector Gutierrez." The four of them silently celebrated. "You will be responsible for creating a case as the prosecution. In our mock trials, you will fight for Donovan's arrest." They nodded in their understanding of the assignment. "Team B will be Paul Westwood, Dylan Richards, Janice Marshall, and Talia Tate. The four of you, along with me, will build a case for the defense. I want you to know everything there is to know about Donovan. I want to put as much doubt on the officer's actions as possible."

Talia Tate.

I was put on one of the most prominent cases of the year in my first year as an associate lawyer. Granted, I would be on a team, but this would still be a massive milestone for my career. My father could have picked *anybody* to fill that fourth spot, yet he chose me. I could tell the choice rubbed some people the wrong way as many of them, not too discreetly, eyed me with looks of envy.

"I want both teams to meet me upstairs in the courtroom. We will watch the live video and the press conference held by the lead detective. I've also already requested the officer's body cam, but we all know how police stations are about handing those over. I've put in an official warrant request with the court if they don't willingly hand it over."

Daddy talked a little longer, explaining the process and thanking everybody for listening to the case. He said the next few weeks will be focused on the Donovan Duncan case. The other partners will delegate all other cases, and this is an excellent opportunity for everyone to show initiative if they plan on remaining at the firm.

After the first meeting, we dispersed. I met with Paul, Dylan, and Janice, and we celebrated being chosen. They thanked me specifically, and then I realized the conversation I'd had with my father a few months ago may have contributed to how he picked the teams.

We moved to the smaller conference room further down the hall. The room was smaller and had a projector at the front. On the screen, the live video from Donovan's friend, Jeremy, was on pause. We sat in a semicircle. Everyone had their various forms of writing options in hand to take notes on everything we saw in the film.

It took maybe ten minutes for my father to join us, but when he did, he came in without the jacket to his suit and his stainless-steel water cup in hand. He drank the contents before setting aside the cup and greeted us with a bright smile.

"The dream teams," he announced in a proud voice. "With the public eye trained on this case, we have no room for mistakes. I want nothing but the best from each one of you. I know for a fact all eight of you can produce thorough work."

He spoke for a little longer, letting us know that until the case was complete, we'd be spending a lot of time together. He told us to exchange phone numbers and emails. I was excited to be on my first big case with such talented lawyers.

"We're going to watch both videos—the live from Mr. Charles and the press conference with Detective Reed—several times. I want y'all to pay close attention to verbiage, body language, and scenery. I want y'all to find any and all things we can use against the officer or from the situation itself to create reasonable doubt."

The live video played first. My heart ached at the tremble and fear in both young men's voices as Officer Mitchell pointed his gun at them. I noticed immediately the slight hesitation in the officer's actions. If he was positive he'd gotten the correct suspect, his movements should have been precise and fueled with confidence. The more the video progressed, the angrier I got. The officer was *sloppy*, to say the least. I hoped I was the one to question him because I had some heated words for him.

As a Black woman, I stood ten toes down behind Black men, especially *young* Black men. We were in an era of social justice warriors and blatant racists. Unlike other minorities, Black Americans spent every day with terror embedded in our beings at the possibility of stumbling into the wrong officer on the wrong day.

Too many times, other races looked upon our *beautiful,* diverse shades of brown and only saw *criminals, thugs, and ghetto-hood rats.* Black men and women had to work ten times as hard to get a fraction of respect in the country. The countless names of Black people who were killed by police for simply existing while Black fueled my need to get into a position to hold the officers accountable while also saving the wrongfully accused.

I had filled three pages of notes by the time Jeremy's video ended. The routine was to review our notes at the end, so I turned to a clean sheet and labeled it *Press Conference Notes.* The video started. I looked up . . . and froze.

"Ladies and Gentlemen, please step away from the suspect." The voice I'd fallen in love with over the last three months addressed the swarm of news reporters. He looked . . . different in his slacks and button-down. He wore his badge with pride and his gun holstered at his hip.

"We will do our due diligence to ensure justice is served." His voice sent an unpleasant chill down my spine. *"We stand with the decisions made by Officer Mitchell, and we trust in his judgment. As the investigation continues, we will turn to our media coordinator to keep the public informed."*

A lump formed at the base of my throat. It made it difficult to breathe, see, think—to exist. The man I'd fallen in love with was the lead detective on my first big case . . . How could I look at him when he was on the side of the corrupt police force who would be working their scheming asses off to put a young man in prison for a crime he didn't commit.

"I'll be right back," I blurted out before bolting out of the conference room and heading directly to the elevators. I had to get some fresh air before I hyperventilated.

Once the elevator took me to the bottom floor, I stepped out into the warm afternoon air. My back pressed against the brick wall of the front of the building as I rubbed my clammy hands against my thighs, ridding my skin of the unwelcome moisture.

The confusion coursing through my blood made it difficult to decipher why I was going through the current existential crisis. It wasn't the end of the world because I was dating a . . . cop . . . right? However, there was no way in hell I could introduce this man to my father. *"Daddy, this is my man . . . who also happens to be the lead detective in the Duncan case."* I could see his hypothetical reaction as clear as day. He would be *disgusted*. My father didn't play about his baby girl, and to bring home a man on the opposite side of the justice system would be World War Three in the Tate household. Hell, my father has probably had several cases where he'd interrogated the detective . . .

Maybe Monique was right. I was foolish to think what Maddox and I were doing was smart. I was navigating in delusion land. Now, reality had gripped me by the nape of my neck like a new puppy, revealing all I was too blind to pay attention to.

I closed my eyes and took several calming breaths. *It isn't the end of the world, Talia. Get a grip.*

"Hey, are you okay?"

My eyes remained closed at the sound of the voice. I chewed on my bottom lip before clearing my throat and swallowing several times until the lump lodged there finally lost the battle and traveled down to the pit of my stomach.

I gave a slight nod before my eyes opened, and I met Janice's worried gaze.

"I'm okay," I replied. "I got overwhelmed with everything."

It wasn't a complete lie. Everything *did* hit me at once, which urged my need for fresh air.

"This shit isn't easy," she commented, "but you're strong enough to handle it, though. We all have our moments, but you got to know how to bounce back from those hard times."

"You're right. I do need to know how to handle those moments." I stood up straight and offered a tight-lipped smile. "Thank you for checking on me. It means a lot."

"I've dubbed you my new work best friend, so, of course, I had to make sure my girl was all right," Janice explained. She bumped her shoulder with mine, and we shared a gentle laugh. "We've got a long day ahead of us, so if you're ready to get back to work . . ."

"I am," I responded. "Let's go."

Janice grinned and led me back through the building to the conference room. The video was no longer on the projector as everyone held various conversations. Upon our return, side conversations halted.

"Sorry about that, y'all," I apologized. "I needed a break from the case. Sometimes, I get a little too passionate, and my emotions can be a bit overwhelming."

Daddy made eye contact with me, and I offered a reassuring smile. He took it for the time being, but I knew he'd send my mother to milk me about why I turned into Forrest Gump earlier.

"I'm going to have Paul and Bernadette join me in meeting with Donovan this afternoon at three. I explained to him and his family the process would be long and tiring. I also told them others would fund this, and not a penny will be paid out of their pockets." Daddy's face glowed with pride. He had built an empire, which made it possible for families in dire need to have the ability to get legal aid without going bankrupt to do so.

"We'll rotate a Team A and Team B member with each meeting. I want the world to know just how strong Donovan's defense team is."

The rest of the conference was the nine of us working on a plan of action moving forward. We'd have a solid case before the pretrial hearing and, hopefully, have all charges dropped. My father shared everything he'd learned in the interrogations before they booked Donovan. He confirmed what we all knew: HPD didn't have solid evidence other than the word of a veteran cop.

"Did the police get the footage from the gas station?" I asked.

"The gas station cameras were conveniently down. We have issued warrants from the cell phone companies to give us access to the GEO tags of Donovan's phone location during the 9-1-1 call and arrest," Daddy answered.

I rolled my eyes. "Of course, it might take them forever to get that back to us."

"I have some contacts in high places. I might be able to expedite this process," Hector explained.

"Tread lightly. We don't want anything labeled inadmissible in court," Daddy warned.

"Yes, sir," Hector replied, pulling out his cell phone and dialing a number. He stepped out of the room.

The room fell back into planning mode as we awaited Hector's return. I'd have to face Maddox eventually, but for now until the end of my workday, he did not exist as my boyfriend. Maddox Reed was the lead detective in a case I was working on and nothing more—even if my heart ached to hear from him.

CHAPTER TEN

Maddox

Staring at the black coffee in my plastic cup, I frowned deeply. The smell of the brew mixed in with the day-old pizza made my stomach churn. The police station was a mess, the streets around the station were crowded with protestors, and the phone had been ringing off the hook for hours. It was so bad I turned my phone off last night and haven't turned it back on yet.

The Donovan Duncan case went viral before the kid even entered the precinct. Now, we had more eyes on us than viewers of the Super Bowl. Of course, I made an initial statement as ordered by my captain, but I hated the situation Officer Mitchell put the department in.

We got bombarded by Tate and two of his associates literally moments after we pulled Duncan into an interrogation room.

◆

Disheveled and scared, Donovan's body language was frigid, closed-off, and resembled a cornered alley cat. He was defensive yet reserved. He didn't attack, but I could tell he was on the defense as he waited to see what tactics we would throw at him.

I greeted Donovan first. "Good evening. I'm Detective Reed, and I'm the lead on your case. Can you tell me what happened tonight?"

Donovan silently stared at me. His lips remained tight-lipped, and his eyes bore holes into mine.

Chavez shook her head and folded her arms across her chest. She squinted her eyes accusatorially at the younger man and leaned into his face. "You're quiet now? After you held a woman and her family at gunpoint and stole all of their belongings? You're quiet now because you didn't think you'd get caught in your web of crimes?"

Donovan's eyes watered, and as his lips parted to speak, the door to the interrogation room opened to reveal Stephen Tate and two of his lapdogs.

"Detectives, I know you are not questioning my client without me present. Sloppy work, don't you think?" Tate questioned with a raised brow. He sat down in the seat beside Donovan, and the two other associates stood close by, eyeing Chavez and me.

"Tate," I seethed. "Didn't expect to see you taking on such a cut-and-dried case. You lookin' to add a loss to your precious record?"

Stephen Tate was one of the best lawyers in the state. His record was as pristine as the suits he wore. He gave the prosecution, as well as the police department, a run for their money. He left no stones unturned, and nothing was left in the dark. Having Tate on the defense team was a guaranteed fight to the death for us. However, I was confident in my officers and the police force. As long as Officer Mitchell did everything by the book, I'd stand ten toes behind him and ensure his good name was not tarnished by the lights and cameras Tate and Associates brought.

"And he brought the Tate Brigade," Chavez added with a chuckle. "A literal pain in my a—"

"Will you two give us the room? We have a right to talk to our client." Tate spoke with a calm voice as he ignored the comments we'd made.

Chavez chuckled and began walking out of the room. I looked at Donovan, who looked relieved to see us leave, but I remained a moment longer. "No matter what dream team you have on your defense, the truth will come out."

The stacks of paperwork on the desk greeted me as I returned from the break room. My coffee was long forgotten as I stared at the workload that awaited me. Chavez, Barnett, and Parsons were all rummaging through their own stacks of files. Carruthers sat at his desk, animatedly talking to someone on the phone. After sitting at my desk, I rubbed my hands down my face and let out a frustrated breath.

"I hate how much work *we* must do to prove Mitchell's actions were clean and in his best judgment. I hate how we have to work every angle to protect our own and prove without a doubt the young man currently awaiting arraignment is guilty of the crimes he's accused of." My frustrations came because, deep in my gut, I felt like something was *off* about the case. The captain hadn't released the body cam footage yet, which meant what was recorded may not have aligned with the officer's statements.

"It's all a part of the job," Barnett sighed.

"It sucks," Parsons added. "I'm missing my kid's recital because of this crap."

Captain Torres stepped out of his office with a cold expression on his aged face. He offered his daughter, Barnett, a reassuring smile before his face returned to the stonelike mask. "Everybody, go home for the day," the captain ordered. "We've all been here for over twenty-four hours, racking our brains and exhausting our resources. Take the rest of the day off and attack this case in the morning with fresh eyes and minds."

"You don't have to tell me twice," Chavez exclaimed as she stood up from her chair and grabbed her jacket and purse.

"Right behind you," I cheered as I mimicked her motions.

We all knew we'd take the file home and stress about it into the night, but it beat being trapped in the police station with the vultures in the press ready to attack. After saying goodbye, I entered the parking garage and got into my car. For the first time in over a day, I finally inhaled and exhaled a breath of relief. I turned on my phone and expected several messages from Talia, but I was only greeted with texts from my mom and sister, who wanted to check in on me.

Ignoring the disappointment creeping into my chest, I dialed my mother's number, placed the phone in the dash holder, and brought my engine to life.

"Hey, baby," Mama greeted me with a gentle tone.

She'd been doing better and had managed to stay out of the hospital. She's been staying up to date with her medication, and I even brought on a new in-home nurse to help regulate her diet. Nurse Katrina would clock in at seven o'clock in the morning and clock out around eight p.m.—right before breakfast and right after dinner.

"Hey, Mama," I replied. "How you feeling?"

"I'm fine. How are *you* feeling? You're all over the news. People are saying that the officer made a bad arrest. I hope and pray y'all aren't about to take away the life of a young Black man in college trying to survive in this world." Her voice was filled with compassion.

I let out a frustrated sigh. "Mama, you know I can't discuss this case with you. I didn't call to get into that with you anyway. I just wanted to check in and let you know I was okay."

"I know you're okay. I'm worried about the young man sitting in a holding cell and can't go home to *his* parents tonight," she rebutted.

"Trust the justice system. If he didn't do it, the truth will come out. If he did it, he'll receive the proper consequences for his actions. I have to go. I love you, Mama."

"Please stay safe," she warned. "You know how the community gets when a young Black man is wrongfully accused. Protests and rallies happen. I don't want you or anyone else getting hurt."

"I know."

The call ended, and my phone connected to the Bluetooth on my car. My music filled the space as I let out another frustrated breath. The pressure on me would be magnified because I was the lead detective on this case. Being a Black detective put a target on my back when it came to the press and procedures. In the eyes of the community, I owed them more loyalty than the badge I wore. It was a double-edged sword, but I tried my best to be a just officer—when I wasn't doing favors for Diablo.

After the call with my mother, I tried to call Talia, but she didn't answer.

"No calls or texts, and now I'm getting sent to voicemail," I mumbled aloud. "Did I do something wrong?"

For the entire thirty-six minutes to my home, I rattled my brain to figure out what I could have done to upset her. We've been doing well these last few months. She was everything I needed in a woman. She brought me joy, peace, and orgasms off the charts. She was the type of woman I could settle down with and marry one day. The sudden lack of communication confused me more than anything else.

When I got home, I tossed my things on the dining room table before going down the hall to my bathroom for a shower. The water was hot against my skin, while the soap was a calming remedy. After the shower, I pulled on some boxers and grabbed the takeout menu to order some fried rice. The ding of my phone made me pause as I slid the notification screen down and read the message.

Talia: We need to talk.

The beating of my heart within the cage of my ribs was louder than the volume on my television. My thoughts swirled in disarray as I rattled my brain for the second time, trying to make sense of what I could have done wrong. It took me almost ten minutes to reply.

Me: Okay. Do you want to meet at the hotel? Somewhere else?

Talia: I don't want to meet at the hotel. If it's cool with you, I'll send the address to this ramen shop I like. I haven't eaten all day, so I'm a bit hungry.

I liked the message, and a few moments later, she sent the link to the location of the ramen shop. I went into the closet and pulled on some sweatpants and a hoodie. I didn't want to be recognized by anyone while I was out, so I wore baggy clothes and placed a hat on my head. Finally, I tied up the laces of my Nikes and looked in the mirror.

A simple outfit worn by many men of color, yet if I were to be at the wrong place at the wrong time, *I* could fit the description of a suspect. The double standard, the unconscious biases, and the deep-rooted racism followed Black people everywhere we went. It was ironic coming from a detective, but I understood both sides of the spectrum and tried my damnedest to remain in the middle.

The small mom-and-pop shop had only four booths, a bar, and a small kitchen. It wasn't hard to spot Talia seated in the booth furthest from the door. She was dressed in a pencil skirt and blouse. A briefcase and jacket sat beside her. Her hair was pulled into a ponytail as she looked over the single laminated menu. The chimes on top of the door made my presence known as she looked up from the menu. The slight smile which tugged at her lips fell into a deep frown once her eyes landed on me—a confirmation that this discussion would *suck*.

"Um, hey," I greeted her. My confidence in where we stood was nonexistent as I watched her grimace at the sound of my uncertainty, especially since she hadn't even given me a proper greeting in return. I slid into the booth seat across from her and lifted the menu. "Do you know what you're getting?"

"I get the same thing every time I come here: spicy miso ramen with an extra egg," she responded. "Everything is good here, so you'll enjoy whatever you order."

"I'll have the same thing you're having then," I confirmed.

A petite Asian woman walked out of the back room. She greeted us with a gentle smile. "What can I get for you to drink?" Her voice was laced with a deep accent.

"Water for me," Talia replied with a grin.

"Same here," I added.

"Are you ready to order?" the older woman asked.

"Yes. Two orders of my usual, please." Talia gathered both menus and held them out for her to make space.

The woman nodded. "Of course. I'll bring out the drinks soon." She took the menus and disappeared into the kitchen.

"She didn't write down the orders," I observed.

"Miss Emma is a pro at this. The menu is simple, and her memory is impeccable. It also helps that I used to come here probably four times a week back in the day," Talia explained.

I smirked. "You love ramen, huh?"

"I do. This place was my escape after classes. The calmness in this comfortable shop brought me a sense of peace when I walked through that door."

My head tilted. "Why are we here?"

Talia looked away for a moment and closed her eyes. She fiddled with imaginary hangnails as she gathered her thoughts. Miss Emma awarded her a brief distraction as she placed our waters on the table.

"Thank you," Talia spoke.

"Your orders will be out in about fifteen minutes," Miss Emma informed us before she walked away.

Talia took the bottle of water and untwisted the cap. She gulped down half the bottle before twisting the cap back on and setting the bottle back on the table.

"Whatever you have to say must be detrimental to our relationship," I assumed. "You've been beating around the bush and prolonging the inevitable. What did I do wrong?"

Talia sighed. "You chose the wrong profession."

"Huh?"

"You had to have known your press conference would have circulated like wildfire after the virality of Jeremy's video of the officer," Talia explained in a robotic voice.

My heart lurched against my chest like a body moving forward after someone slammed on the brakes. The realization of my entire identity being revealed before I was ready to do so hit me harder than I imagined. The stress of the case made me forget about the press and the brief statement I'd made on behalf of Officer David Mitchell. The weight of the investigation and Tate's involvement pushed my arrangement with Talia to the back of my mind. As the thoughts came hurling to the front, I felt nauseated and ill-prepared for this meeting with Talia.

I thought she was different. I thought she'd be the exception. I thought getting to know me first would diminish the biases and prejudice surrounding me being a detective.

"Look, I know dating a cop isn't for everyone. My job is dangerous, and my responsibilities are heavy, but I thought you were different. I thought we were really building something beautiful," I defended.

Talia chuckled. "It's not the fact that you're a cop, Maddox."

"Then what's the problem? Why are you looking like you want to break up with me and block me from your life forever?" I asked.

"Dating you would be a conflict of interest," she stated in a monotonal voice.

"Conflict of interest?" I repeated. "What do you mean?"

"I wish we had disclosed more about our personal business before getting this deeply involved. It was irresponsible of me to blindly fall . . . to blindly engage in a potential relationship with someone I hardly knew."

"You know me," I countered. "You know me better than anyone I've ever been with. You see me, and I see you. I'm not understanding the issue."

"Stephen Tate is my father."

The final blow released all of the oxygen in my lungs.

Breathless.

Confused.

Angry.

"Stephen Tate is your *father*?" I repeated the statement in total disbelief. "Stephen Tate is your father."

The woman I'd foolishly fallen in love with was the daughter of one of the best lawyers in the state. He'd won more cases than any other lawyer to step foot in my precinct, yet I never knew he had a daughter . . . especially a daughter as amazing as Talia. Talia *Tate*. It was a cute name—a powerful name, even. To know the woman I'd fallen in love with was related to a powerful man like Tate felt like a setup.

"I'm on the defense team of the Donovan Duncan case. I'm tasked with leaving no stone unturned. With you being the lead detective, I have to end things before the court gets messy."

"It's not a crime to date me," I informed her. "There's no rule saying we can't continue to build what we started while you work on this case."

She stared at me for a moment. Her face was stoic and didn't reveal any emotions. She'd purposely molded her face to prevent me from discovering what her heart truly felt at this moment.

"One of us would have to step away from the case. This is a *huge* case. Donovan Duncan is front-page news. There's no way either of us should want to back away from this. You're literally the face of the investigation, and I'll be on the defense team, might even be the second chair depending on how my father feels about my work on the case," she rambled. "This isn't my first case, but this is my first *big* case. I've won three small cases and a midlevel case, but this case would put me on the map with the heavy hitters in the legal world. I can't step away so early in my career."

"I like you a lot, Tee," I confessed. I reached across the table and held her hands in mine. She looked away and sniffed.

"I like you too," she confirmed.

"Maybe we were foolish to continue this romance without revealing every part of ourselves to each other. That was a mistake, but I can't walk away from these feelings, Tee. I can't."

She pulled her hands away from my grasp and set them in her lap. She looked down, unable to meet my gaze. I wanted to snatch her up and press my lips against hers, but I doubt she would have submitted to my desperate attempt to ease her worries.

"Maddox . . ."

She trailed off as the food was brought out. Miss Emma set the large black bowls filled with delicious ramen before us. My stomach growled, ready to devour the meal, even if the rest of my body was aching for the woman a few feet away from me.

We thanked Miss Emma for the meal, and she bowed her head before giving us some privacy. Talia picked up her chopsticks and soup spoon after she mumbled grace and dove into the noodle dish. I mimicked her actions and closed my eyes to enjoy what may be the last meal I shared with the love of my life.

Three months with Talia felt like forever. Now, as I sit with the weight of her proclamation resting on my shoulders, it seems like "forever" is approaching quickly. Was there any way I could salvage the situation and walk away with our relationship still intact? Could we hide our romance until after the trial—if it even *went* to trial?

"Can you tell me one thing?" I asked after eating most of my meal.

Talia set her chopsticks against the bowl's rim and dabbed her mouth with a napkin. "What?"

"Were you looking for a way out?" I asked.

"What do you mean?" Her eyebrows merged in confusion.

"Were you looking for a way out of this relationship with me, and this was your route? Being a detective doesn't change the man I've been since we met. My being on this case doesn't negate the months we'd spent getting to know each other. Are you using my occupation as a cop-out?"

She blinked. "No."

"Then did you never really like me to begin with? There's no way you can walk away from what we started building because of this case. It's not that serious—"

"That's the thing. It *is* that serious to me. I believe in my entire being that Donovan Duncan is innocent of the crimes y'all arrested him for. I see a scared, targeted young Black man, and you don't. That's why I have to put distance between us. I have to put my client's interest before my flesh's desires."

"Desires of the flesh?" The chuckle came from deep within my gut. It wasn't humorous in the slightest. "That's all I was to you? Desires of your flesh?"

"I . . ." She cleared her throat. "I think it would be in the best interest of both of us to cut ties. I enjoyed our time, but my career comes first, and you are on the *wrong* side of the law."

If we were in a boxing ring, I'd be laid out flat on my back after the fatal blow to my heart. She'd hit me deeper than I anticipated, as I felt breathless after she attacked my character. "Wrong side of the law . . ."

"Look, I—"

"Nah, you've said enough. I get it. This was a shock to you, but you have no idea what kind of detective I am. You don't know what I've done in my ten-plus years wearing this badge. I'll be damned if I'm going to sit here and allow such blatant disrespect of my character." I slid out of the booth and stood to my feet. I reached into my pocket and pulled out a crisp hundred-dollar bill. "Good luck on your case."

"Maddox, wait."

"Wait for what?" I questioned. "Wait for you to say what you've already insinuated? You're breaking up with me, that's clear. What more do you have to say?"

She remained silent.

"Exactly."

I turned toward the exit and left without another word. I wouldn't cry, but I wasn't sad about the situation. I was *pissed*. How could the best woman to enter my life switch on me at the first sign of hardship?

I'd make it my personal duty to prove Officer Mitchell's actions were just and unbiased. I'd prove it to Stephen Tate and his daughter as well. Donovan Duncan would pay for his crime, and I would rejoice at the loss the Tates took because of it.

Talia Tate made an enemy out of me when she attacked my character. Now, she'll pay.

CHAPTER ELEVEN

Talia

"We were getting snacks from the gas station. It was late, and we probably could have gone to a grocery store instead, but the gas station was the closest to the house. I didn't know it was a crime to buy snacks." The tremble in Donovan's voice was unmistakable. The unsteady tone reaffirmed the fear he felt at the moment.

"I am truly sorry for what you went through. Sadly, in this country, doing anything while Black can put a target on our backs. Statistically, minorities are targeted at a far higher rate than their white counterparts. It's a tragic truth we have to face every day we exist in this world," I explained gently.

"It's not fair," Donovan exclaimed. "It's not right. Existing while Black and being subjected to demoralizing conditions is unfair. My life rests in the hands of an officer who only saw the color of my skin. The tapes from the gas station and his body cam should be more than enough to protect me from the wrath of the judicial system."

Janice sighed beside me. "Everything you feel, we feel as well. I can guarantee we are doing everything possible to dismiss this case."

"Standing in front of the judge in arraignment court was humiliating. Having no control . . ." Donovan balled his hands into tight fists and slammed them against the table.

We'd finally gotten his bail money in order and were waiting for his release to process in the system. Janice and I were tasked with taking him home to his parents and getting some statements from them to help build his character profile for the courts.

"I can't possibly imagine what you've been through these last few days. We will do everything in our power to avoid going to trial. We're going to build your case, and in the pretrial in two weeks, we'll have more than enough evidence to warrant a dismissal," I explained.

"How can you be so sure?" Donovan asked.

"You're not guilty, right? You didn't commit the crime, right?"

"Right," he replied.

"Then trust in your defense team to make the judge see that for you," I finished.

Donovan nodded. "Thank y'all."

I offered a smile while I flipped through my case file. Janice engaged in a trivial conversation with Donovan to keep his mind out of the dark while I got lost in my thoughts. He was another young Black man caught up in a corrupt justice system. He reminded me of why I fought so hard in law school to reach this point. I was only seventeen when Trayvon Martin died. His death and the way the justice system failed him radicalized me. For them to find Zimmerman not guilty of taking the law into his own hands broke something within me and ignited a fire so fierce that even my father was surprised at the passion I showed for making a difference.

It took over three hours for them to release Donovan and then another hour and a half for us to drive to his home. His parents were waiting on the front porch. When we pulled up to the house, they stood up from the porch chairs and met us in the driveway. When the engine turned off, the doors unlocked. Donovan hopped out, and they embraced him in a tight hug. His mother broke down and sobbed. The three of them held each other at the reunion.

Janice and I waited a few minutes in the car to allow them some privacy before we emerged from the vehicle.

"Good evening, Mr. and Mrs. Duncan. We hate to be here under these circumstances, but before we go, can we please record some statements for the pretrial?" I asked.

Mrs. Duncan wiped away the tears from her eyes but held on to her son as if she were afraid to let go. I wasn't a mother, but I could imagine the pain she felt each day that passed with her child in a jail cell and not at home for her to protect.

"We want to thank you and your firm for all of the work y'all are doing for our family," Mr. Duncan began. "We make decent money, but we wouldn't have been able to pay for the bail and the court fees on top of everything else. The fact y'all are working so hard . . . God is good."

"It's really what we work so hard to do," I explained. "With the truth on our side, we have nothing to worry about."

"If y'all don't mind, can we sit on the porch and record the statements?" Janice asked.

"Of course," Mr. Duncan replied.

"What kind of person is Donovan? Is he capable of doing the crime he's accused of?" Janice asked in a gentle tone.

Mr. Duncan shook his head. "No. Donovan was always reserved. He stayed out of trouble, avoided drama, and always respected law enforcement."

Mrs. Duncan nodded. "My baby would never steal from *anybody*. We would make sure he got anything he wanted. He worked hard to avoid trouble because he didn't want to jeopardize his schooling."

"The night of the incident, I didn't do anything but go into the store and get some snacks. If I could go back and change anything, I'd go to a different store." Donovan let out a small chuckle.

"Again, we're so sorry this happened to you," I reaffirmed.

We spent the next hour listening to the Duncans describe their family dynamic, Donovan's schooling, childhood, current life, and his friends. I sent the team a message to ensure we gathered statements from Jeremy and the other friends Donovan spent time with. We knew the prosecution would have Jeremy testify and crucify him on the stand, but we'd coach him through the process.

After we got all the information needed for the day, I dropped Janice off at the office and headed home. I was exhausted. My body moved on autopilot from the moment I hopped on the highway until I climbed into bed. I didn't even remember taking a shower or eating dinner, but I did.

My mind was elsewhere as I lay in bed watching some old '90s show playing on the TV. It had been two days since my last conversation with Maddox, and every night, I still *yearned* to be in his arms. My mind was set on cutting ties, but my heart hadn't gotten the memo. My heart begged to be near Maddox. My heart cried out to him every night. Maddox had infiltrated the organ, and she wasn't happy with my mind's decision.

My mind replayed the conversation anytime I had some quiet time to reflect on the events.

"I have to put my client's interest before my flesh's desires." As the words left my mouth, I instantly regretted them.

"Desires of the flesh?" As the words left his mouth, my ears rang at the humorless chuckle that followed. "That's all I was to you? Desires of your flesh?"

Of course not, I wanted to say, but instead, I cleared my throat and croaked out a hasty response. "I think it would be in the best interest of us both to cut ties. I enjoyed our time, but my career comes first, and you are on the wrong *side of the law."*

———◆———

My gut churned at the way "wrong" left my mouth. It slapped Maddox in the face while it punched me in the gut. I didn't mean it to come off as cruel, but it was the only way to drive urgency into the fact we couldn't date anymore.

We could have continued to date, but you're afraid of the attention it would garner.

"No," I replied to my thoughts. "I did what I thought was right."

Then why does it feel so wrong?

The question evoked a wave of nausea so intense bile almost erupted from my mouth. The ringing of my phone broke my inner turmoil. I picked it up and swiped the screen.

"Hey, SJ," I greeted my brother.

"What's wrong, kid?" he asked as soon as the camera connected.

"What?"

"I can see it in your face. You look like you're about to throw up. What's wrong?"

I frowned. "There's nothing wrong."

"You might can get away telling that lie to Mama and Daddy, but you can't lie to me. What's going on?" he asked again.

My bottom lip trembled as I felt the itchiness in my throat as I swiped at my teary eyes. "Junior . . ."

"I'm here, kid."

"I fell in love and got my heart broken . . ." I explained in a strained tone.

"He broke up with you?"

I shook my head. "No. I broke up with him."

"If breaking up with him would hurt you this much, why did you do it?" SJ rubbed his fingers through his thick beard.

He looked just like our father, with my mother's eyes. SJ was the best brother any girl could ever ask for. He let me talk to him about anything. It was funny because he let me vent to him, even about girl stuff. There were numerous times in high school when I came crying to him because of boy problems. SJ would threaten to beat them up while giving me the best hug ever. It had been several years since I had a good hug from my big brother.

"I did it because it was the right thing to do. I can't date someone involved in the biggest case of my career. Not only would it be bad for me, but also Daddy wouldn't—"

"There you go, making decisions based on our father's approval."

"SJ—"

"Nah, Tee. You know your life is your own. You have a right to live the life you want to. Do you think they approved of Kiara? Not only was she the complete *opposite* of the type of woman they wanted for me, but she also wasn't in one of the *prestigious* careers they hinted at."

"I remember those arguments," I chimed in.

"But I fought tooth and nail to make sure they respected my relationship at the end of the day because what Kiara and I have together is magical. I wasn't going to block the blessing God put in front of me because of the disapproval from our parents. My marriage ain't none of their business."

"It's easy for you to say," I whined.

"It's easy for you to *do*, but you're too scared."

"I'm *not* scared. You just don't understand. It's different in my career. Dating the wrong person can ruin everything I worked so hard to establish."

"I'm confused, kid." SJ let out a deep breath. "Were you dating the wrong person, or did you break up with someone you cared for because of your fear of standing firm on that love?"

"Here you go, sounding like Daddy," I mumbled. "You're making me feel worse than I had before you called."

"I'm sorry," he mumbled. "I just hate seeing you sad and hurt. We don't have to talk about this anymore, but just tell me one thing."

"What?"

"After the case, do you think you could get back together, or would it be over forever?" he questioned.

"I don't know," I sniffed. "The way things ended, I don't think we'll come back from it."

"If it's meant to be, it'll come back around," he prophesied.

I wiped my eyes and smiled sadly. "What did you call me for? I know my sad love life wasn't on your mind."

"I wanted to know if you could babysit your niece this weekend. She misses you, and we need a date night."

I smiled. "I'd like that a lot."

"Cool. We can drop her off, or you can pick her up from your parents' house."

"*My* parents? Like we don't *share* them?"

"They yo' parents today."

"And they'll be yo' parents tomorrow, *loser*."

We laughed together and caught up for a little while longer. He asked me about settling into my job, and I asked how his life had been going. The distraction was a blessing because once the call ended, I welcomed sleep with open arms.

"Good morning," I greeted the room of seven other lawyers. Various responses followed. I took a seat next to Paul, and he offered a smile. I returned the gesture before pulling out my iPad and case files.

"What's on the agenda today?" I asked.

"We're going to review all of the information we've gathered and discuss interviews with the officer in question. Your father is out trying to get the body cam footage. If the station doesn't turn those over, they'll be fined," Dylan explained in a low voice.

I nodded and loaded the recordings from the Duncans. All eight of us explained what we'd done over the last few days and our expectations for the upcoming weeks. It was surreal to be involved and working beside such talented individuals. I went from dreaming about a moment like this to actually living in it.

"Hey, Tate."

I looked up at the sound of my last name being called. "Yeah?" My gaze met Calvin Lyons as he approached me.

Calvin was an older man, probably in his midthirties. He had a low-cut fade, a dazzling smile, and always came dripped down in his expensive suits. A lawyer had to hold a certain attractiveness. People wouldn't admit it, but they trusted attractive people much more than anyone they deemed unattractive. Calvin used to work as a public defender before he came to T&A.

"You said you got to see the real Donovan Duncan. Do you think he's telling the truth?" Calvin asked.

I nodded. "I'm positive about his innocence. I know when the camera footage comes back, it'll support everything we have gathered."

Calvin nodded. "I've been doing this for a couple of years, but I still have my doubts about the justice system. Seeing innocent people get locked up breaks something deep in my soul."

Bernadette hummed, "I've been in this industry since before some of y'all were born, and it's been the *same* cycle. Cases like these bring out the worst in people. Remain firm in your trust in the justice system. Remain firm in your trust in each other. Without unity, we will fail. The prosecution will try to derail all we work hard to do, but we have to remain strong."

Bernadette was in her late fifties. She was a few years younger than my father. They went to the same college and graduated a few semesters apart. Bernadette had back-length gray hair that she always wore in loose, neat curls. She was on the heavier side but always wore the nicest pantsuits that complemented her body. She was sweet but a beast in the courtroom. Her record was iconic. Everyone in the legal world respected her because she was thorough and always had the clients' best interests at heart. She was an awesome mentor during my internship days.

We all nodded in solidarity.

"Sorry for my tardiness," Daddy stated as he entered the conference room. "You'll never guess what HPD is claiming."

"Don't tell me they're not giving out the body cam footage," Dylan grumbled.

"Worse. Officer Mitchell states his camera *malfunctioned* during the chase. There's no footage of the foot chase or the gas station arrest," Daddy explained.

"That's bullshit!" I slammed my hands on the table. "Do they think we're stupid? He must have deleted the footage, which is why it took them so long to hand it over. It's been tampered with."

"Hold off on the accusations," Daddy advised. "We're working on the geotags through Hector's contact. We also have a description of the original suspect."

Daddy inserted a disc into the computer's CD player. A few moments later, a first-person perspective of the incident began to play on the projector. It was weird watching from this view, but it provided a lot of insight into what Officer Mitchell saw.

We paused it right before he came to a split in the alley. The back of the suspect's body was on full display. He wore a hoodie, jeans, a backpack, and designer shoes. I pulled up the mugshot Donovan had taken while he was processed. He also wore a hoodie, but his pants were darker, and his shoes were completely different.

"I don't know how fast someone can change shoes, but the shoes are a dead giveaway," I pointed out.

"I noticed that too," Rashad agreed.

Rashad was also a veteran lawyer. He'd had well over ten years under his belt and had his fair share of wins. He reminded me a lot of my brother by how he spoke and carried himself. He was an easy guy to communicate with.

"We're going to present this at the pretrial. What other things show discrepancies in the officer's statement and actions?" Daddy quizzed.

"I believe if we use some computational analysis, we'll discover the height differences in the suspect seen in the footage and Donovan. And I think they have different builds," Dylan answered.

We spent nearly an hour dissecting the differences. We also noted the hesitation in Officer Mitchell's movements when he ran up to Donovan. I looked away when he pushed Donovan to the ground and pressed his knee into his back. It was triggering. Luckily, Donovan gets to live to tell his truth . . . unlike other unfortunate Black people who were killed by law enforcement.

"We're going to break for lunch. Y'all don't have to return to the conference room if you don't want to, but I would like a written opening statement for pretrial. The best opening statement will be the second chair." Daddy dropped the incentive before he walked out of the conference room.

"Anybody else want to go to Chili's? I have a taste for a triple dipper," Dylan offered.

"Chili's does sound good," I agreed.

"I'm in," Paul and Janice said in unison before chuckling.

"I've got plans with my wife," Hector informed us as he gathered his things. The other Team A members had similar arrangements with their significant others. I shrugged and led the group out of the conference room and toward the elevator.

"I'm not even going to lie," I began. "I didn't expect life to move so fast after getting hired here."

"Girl, you got lucky, for real." Janice chuckled. "A lot of first-year lawyers don't get *any* action. You chose a great firm to be an asset to."

"Granted, the position probably would have been here for her regardless," Dylan pointed out. "I doubt Stephen Tate would have wanted his daughter to work for any of his competitors."

"Valid point," I chuckled.

The work environment at T&A was perfect. During this case, they were the ideal distraction to keep my mind off Maddox. Any time one of us had to go to the police station, I was the one to remain quiet. I didn't want to see him until after the trial to protect my heart and sanity.

CHAPTER TWELVE

Maddox

"Uncle Maddy!" Brielle exclaimed as I walked into the house.

"Hey, bighead," I teased. "How are you?"

"I'm okay. I saw you on TV last night. You're famous now," she explained.

"Barely," I retorted with a snort. "I just do my job."

"Well, everybody at school is talking about it," she explained.

I frowned. "Aren't you in third grade? What the hell are a bunch of third-graders doing talking about this?"

Brielle smacked her lips. "Uncle Maddy, *please*. You know I'm in *fifth* grade. Next semester, I'll be in *sixth* grade. I'm almost a middle schooler. We're very sophisticated."

"Sophisticated? What do you know about sophisticated?" I asked.

She beamed with joy. "It was a vocabulary word last week. I got a ninety on it, by the way. The only word I got wrong was illegible. I spelled it with an *i* instead of an *e*. I'm still upset about it."

I patted her shoulder. "When you get a hundred on the next one, I'll slide you a hundred-dollar bill."

"Really?"

"Yes. You got my word."

"I won't let you forget," she grinned and went to her room.

"She's going to bug me about the hundred dollars," Brittney complained as she came into view from the kitchen. She cleaned while Mama ate honeydew melon at the dining room table.

"I'll give it to you now, so you have it to give her when she takes her next vocabulary quiz." I reached into my pocket and pulled out my wallet. I unfolded the flap, retrieved a crisp hundred-dollar bill, and placed it on the counter.

"Oh, you're big money now?" Brittney questioned with a raised brow.

"No. I just want to encourage my niece to stay in school, focus on her homework, and avoid trouble. Monetary incentives seem to do well with girls. Y'all like to buy shit." My shoulders lifted into a short shrug.

"You're annoying, you know that?" Brittney asked.

"So I've been told."

"What brings you by today?" Mama asked.

I rubbed my hands together and claimed the seat across from her. I wanted some of her fruit because it looked good, but I refrained from taking her healthy snack. The nurse had gone to refill Mama's prescription, so she wasn't here at the moment.

"It's been a few days, but I'm quickly losing my mind. I miss this girl so much but can't communicate with her." I explained.

"Who is this girl again?" Brittney inquired.

"Talia Tate." Saying her government name still sent a shiver down my spine. "I met her on a dating app, and we clicked instantly. From the moment we . . ." I trailed off. I wanted to divulge my love life to my sister and mother, but not in a vulgar way. Censorship of my words was key in keeping the focus on my pain and not the sins I'd committed over the last few months.

"From the moment y'all *what?*" Brittney urged. "You can't get quiet before the story gets good."

"From the moment we *connected*, it was like my soul had found its mate. It was like God had opened my eyes to a love I never knew existed. Talia was . . . Talia is someone I see myself settling down with, but at the first sign of difficulty, she dumped me like a sack of rotten potatoes." I grumbled the last part as images of her seated across from me at the ramen shop replayed in my mind. The hurt I felt still lingered in my heart. It was like her words branded me and left an infected scar that oozed at the mention of her.

"Do you blame her?" Brittney queried.

"Excuse me?"

"What she's trying to say is y'all went about the relationship wrong," Mama clarified.

"How?" My eyes were as wide as the sun as I looked at the two of them with shock.

"Hiding, lying, and sneaking around. Anything you can't do in the public shouldn't be done," Mama preached.

I smacked my lips. "I don't agree with you, but I respect what you say."

"She's right," Brittney added her two cents.

"Is she?" I countered. "Because I don't feel like she is."

"Yes," Brittney reaffirmed.

"All I'm saying, baby, is that you hid this girl, you withheld facts about yourself, and snuck around in hotels to keep the delusion going. If you really love this girl and want to be with her, you would have shown her every part of you months ago and not tiptoed around your career, your personal life, and what you do in the streets of Houston." Mama took a bite of her last piece of honeydew melon before she crossed her arms over her chest.

I pressed my pointer and middle fingers against my temples and rubbed firmly, desperate to relieve the headache creeping into my head. "Y'all don't understand."

"Help us understand," Mama encouraged.

"It's hard to find someone who isn't afraid of dating me. Dating a cop—let alone a detective—is scary. We put our lives on the line and encounter some very dangerous people. Not only that, but also the optics of dating a cop when public views on police in general are radical all over the world . . . it's a lot . . . especially for a first-year lawyer whose father is leading the defense team to a front-page case."

"C'mere," Mama ordered. She opened her arms and motioned with her hands for me to close the space between us.

Without hesitating, I stood up and got down on my knees in front of her. She pulled me into a tight hug and rubbed my back. My eyes closed as I inhaled her warm, inviting scent. Mama smelled like expensive perfume and shea butter lotion.

Brittney chuckled. "Yo' Mama got you spoiled beyond belief. You act more like a little boy than an almost forty-year-old man."

I gasped. "Don't ever disrespect me like that again. I'm *thirty-three*. I ain't *nowhere* near forty."

It might've been weird to some people to see a grown man clinging to his mother and telling his mother and sister details about his love life, but these two women were my best friends. Despite how much we may bicker or get on each other's nerves, our love was stronger than anything else. I trusted them with my life, and they felt the same way regarding me.

"We could all sit around here and go back and forth about the should've, would've, and could've, but none of us have the time for that. What do you want to happen with your relationship with Miss Tate?" Mama asked.

Brittney chewed on her lip. "He's going to hide and ruin his chance to make it right because he's terrified of falling in love."

"*What?*" I frowned. "Not to be disrespectful or anything, but you're wrong, Bri. I'm *not* afraid of falling in love. In fact, I want to. I want to fall in love and live happily ever after, but this isn't a fairy tale. This is *real* life, and in real life, people get their hearts broken. My fear is my heart will shatter beyond repair, and I lose myself in the process. I don't want to assume the worst, but is fighting for her love worth the risk?"

"You'll figure it out," Mama concluded. "Have faith in yourself and in God's ability to assign our soul mates. If Miss Tate is yours, you'll get your happily ever after; if she isn't, you'd better be grateful you cut your losses early on."

"Okay," I agreed in defeat.

My phone rang before I could say another word. I pulled it from my pocket and looked at the screen. My captain's name was on full display.

"I have to take this."

I stood up and swiped the screen to answer the call as I stepped onto the front porch. Then I closed the door behind me and sat on the porch swing.

"Hello?"

"Reed, I need you to escort Officer Mitchell to the law firm of Tate & Associates," Captain Torres instructed.

"Um . . . Can't someone else do it?" I asked. "It's my day off, and I just want to enjoy some downtime and family."

"No. It has to be the *lead* detective on the matter. You can trail him in his car, but I don't want one of my officers in the lion's den without backup. You're the lead detective on this case, and you need to have the backs of your fellow officers."

I smacked my lips. "Okay. I'll text Officer Mitchell and let him know to meet me at the firm."

"Thank you, Reed," Captain Torres stated. He hung up the phone without another word. A frustrated breath escaped my lips as I rubbed my hand across my head.

My mother lived at least forty-five minutes from the T&A building, so it would be in my best interest to head out now. I went back into the house and bid my goodbye. I could see the skepticism in both my mother's and sister's faces. I reassured them the meeting wasn't bad and I'd call them when I made it home.

An indescribable feeling settled into the pit of my stomach as Officer Mitchell and I rode the elevator to the floor where the meeting would take place. We were escorted by one of the associate lawyers. His name was Dylan, I think. When the doors opened, I followed behind the two other men and looked around the firm.

Will I see her?

I shook the thought out of my head. I wasn't here to see Talia. I was here to protect Officer Mitchell from the vultures, also known as lawyers. Anyone on Tate's team would be just as vicious and accusatory as he was.

"Wait right here. Mr. Tate will be with you shortly," Dylan explained.

Officer Mitchell looked like he was about to shit a literal brick out of his ass by the way his forehead glistened with a thick layer of sweat. I offered him a napkin from my pocket, and he dabbed at his face.

"Look, Mitchell," I began, "You need to take a breath and calm down. You're acting guilty, and they are going to eat you alive."

"I-I . . ." Mitchell stuttered and stopped. He cleared his throat and looked at me with certainty in his eyes. "I didn't do anything wrong. I made a clean arrest and used the right amount of force. The only reason I'm getting any blowback is because of that fuckin' viral video."

Though his eyes held certainty, his voice was laced with fear and apprehension. I rubbed my hand against my chin and looked at him while I searched for the proper words to ease his worries.

"Look . . ." I paused and stood up. "What's done is done. You can't dwell on the past or someone else's actions. As long as you know you did everything by the book and made a clean arrest, stand on it. Don't let them break you, Mitchell. You're stronger than that."

"Thanks."

We waited only a few more minutes before the conference room door opened, and Stephen Tate strolled in like he was the man of the hour. I'd refrained from a snarky greeting when my eyes landed on the woman trailing a few steps behind him. *Talia.* She looked a lot like her father. The resemblance was uncanny. I almost felt foolish not to see the similarities before the big reveal.

When our eyes connected, it was as if the whole world had slowed down. It had been too long since I'd felt her body against mine. It had been too long since we pressed our lips together. My heart . . . Oh, my heart yearned to scoop her up in my arms and wake up from this nightmare.

"Good afternoon, gentlemen. I wasn't expecting your presence in this meeting, but I appreciate the visit, Detective Reed," Tate spoke. His face held amusement as he gestured for us to take a seat. "I'm unsure if you are aware, but this is my daughter, Talia. She'll be on the defense team alongside some other great lawyers."

I licked my lips as Talia reached out to shake my hand. "Hello, *Talia.*"

"Hello, Mr. Reed," she replied as I placed my hand around hers and gently shook it. She took her hand back and diverted her eyes.

"Will Officer Mitchell need a union rep?" I questioned. "I don't want him to incriminate himself by any questions the two of you may throw at him."

"We can promise you the line of questioning isn't incriminatory," Tate confirmed. "All we're doing is corroborating the night's events for our own notes."

"Cool." I took my seat and crossed my arms over my chest.

My eyes trained on Talia, who had her iPad and pencil on the table. I guess her job was to record the conversation and take notes. It was nice to see her in her element. She was beautiful as hell in her work outfit. The skirt hugged her hips and thighs perfectly. Her blouse allowed a sliver of cleavage to pop through. Visions of the countless nights I'd spent with her nipples in my mouth filled my mind. I adjusted in my seat to calm down the elevation of my arousal. The last thing I needed was to get an erection in the middle of a conversation with her father.

"Everything said in this room from this point forward will be on the record," Talia announced. She placed the device on the table and pressed record.

"We want to go over the night of the incident. Can you tell us when the call came in and what you were doing in the neighborhood?" Tate asked.

Officer Mitchell folded his hands on the table and nodded. "I was in the car with my partner. We were doing patrols as usual when we took the night shift. Crime rates have increased in the area, so our captain increased the police presence to be proactive in stopping crime."

I'd zoned out of the conversation and stared unapologetically at Talia. She was in her element. She wrote animatedly on her iPad. Despite how things ended between us, I couldn't deny my immense attraction for her. I pulled out my cell phone and sent her a text message.

Me: Can we talk?

Her phone chimed on the table. I pretended not to notice as I scrolled mindlessly on my phone. I watched her pick up her phone and read the message. My phone was muted, so the reply didn't make any noise as Tate and Mitchell conversed.

Talia: There's nothing to talk about.

Me: Actually, there is. Quite a lot, I might add. You owe me a final conversation.

Her eyebrows knitted together as she read my response. This time, the phone didn't make any noise. She shot a glare my way before she typed a quick message in response.

Talia: Owe you? No. Communicating with you during an active case could ruin my career. Move on. I have.

I licked my lips as I read the message. There was no way in hell she'd moved on after only a few days. If she could move on after the fantastic time we'd spent together, then it was all an act.

Me: That's a lie. What we had was special . . . or at least I thought it was. If you can throw all that away just like that, then damn, I ain't mean shit to you for real, huh?

I rubbed my fingers against the space between my eyes and deeply breathed. She was affecting me more than I planned to allow. The conversation was supposed to be light and flirtatious, but the more we communicated through text, the more her words from the other night haunted me.

Desires of the flesh.

Wrong side of the law.

She disrespected me too many times that night, and a part of me wanted to get my lick back. I wanted to hit her where it hurt as well. I just had to find a way to get her alone to do so.

Talia: Room 310 after this meeting.

I fought the urge to smirk as I pocketed my phone. The rest of the meeting with the Tates passed in a blur. My mind was hyperfocused on what I would do to Talia when we were alone again for the first time since the breakup.

"Thank you, gentlemen, for taking the time out of your day to come answer some questions for us. We will be in touch," Tate concluded. He walked us to the elevator and smiled before turning to Talia and whispering something in her ear.

"Okay. I'll get right on it," she replied aloud as the elevator doors closed.

"That didn't go as bad as I thought," Officer Mitchell commented as we took the elevator to the first floor.

"I told you there was nothing to worry about. I'm going to go to the restroom. I'll be sure to tell the captain how the meeting went."

"Great. See you." Officer Mitchell saluted goodbye before walking toward the exit. I hopped back on the elevator and pressed the button corresponding to the third floor. Once the elevator opened on the designated floor, I walked the short distance to room 310 and stepped inside. The room seemed to be an old file room. Boxes covered the room from top to bottom in rows along the 200 square foot room length. There was only one door from which to enter and exit. A small window in the far corner provided just enough light to see. I leaned against one of the walls and stuck my hands in my pockets while waiting for Talia.

Finally, the door slid open and closed almost as quickly. Talia came into view and turned on the light to illuminate the room better. The room instantly felt smaller than what it was.

"What do you want?" she asked in a hushed tone. Her arms crossed over her chest as she glared at me.

"I want the truth," I retorted.

"What truth?"

"Did you even love me for real?" I asked.

Talia paused. "Maddox—"

"I want an answer," I demanded in a deep baritone. "I deserve the truth. I spent months opening up to you, sharing parts of myself, and giving you all I could. Did you love me? Why was it so easy for you to end things? Why didn't you try to make it work?"

The questions came too fast. I couldn't stop myself. The raw emotions I felt of losing her so abruptly had taken over at this moment. I wasn't the type of man to accept things at face value. I wanted to know the *why* every time. For the first time in my life, I felt a strong connection to a woman. It didn't sit right in my spirit to accept the breakup without understanding the full scope of the situation.

Talia's lip trembled. "It's the only way—"

"It's not, and you know it!"

She stepped closer and placed her hand over my mouth. "Look, I am already breaking several regulations to have you in this room as it is. Please lower your voice so we don't draw any attention to us . . ."

I moved her hand and held it in mine. "Okay. I'll try to hold in my anger."

She didn't immediately snatch her hand away as I'd anticipated. She held my hand back and looked away for a moment.

"Everything we shared over the last three months was very real to me. The love I began to feel for you was genuine. However, my career comes first. I would never throw away everything I worked so hard for because of a man."

"Why do you think you had to throw anything away for me? Just because I'm the lead detective didn't mean anything. I wasn't the officer who made the arrest. I just happen to be the voice of the police department for the case."

"And that alone is a red flag. Protecting the officer in question instead of the young Black man doesn't sit right with me," she admitted.

"Baby," I whispered, "it's my job to protect this city. If Donovan is guilty of the crimes committed on the night in question, then I will see that justice is served." I cupped her face in my hands and pressed our foreheads together. "I miss you."

"I . . ." Talia closed her eyes and slowly placed her hands on my back. She pressed the pads of her fingers against the cotton material of my shirt. "Maddox . . ."

The crack in her voice tugged at my heartstrings.

"I need you, baby." I tilted her head up and gazed into her chocolate orbs. "I need you so badly."

"I need you too," she whimpered as tears pooled at the rims of her eyes.

The temperature rose in the room. Our bodies could no longer fight the inevitable. I could see the pain and the arousal competing behind her teary eyes.

"I'm yours," I proclaimed. "I'll always be yours."

"Maddox . . ." The way my name sounded from her broken voice sent a shiver down my spine.

"Let me fill you," I offered. "Let me fill you until the pain turns into pleasure . . . even if for a brief moment."

"Please," she panted.

I dipped my head down and pressed my lips against hers. Fireworks would have lit up the room had this been an animated movie and not real life. The fire between us ignited in wild flames. There was no denying the power of our connection as our lips parted and our tongues met.

I pressed her back against the wall and slid my hand underneath her skirt. The seat of her panties was drenched from her arousal. I slid the material to the side and rubbed her clit.

"I've missed my pussy, Talia. Promise me you won't keep her from me anymore." I pressed my hand free hand against her neck and squeezed gently.

Talia's eyes lulled shut as she relaxed against my touch. "Mmm."

My grip tightened. "Promise me."

"I promise," she moaned.

"Good girl."

I hiked her leg up and welcomed the sweet scent of her pleasure. She smelled like home. I could get lost between her legs and find euphoria. I had to get a taste. I had to dive deep into the warmth.

"Relax," I instructed as I cupped my hands on her thighs and lifted her into the air. Talia yelped in surprise as she instinctively wrapped her legs around my neck. Her moans were quiet as she desperately tried to contain herself while I ate her pussy until her juices dripped down my chin. I licked her clean before I placed her back on her feet and unzipped my pants. The relief I felt as my dick moved freely was only appreciated for a moment.

"I don't have a condom," I swore under my breath.

"I don't care. I need you."

"Are you sure?" I asked for consent.

"Yes."

I ripped her panties off and rubbed the tip of my dick against her wetness. She lifted one leg and hooked it around my waist. Her juices were the perfect lubricant to help ease me inside of her warmth. I took my time, inch by inch, until I completely filled her.

CHAPTER THIRTEEN

Talia

How did I end up here? What the hell were we doing? Every defense I'd set up since cutting ties with Maddox came crumbling to pieces the moment my eyes met his during the questioning of Officer Mitchell. Why had he come? He didn't serve any purpose other than to distract me from paying attention to the words the man in question was saying.

"Maddox . . ." I moaned. My fingers dug into his skin as he stroked slowly into me. Each thrust was calculated and intentional. His breath blew against my neck and ear, sending an erotic wave of pleasure through my brain.

"I don't care what you say," he explained in a grunt. "We're meant to be together. You can fight it all you want, but my soul picked you."

"Maddox . . ."

I could no longer form words. He made me feel unexplainable pleasure. How could I move on when he turned me on to this degree? How could I look him in the eyes and tell him we couldn't be together when the euphoria was blinding?

"I want every part of you, Talia," he informed me. His eyes bore into mine. I was hypnotized by the fierce flames dancing against his orbs. He meant every word he expressed.

"Please," I whimpered. "I'm so close."

Maddox lifted one of his hands to my neck and squeezed. His grip tightened as I neared my peak.

"Hold it in," he demanded. "You can't cum until I tell you."

My legs shook. "I can't . . ."

"Tell me you want me just as much as I want you. Tell me you love me just as much as I love you." He pounded into me. The calculated strokes turned into powerful thrusts. His purpose had gone from pleasure to domination. He wanted me to submit to him. He wanted to break down my barriers.

"I . . ."

I couldn't. When the postnut clarity came, I'd regret making those promises to him because despite how much my heart and soul yearned to be by his side, I couldn't do so with this case in the way. It was unethical for me to sleep with a *detective*.

"Talia, *answer me*," he demanded in a deep, authoritative voice. I felt like a scolded child—vulnerable and scared.

"Maddox, *please*," I pleaded. "I'm so close. Don't deny me my orgasm."

"Would it be a lie?" he asked. His thrusts became more sporadic. They were strong, frequent, and . . . messy. He was unraveling inside me while I tried to hold myself together. "You don't love me? You don't love this dick?"

Tears streamed down my face as my nails dug into the material of his shirt. My legs shook from the pleasure while my heart ached from the pain—the pain of being in the arms of a man I had no business being with. The pain of wishing I'd remained ignorant of our misconstrued love. No matter what I chose, the consequences would be severe. Staying with Maddox during this trial meant the potential of having my business aired out in the streets. Neither one of us needed the spotlight on us right now. Staying with him meant having to recuse myself from the case because it would be a conflict of interest.

On the other hand, not being with Maddox meant a void in my heart unable to be filled. Ending things with him meant my soul would wallow in the sadness for eternity—missing the only being ever to make us feel . . . whole.

"Baby," Maddox mumbled. His voice revealed every emotion he held within the confines of his love organ. His body penetrated me in a desperate attempt to get the words out of me. His knees almost buckled underneath him. He growled as he gripped my waist and leaned me against a stack of boxes. He pushed my body down as he pounded into me. He hit my spots repeatedly.

"Talia, I'm not complete without you. We can make it work."

"No, we can't!" I sobbed. The dam burst. As my sobs erupted, my legs quaked as my body released a powerful orgasm. I convulsed . . . and sobbed.

Waves of my orgasm swirled with Maddox's as he held on to my waist as if when he let go, I'd disappear in the wind. I wish I could. I wished I were lighter than the air so I could fade into the void. Three months with Maddox felt like an eternity. It was the only explanation for why I felt so broken at losing him.

"Talia . . ."

Maddox pulled out of me, and loneliness entered in. I was empty from him removing himself from inside of me. How was that even possible? Why was our connection so strong?

"Talia . . ."

"You need to leave. I-I . . . I have to get back to work before someone looks for me." I stood up and placed a hand on the wall to steady my movements. I fixed my clothes and wiped my tear-stained face.

"I'm not done fighting for you," Maddox proclaimed. "You're meant to be the love of my life, and I'll fight tooth and nail to make you realize it too."

"Please, just go," I begged.

Without another word, Maddox adjusted his clothes and exited the room. Left alone in the room, my heart pounding like an HBCU drum line against my chest, I shook. The tears poured from my eyes. My soul cried for Maddox. She wanted him, and my stubbornness brought her pain and anguish.

"Mama," I croaked out.

The tears had burned the rims of my eyes for hours. I'd told my team I'd caught a stomach bug and would work from home the rest of the day. After spending two hours in my car sulking and crying like a lovesick teenager, I drove to my parents' house and walked in with the weight of the world on my shoulders. I was almost positive I'd fall through the floor if I stood in one spot for too long.

"I'm in the den!" she called out.

With heavy feet, I walked down the hall to the den and saw her seated on the love seat with a mug full of warm green tea in her hand. The smile on her face fell into a deep frown the moment she took in my appearance.

"Oh no. What's wrong?" she asked as she placed her mug on the table and patted the spot beside her.

"Mama . . ." I whimpered and closed the distance between us. I fell into her open arms and sobbed. Gut-wrenching cries filled the air as she squeezed me in her warm arms.

"What's wrong, baby? Tell me how I can help ease the pain. Does your dad know you're having a bad day?"

The mention of Daddy only increased the power of my weeping. My heart was holding on by a single thread. What would my father think if he saw me broken? Would he take me off the case? Would he think I was unworthy of working at his firm?

It took me almost ten minutes to finally calm down. The tears lessened to a mere whimper as I wiped my eyes and nose from the uncontrollable leakage of tears and snot. The sight was humiliating, but because my mother didn't judge, she just held out a box of Kleenex until my face was clear of the bodily fluids.

"Are you hungry?" she queried. "I can fry some chicken legs and make beans and rice for an early dinner. I know that's one of your favorite comfort meals."

"Please."

"C'mon." She stood up and held her hand out for me. Once I was firmly on my feet, I rolled my shoulders back and followed her into the kitchen.

"What do you need me to do?" I asked.

"Do you want to help cook?" she quizzed with a raised brow.

I shrugged. "Yeah. I can."

"Okay, let's wash our hands and get everything we need."

We moved around the kitchen like a well-oiled machine. Before I washed my hands, I turned on the speaker on the bar and pressed *play* on my oldie's playlist. The calming sound of the Isley Brothers filled the speakers. Once all the food and ingredients were clean and in order, Mama instructed me to put the rice on and prep the beans in a separate pot.

"Are you ready to talk?" she asked.

I sighed. "I guess."

"You know your father and I have always stressed to you and your brother that we are a safe space for y'all. Whatever you're going through can be shared with us," she reminded.

"I know, Mama," I replied. "It's just . . . I'm not ready for Daddy to know. Can you promise not to tell him what's bothering me? I'll tell him when I feel the time is right."

"I promise." She looked at me with so much concern in her aged eyes I felt an ache in my chest.

I rinsed the rice until the water was clear and sprinkled some salt into the pot before placing it on the stove and turning it on. I repeated the process with the beans and then washed my hands.

"I was in a relationship with a man for three months," I confessed. My method was always to rip the worst news off like a Band-Aid.

"Hmm," she responded as she cleaned the chicken while I turned on the burner where the chicken would be fried.

"It was my little secret. Something exclusively mine without any outside interference. We would have celebrated our three-month anniversary a week ago, but things happened."

Mama raised her eyebrow as she grabbed the onion and garlic powder. "What happened?"

"He turned out to be the lead detective on the case Daddy and I are working on," I revealed.

"Detective Reed?" she asked.

His press conference had been on every major news channel, so I wasn't surprised she knew who the man was. I reluctantly nodded. "Yes."

"He's a handsome man. Real strong looking," she commented.

"Mama!" I exclaimed while covering my face.

"Sorry, but he is," she chuckled. "But this is bad because it's your first big case, and you don't want anything or anyone to get in the way of you making your father proud on such a viral case."

"Yes, exactly. I have the chance to be a part of history. I don't want my relationship with Maddox to overshadow all the hard work I'm putting in for this." I stirred the rice to calm the boiling water and sprinkled salt and pepper into the beans.

"You are your father's child," she commented.

"What do you mean?"

"You'll jeopardize your happiness for your career. If I hadn't held on to your father like I did, he would have ruined the best thing to ever happen in his life. Being a lawyer is a lot of work, and it gets lonely at the top. However, you have to find the balance between career and love at a certain point in your life."

"But, Mama—"

"There are no buts. The balance exists. You have to find it. It's clear from your breakdown that the young man is someone you really care for and could see yourself being with in the long run. This case is temporary; love is forever," she explained.

"I hear you," I replied while I hung my head.

"Lift up that head, baby girl." She seasoned the flour and coated the first batch of legs before dropping them into the hot grease. "You have always been book smart with your mind set on being the best lawyer you can be. Now that something else has caught your attention, you panicked and pushed it away before finding a solution to have the best of both worlds."

Mama turned to the sink and washed her hands as I turned down the temperature of the beans and rice. Once the lids were on the pots, I sat at the bar. Mama put the dirty dishes into the soapy water. She washed them and set them on the rack to dry.

"It wouldn't have been hard if he wasn't a detective. He's on the opposite side of the law. He's arresting innocent Black men," I defended.

"He does his job, and you do yours. I don't understand why you find fault in that."

"It doesn't matter now," I concluded. "What's done is done. I broke up with him, and that's that."

"Stubborn, just like your daddy," she commented.

"Well, Daddy got his happily ever after with you . . . I'll get mine too."

"I hope so," she mumbled. "Go ahead and get your plate out of the cabinet. The first batch of chicken is done. I won't drop the rest until your father gets home. I want his food to be nice and hot when he gets off work."

Mama used the metal tongs to get the chicken legs and set them on the drying tray. She made my plate once the chicken was no longer drenched in oil. She held it for me to take, and I uttered a quick prayer before I dove in. Homemade meals were appreciated. The juiciness of the chicken made my heart happy for the first time all day. The savory seasoning of the rice and beans remedied the pain my soul felt.

"This is delicious, Mama," I commented around a mouthful of the sumptuous food.

"Thanks, Tee."

For a moment, the smooth R&B filled the silence in the air. Mama cleaned around the kitchen while I cleaned my plate. I knew my departure was close because I glanced at the time on the microwave. It read 6:07 p.m. Daddy would be home soon.

"Thank you for dinner, Mama. I have to go soon. I'm not ready to talk to Daddy, and I know he's driving home," I explained.

"Are you sure you don't want to spend the night?"

"I'll be all right. Unloading and cooking with you helped a lot. Now, I only need a warm bath, a hot shower, and sleep."

"You know I'm here for you through everything. Call me if you need to talk, and I'll answer."

"I know, Mama. I love you so much."

I washed my dishes and hugged and kissed her before I left. I was so grateful to have a mother as kind and caring as the one I was gifted with. I know we didn't get to pick the family we were born into, but if I had the choice, I'd still pick them. I had a lot to think about tonight, and my mother's input helped me immensely.

Everything will work out as God intended.

CHAPTER FOURTEEN

Maddox

"P*lease, just go.*"

Talia's words haunted me. They rang through my ears as I walked out of the file room. They rang through my ears as I took the stairs to the ground floor. They rang through my ears as I drove home, showered, and climbed into bed.

"Talia, I'm not complete without you. We can make it work." I pleaded.

"No, we can't!" she sobbed.

Why would God punish me? Why would he put her in my life for us to end so tragically? Why would we build this beautiful soul tie for three months and have shit crash and burn like a highjacked plane? How much begging and pleading would I have to do to get my woman back?

Is she worth the begging and pleading? At what point does it go from persistent to pathetic?

I gulped as I rubbed my hands down my face. "Dammit!"

"Reed?"

My eyes lifted to the sound of the voice. Carruthers was standing outside the car.

"Yeah?"

"You okay, man?" he asked with worry lines indented on his forehead.

I nodded. "Yes." I exited the car and stuffed my hands in my pockets.

"We need to speak with Karmen. I know you've got a lot on your mind, but I think this will be a good distraction," Carruthers explained.

Despite feeling gutted by Talia, life continued. My workload multiplied before I had the chance to breathe. Between Talia, the Duncan case, and the plethora of new cases piled on my desk, I was overwhelmed and exhausted. Not to mention, Talia's words haunted me every idle moment I had. Luckily, due to my full schedule most nights, I was too tired to allow my brain and heart to miss Talia. After spending hours in the field, by the time I came home, I'd pass out on the couch before I got the chance to allow Talia to plague my mind.

"The victim is thirty-six-year-old Carlos Thomas. Thomas suffered multiple gun wounds and lacerations to his hands and ankles. He bled to death in the spot he lay," Karmen explained. She lifted the white sheet to reveal the victim's face.

Instantly, my stomach churned. The queasiness intensified. I recognized the man as one of Diablo's crew. The phone call would come before I left the scene. The more I continued with the corruption, the worse I felt. The guilt started to set in the deepest part of my core and spread like wildfire.

"Thanks, Karmen," I replied. "We'll need copies of the reports."

"On it." Karmen walked over to another crime scene investigator.

Detective Carruthers stayed behind to talk to both of them and ask a few follow-up questions while I looked around the vicinity for any security cameras. I'd have to personally request to retrieve the footage to vet the recordings before I turned it into the evidence. As if on cue, my phone buzzed in my pocket. I made eye contact with Carruthers to signal my call and moved to a discreet area to answer.

"Hello?"

"You know the deal," Diablo stated.

"Look, this is the last one. My squad is under heavy investigation because of the viral Duncan case. I can't afford to get caught up in this mess," I explained.

Diablo chuckled sinisterly. The sound made the hair on the back of my neck rise. "You do *what* I say *when* I say for as long as I say."

"No. I'm done after this." My voice was clear and void of any fear.

"Excuse me?" Diablo quizzed. "What did you just say?"

"You can beat me up, kill me, or whatever else you want to do, but I'm not doing this shit anymore."

Diablo laughed. "We'll see."

The call ended. Deep within the pit of my stomach, I knew I'd made a grave mistake, but I had to clean up my life if I wanted to be a better man for Talia . . .

Talia.

Am I delusional? I must be.

Every action I made somehow circled back to the woman who continued to rip my heart out of my chest. I hadn't planned on having sex with Talia when I requested to speak to her, but the desire was powerful. The initial conversation was supposed to be nothing but answers to my questions. Our connection was too real to ignore the call of her body. Her soul cried out to mine, and unlike her, I wanted to reunite the star-crossed lovers.

"Everything all right?" Carruthers asked as he walked over to me.

"Yes," I dismissed. "I'm going to enter the businesses around the area to see if they'll give us footage over the last forty-eight hours."

"Sounds good. I've talked to Karmen and Helen. They're compositing samples for the report. Karmen said it should be sent back within the next two weeks. She said the labs are backed up, and everything is delayed."

"I don't doubt it," I agreed. "All of my open cases are backed up from labs not being ready to court dates being rescheduled. The world is a mess."

"You got that right," Carruthers agreed. He walked over to the body again and examined the area around the corpse.

With a few quick strides, I walked over to the furniture store adjacent to the crime scene. The door chimed to announce my entrance.

"How may I help you?" an older white man with a gray mustache and balding hairline greeted me.

"There was a murder in the alley next door. I was wondering if your security system works."

"It's an older model with grainy footage, but I can pull up the tapes for you."

"Please."

He nodded and walked off into a back room. While I waited, Talia plagued my mind for the umpteenth time today. It was like I was drowning in the middle of the ocean with no vest to keep me afloat. I was grasping for help with no rescue team in sight. How could I take control of my life when everything felt out of whack?

Could I put my career on the line to make things right with Talia?

Do I come clean to my captain and see what he suggests? Do I risk public backlash and an investigation into *every* case I was a part of for the sake of doing the *noble* thing? Or do I wait until it crashes and burns in my face?

I weighed the pros and cons of all the decisions I had to make in order to breathe without strain. I had to cut ties with Diablo because the longer I stayed under his control, the harder it would be to live in my truth. Talia deserved a man who wasn't working with criminals. She deserved someone man enough to do the right thing regardless of the blowback it would bring.

Talia deserved a man on the *right side* of the law.

Even though her words haunted me, her assumptions of what I did in my job weren't too far from the truth. If the other day in the file room told me anything, it was that she loved me just as much as I loved her. However, she was fighting her feelings harder than I was. I'd come to terms with the fact I wanted to spend the rest of my life with her. She'd come around in due time.

I hope.

Talia would be a more challenging mission. I had to remove myself entirely from Diablo's control. He was my biggest obstacle in going legit and living a meaningful life. Where did it all go wrong? How had I gotten involved so deeply?

As my mind thought back to the first time I was presented with the option to stay legit or fall into the world of corruption, my head began to ache.

———◆———

It was my first day on regular patrol after my undercover job fell through. I was on patrol with Officer Stanton. Three years on the force still made her somewhat of a rookie. She was a short woman, about five foot four. She had short black hair in a pixie cut and always wore dark makeup with signature plum-colored lipstick. She was cool as hell, though. From the short time we'd gotten to know each other, she seemed like great company.

"Before this, I wanted to be a fashion designer," she confessed. "All through middle school and high school, I took designing classes. I even made clothes during my junior and senior years. I was all set to go to fashion school when I witnessed my mother get shot and killed in front

of me. She'd been dating this abusive man. She finally got the courage to leave him, and he shot her in the heart." Stanton's tone was void of emotions.

I assumed witnessing something as tragic as the unjust murder of a mother would create lasting emotional issues.

"Damn." *I rubbed the back of my neck.* "I'm sorry you had to go through that."

"It's okay. I've been through counseling and therapy. I've learned to live with the grief of witnessing something so traumatic."

I licked my lips. "Maybe counseling would help me."

"Similar experience?" *she asked.*

I nodded and added a quick shrug. "I watched my best friend get shot by the police during a raid. He was hit by stray bullets. The pain was extremely hard to process because we were only teenagers. I promised him I'd be the change in the system for him."

"That's beautiful," *she replied.*

The radio beeped, and dispatch signaled in. "We have an active robbery in progress."

I sat up straight in my seat and turned on the siren as Stanton communicated with dispatch. We moved through the dark streets of Houston until we made it to a jewelry store.

"Proceed with caution," *I advised as we exited the car.*

"I'll go around the back. You go through the front door. We'll meet in the middle. Backup is ten minutes away," *Stanton instructed.*

I nodded and pulled my gun from the holster. I took the safety off and got into my defensive position as I pushed through the broken front door. Stanton disappeared around the building. I'd taken all of five steps into the building when my cell phone buzzed in my front pocket.

The hair on the back of my neck rose as I pulled the phone out of my pocket and read the notification. It was the first time I'd gotten a text message from Diablo.

Diablo: Kill him.

How did he know I was here? Does he have a tracker on me? Is he responsible for the robbery?

I looked around the room and noticed the security cameras throughout the building. The red light revealed someone was watching live from somewhere.

Can I kill a man in cold blood? When the moment presents itself to me, can I willingly pull the trigger at the command of a notorious criminal?

I had three just shootings in my career. Would this one change me? Would God condemn me to hell for killing a man?

My phone buzzed a second time. This time, it was a notification from my bank. Six thousand dollars would be available in my account in one to three business days upon processing.

I gulped down the lump that crept up my throat.

This man's life was worth six thousand dollars. I was about to kill a man for six thousand dollars. On the other hand, the money would help pay off some of the debt I'd acquired from Mama's medical bills. If I didn't go through with the killing, it would most definitely guarantee my untimely demise. I imagine Diablo would have his goons chop me up and feed me to the swine. With a somber nod, I moved deeper into the store.

The suspect came into view as he tried to break into the safe. He couldn't have been older than his midtwenties. He'd broken into the wrong business, and now, his life had to end.

"Freeze!" I shouted. "Let me see your hands!"

The suspect jumped with fear as a gun slid out of his grasp.

"Gun!" I shouted and pulled the trigger.

Bang!

Bang!

Two quick shots rang through the air as the bullets penetrated his chest. My hands shook from the pure adrenaline coursing through my body. I watched in horror as his body fell limp against the safe he'd tried to open.

"Reed!" Stanton called out.

"In here," I shouted my reply.

"Are you okay?" she asked as she entered the room with her gun pointed. She looked at the suspect on the floor and placed her weapon into the holster.

I exhaled. "Suspect pulled out his gun and attempted to shoot me. I shot first before he could get me."

•——•••◆•••——•

The ease with which I curated the lie scared me. Maybe I was as bad as Talia assumed. For most of my career, I lied with ease to protect Diablo and keep the cash rolling in. Killing the man— Jamison Greene—had haunted me for years, yet I continued to do what Diablo asked. Diablo paid me enough to get out of medical debt. What would happen to my mother's insurance when all of this blew up in my face? Would I be able to pay the expenses if I lost my job on the force and the side hustle from Diablo? The weight of the world would permanently sit on my shoulders until I figured out what to do.

CHAPTER FIFTEEN

Talia

"The entire department is guilty," Paul announced as he entered the conference room. We all turned to look at him. He wore an expensive suit with a smirk on his brown features. He held a stack of blue folders in his arms. The thickness of the folders piqued my interest.

"What did you find?" Dylan inquired.

"Reports of wrongful arrests, complaints, and open investigations dating back *ten* years. Officer David Mitchell has disproportionately targeted minorities since his rookie years on the squad." Paul passed out the folders to us as he explained his findings.

Upon examining the first few pages, I discovered incident reports and statistics from all the officers, detectives, sergeants, and lieutenants associated with Captain Torres over the last ten years. This was a gold mine for the defense team. Establishing a pattern of bias, racism, and corruption would be the nail in the coffin to get the case dismissed and all charges dropped. Everyone listened to Paul while I spread out the files before me and grabbed my yellow and green highlighters. At every mention of Officer Mitchell, I highlighted the information in green. I was in a good vibe, noting Officer Mitchell's shady ways, when a name caught my attention.

Detective Maddox Reed.

Once I noticed his name, I doubled back and went through with my yellow highlighter and placed a star next to mentions of his name. The more his name came up, the more nauseated I felt. My brain began to pound against my skull. I knew it was too good to be true. He *was* on the wrong side of the law. He was just as crooked as every other cop in the city. I'd been blinded by the lust and pleasure he brought to the bedroom. I'd been blinded by a man showcasing things I'd never experienced before . . . only for him to turn out to be just as horrible and unworthy as everyone else.

It might not have stung as severely had I only seen his name once or twice, but as I looked over the discreet stars, I'd counted almost ten before I decided to spare my heart any more damage. How could my heart recover from such a travesty? I was foolish to think jumping into a relationship with a man I barely knew would end any way other than heartbreak. How could we ever work? If we could find his corruption so easily, who's to say other agencies wouldn't also look into his bad behavior? Could I be with someone who could potentially spend the rest of his life in prison if these crimes were ever brought to light?

Daddy walked into the conference room with bagels and donuts for all of us. He smiled as he set the boxes on the table and stepped back so we could all dig in. I leaned forward and grabbed a glazed donut and a few napkins. As we all enjoyed the unexpected treat, Daddy spoke.

"Good morning," he began.

"Good morning," we mumbled in unison through mouths stuffed with pastry goodies.

"I've gotten a few updates on the case regarding court dates." Daddy rubbed his hands together. "The court is backed up at least two to three weeks from the original dates. The influx of cases received over the last two months has caused a shift in the logs. We are looking at a date at least fourteen to seventeen days out for Donovan's pretrial hearing with the prosecution. I've taken the opportunity to send the prosecution a deadline of thirteen days to dismiss the case or offer a plea deal to avoid the hearing altogether. I'll keep you all updated on their response."

The bile rose my throat as I desperately tried to swallow. I opened my mouth to detest the idea of allowing the prosecution to offer a plea deal, but Dylan spoke up first.

"With all due respect, Mr. Tate," he began. He cleared his throat and straightened his posture. "I don't want to give the prosecution the ability to propose a plea. We have ample evidence to create reasonable doubt. I don't want Donovan to admit guilt to a crime he did not commit because it's permanent."

"The goal is to see what they offer before we go to court. I don't want to force Donovan to do anything he isn't comfortable doing. Trust me, we're all on the same page," Daddy explained. "I see Paul has shown you all the evidence we found against Officer Mitchell."

"Are we going to go after the whole department?" I asked. "With the amount of misconduct, corruption, and racism running through the department, I can't imagine we'll turn a blind eye."

"Hold on, Little Tate," Calvin warned.

My eyebrows knitted together in confusion. "What?"

"You have to pick and choose your battles. We aren't the top law firm in the state because we make enemies with law enforcement. We go after who we need to while keeping our relationships and connections with other aspects of the criminal justice system intact," Calvin explained.

"So, we're supposed to ignore all of the red flags in these files for the sake of hypothetical connections?" I quizzed. "We're supposed to turn a blind eye to the rest of the bad going on in a department created to protect and serve the community?"

"I feel your passion," Bernadette commented. "However, the officers protect their own before they protect us. We don't need an entire police force against us when their testimonies in cases are so important in trials."

"This is horrible," I whined.

"It is," Janice agreed. "But it doesn't change the reality of it all. We all wish these types of situations were black and white, but everything in the justice system is gray and up for interpretation and discernment."

"Our fight isn't to dismantle law enforcement and start a revolution. It's a noble feat, but not what we should be focused on. Our fight is to prove Donovan Duncan's innocence. We will do so by putting Officer Mitchell's questionable past under a magnifying glass," Daddy explained.

"I guess it does put a few things into perspective. I don't like ignoring all of the corruption happening in a city that I love, but I'll focus on the main goal we set," I explained.

My mind was on a swivel as we discussed the top three points for stacking our defense. I'd zoned out several times with my mind drifting back to Maddox. He'd get to live another day as a corrupt detective because he wasn't pertinent to our case. How could I ever look at him again? Hell, at this point, I prayed I never had to.

I walked into my parents' home as the smell of gumbo infiltrated my senses. The spicy and savory scent of the seafood delight made my stomach grumble with anticipation. It was the first Sunday dinner in what felt like forever, where we could all make it.

"Mama," I called out to signal my arrival.

"We're in the kitchen," she responded.

I placed my purse on the table by the door and hung my coat on the rack before walking deeper into the house. From the sound of laughter, my nieces and nephew were playing in the den. My brother and father were in the living room watching Sunday night football. I'd greet them when the food was ready, and we all sat down to eat. When I entered the kitchen, Mama was rinsing the white rice while Kiara set the table in the dining room.

"Hey," I greeted them.

"Hey, Tee," Mama exclaimed with a smile as bright as the sun. I closed the distance between us and gave her a quick kiss on the cheek. She leaned into it graciously.

"What's up, Talia?" Kiara asked as she set the spoons on the table.

"It's great to see everybody tonight," I confessed. "I should've known none of us would miss Mama's famous gumbo."

My mother's gumbo included shrimp, snow crab legs, sausage, chicken, and an assortment of vegetables served with white rice. This was a southern delicacy, and I only ate my mother's recipe because nobody made it like her. The soulful dish would ease my aching soul for a brief moment. A home-cooked meal was definitely one of my favorite medicines to ease an aching heart.

"Girl, you know it," Kiara snickered. "Nobody makes gumbo like Miss Emilia. I wish SJ had gotten the cooking gene from her, but the man can hardly boil an egg."

"Cooking definitely skipped a generation," Mama agreed.

"That's because SJ and Daddy watched sports together every Sunday while I gravitated to the kitchen with you. It's the natural order of things," I added.

"Speaking of SJ and your daddy, can you tell those football nuts the food is ready?" Mama asked.

"Yes, ma'am," I replied.

I walked through the hall to the living room. SJ and Daddy were seated on the edge of the couch, legs spread open, eyes trained on the huge high-definition television with a bottle of beer in hand. Twins. My father and brother looked like identical twins, except one of them was aged several decades.

"Hi, Daddy. Hey, SJ." I stood to the side as I admired two generations of Tate men. I was proud of them. They'd done a great job in protecting and expanding our family. SJ was the first to pry his eyes away from the game. He offered me a gentle smile before he stood to his feet and pulled me into a warm embrace.

"What's up, kid?" he queried while pressing a kiss to my forehead.

"Mama said dinner is ready," I announced.

Finally, Daddy's eyes met mine, and he mimicked his son's movements. "I'm glad you could join us tonight for dinner, Tee."

"Me too," I agreed.

"I was starting to think you forgot I was your dad," he confessed.

My eyebrows knitted together in confusion. "Why would you think that?"

"Because I only see you at work these days. You have been dodging me like I'm some infamous dictator or something," he explained.

"Aw, Dad. I'm sorry for making you feel this way. I guess it is a bit weird for me to switch between employee and daughter around you, but I will try to do better."

"Thanks. Now, let's go get some of that good gumbo."

SJ and I followed Daddy into the dining room. The kids were seated at a smaller table in the corner where they had their small bowls of gumbo. It amused me to see such young people enjoy the food. Most kids their age were picky regarding certain smells and textures. I didn't start eating seafood until I was almost twelve years old. I had to grow into the fishy smell of shrimp and crab before I finally tried it. Once my taste buds matured, I was obsessed with it.

We sat at the table, hot bowls of gumbo and rice in front of us as we said grace and dug in. For a moment, everyone was quiet. The only sounds in the room were the clicks and clinks of the silverware hitting the bowls.

"I might have to take some home with me," I announced as I sat back in contentment.

"Miss Emilia never misses," Kiara agreed.

"I made more than enough for everybody to fill a Tupperware container for leftovers," Mama informed us.

"But don't be greedy. Leave some for us," Daddy chimed in.

"Baby, let them get as much as they want," Mama told him.

SJ and I made eye contact, and I offered him a smile. His response was a slight frown. I rolled my eyes because he could always tell when something bothered me, even when I pushed my feelings to the back of my mind. He was his mother's son when it came to reading emotions.

"Let me get on up and clean my kitchen," Mama announced.

"I'll help you clean up," Daddy offered.

"I'll get the kids cleaned up," Kiara said as she stood.

Everyone made a move to handle something. I tried to figure out how to be of service, but SJ stood up and pulled me with him to the backyard. It was always well kept. Two trees stood at each corner of the fence, and in between was a concrete section with lawn chairs, a table, a grill, and a smoker. A garden was near the house. We helped Mama set it up a few springs ago. She's been able to grow tomatoes and peppers. SJ and I had a lot of great moments growing up in this backyard. I cherished all of them.

"Talk to me," SJ instructed. He sat down on the lawn chair and crossed his arms.

"About what?" I asked.

"You're a smart girl, kid," he responded. "Don't act dumb now."

"Seriously, I don't know what you're hinting at."

"You've been off all evening. I know you been going through a lot, so talk to me."

My lip trembled as I claimed the seat beside him and rubbed at my burning eyes. "I don't want to cry right now."

"Just talk, and I'll listen."

"There's nothing to say," I tried to conclude.

"It's about ol' dude, huh?"

"How did you—"

"For a lawyer, you sure did fall for that . . ."

I laughed. "SJ, *please.*"

"Girl, c'mon. That sadness isn't going anywhere until you talk to somebody." He tapped my foot with his. "What did you find out about your little friend?"

It was against protocol to share my findings with people outside of the office, but SJ was trustworthy. Whatever I shared with him wouldn't be posted in headlines in the morning.

"The man I fell in love with has been doing some questionable things in his career. His name came up several times during our investigation. I know it's a lot to process because I still have strong feelings for him despite all of the pushing away and running I've been doing."

"Do you know why he put his career on the line to do shady shit? Have you talked to him? Has he shared anything with you that would explain his actions?"

I mulled over SJ's questions. My mind drifted to our conversations in Dallas. He'd shared with me his mother's health issues. Anyone drowning in debt may have been forced to do things for extra money. Even though his choices were illegal, he did what he felt was right to ensure his mother had the best medical care they could afford. As I pieced together the missing parts of the puzzle, my head pounded against my skull.

What had started as a cute whirlwind romance had turned into something chaotic and confusing.

"It's not my business to tell, but it makes sense. If Mama were in a similar situation, we'd both do whatever it took to keep her healthy."

SJ hummed. "I'm going to tell you one thing and then let it be." He cleared his throat and leaned his arms against his knees. His eyes trained on me, and the seriousness of his gaze sent a shiver down my spine. "The longer you hide, fight, and run from this man, the more your life will be miserable. You're working on a life-changing case, yet spending most of your free time wallowing in sadness. Face the demon and move on."

"You're right." I agreed. "Thank you, old man."

"Whatever, kid."

We stood up. He pulled me into a tight hug before playfully pushing me. I pushed him back, which sparked a full-on sibling fight.

"I knew I would find the two of y'all doing something you ain't have no business doing," Daddy's voice stated from the back door.

"Blame yo' daughter," SJ retorted while smoothening the wrinkles in his shirt.

I gasped and placed a hand on my chest. "I am *appalled* at the accusation. If my memory serves me correctly, your *son* issued the first attack."

"Both of y'all get in here for dessert before me and my grandkids eat all the banana pudding."

At the promise of banana pudding, SJ and I jogged into the house and headed straight for the kitchen. Peace was restored once we'd both taken a bowl from the counter. Family dinners weren't as frequent as we all wished them to be, but it was a beautiful experience when we had them. Every moment I shared with my family, I was extremely grateful. Many people's childhoods were riddled with trauma and pain. Many people held resentment against family members. Many people didn't have the luxury of feeling safe with the families they were connected with through blood or marriage. I pray to one day add to the family and provide a safe space for my kids to come to me with anything.

The idea of having kids and starting a family hadn't crossed my mind for twenty-eight years. Since meeting Maddox, he'd changed something inside of me. I started thinking about my personal future more than I had since I was a maturing teenager.

I didn't go through the crazy boy stages. My mind had always been on becoming a lawyer. At the forefront of my mind was getting the grades needed for law school. Then it was to obtain the necessary experience to get the position at the firm. Now, as I sit on my throne at T&A, I want more . . .

With Maddox.

The thought created a pause within me. I almost choked on the dessert in my bowl as I returned to reality to escape further thoughts of the man I'd been trying desperately to forget.

"Thank you for dinner, Mama," SJ said. "We have to head back home and get these kids to bed. They've got school in the morning."

"Thank you for coming." Mama pulled SJ into a hug as Daddy did the same with Kiara. Then they switched. I spent the time hugging Kellen, Kyari, and Stephie.

"I'll take y'all out for ice cream and time at the park as soon as I get some free time, okay?"

"Yes!" Kyari and Stephie exclaimed together.

"I'd like that a lot," Kellen agreed.

We said our goodbyes and helped SJ and Kiara load their car. Once SJ had pulled out of the driveway, I turned to my parents and smiled.

"I'll head out now too."

"Thank you for joining us tonight, Tee," Mama said as she held out the bags with my Tupperware filled with gumbo and white rice.

"It was great seeing my baby girl outside of the office," Daddy added. "I was starting to think you didn't want to spend any time with your old man."

I frowned deeply. "That's not true."

"I know, but the ducking and dodging hasn't gone unnoticed."

My attempts at being discreet with my emotional damage hadn't been great. My father was observant and had all of the same qualities as my brother. SJ picked up on my issues over a FaceTime call, so, of course, my father would notice my quirks and tells throughout the day at work. I respected that he'd given me time to come to him, but I still wasn't ready to let him in completely. I looked at Mama to throw me a life raft, and she graciously stepped in.

"It's been a long day. Why don't we pick this up another time? Tee has to drive home, and we don't need her distracted," she explained in a gentle tone.

"All I'm saying is, I miss my baby girl. I didn't want this job to come between us. I want you to know you can still come to me." Daddy pulled me into a hug and pressed a kiss to my temple. My bottom lip trembled, but I fought successfully to ward off the emotional breakdown.

"I know, Dad. I promise I understand. I love you, but right now, I've got to get through this on my own. I don't want you to regret hiring me." My voice was raspy from the obstructed pathway my vocals had to travel through.

"Never. No matter your issues, I'll always be proud to see your name on the employee registry. You make me proud every day by simply existing." Daddy rubbed my back.

"Thank you."

"Always," he replied.

After another round of goodbyes, they walked me to my car and waited on the porch until I drove off. The ride home was heavy. I was exhausted from the conversation with SJ and the random thoughts about Maddox. I'd be glad when my mind, heart, and soul moved on one accord again.

CHAPTER SIXTEEN

Maddox

"The weather is nice," Mama commented as she crossed her hands over her lap and looked at the scenic view from the park bench.

Today was a good day for my mother. Her sugars were the best they'd been in weeks, and her spirit was high. She wore a permanent smile, and I couldn't let the energy go to waste. We packed up my sister's Toyota Rav4 and made it a family day. We hardly had these anymore, so I was extremely grateful to see the four of us spend some quality time together.

Our first spot was a soul food place downtown. Mama ordered an oxtail meal served with yams, greens, and corn bread, but I made sure she only ate half of the corn bread to keep her sugar down. Brielle ordered chicken wings and fries. Brittney ordered a catfish combo, and I ordered the two-piece pork chop meal served with macaroni and cheese and green beans.

After we ate, we went to Hermann Park. We walked the trail and then went to the playground, where dozens of families enjoyed the weather. Some even lay out in the field with blankets for a picnic.

"It is really nice outside," I said.

Brielle was a few feet away, sitting on the swing and making videos on whatever social media app the kids were all obsessed with these days. Brittney was on the bench across from where Mama and I were seated, speaking on the phone with some man. I playfully bumped Mama's shoulder with mine.

"Who is your daughter over there on the phone with?" I asked like the protective brother I was.

"She met a man at work. I think he's some deliveryman who stocks the vending machines at her job," Mama answered in a low tone. "But you didn't hear it from me."

She let out a genuine giggle as her eyes twinkled under the sun's rays. I rubbed her shoulder and joined her with a chuckle of my own.

"You are something else, Lady."

Mama's gaze went back out into the distance. She looked down at her hands before her eyes met mine. I was trapped in her powerful stare. Her eyes held a tsunami of emotions.

"I want to apologize to you," she began.

My eyebrows met in the middle of my forehead in a mixture of confusion and surprise. "Apologize for what, Mama?"

"I have to admit I didn't take my health issues seriously until it was too late. I didn't take the doctors' warnings until the damage had already done a number on me." Her voice was calm but packed with an abundance of raw emotion.

"Mama . . ."

"I've always been a stubborn woman. It's one of the qualities your father loved about me." She smiled faintly. "I didn't take any of my health issues seriously because I didn't want to seem like a failure to the two of you. I didn't want my health issues to burden you, but ultimately, they did. I'm sorry for the stress I put on you throughout the years."

"It's okay, Mama. You raised us to be selfless. Your health is important to me. I would do whatever it takes to ensure you're doing well at the end of the day."

"I know, but you sacrificed so much," she continued. "You put your love life on hold. You should be married with kids and a beautiful wife right now. You stopped living because of the debt my medical bills put us in."

The sadness in her tone tugged hard at my heartstrings.

"Mama, I made the choice. You have no reason to apologize. Family helps family. You busted your ass for us throughout my entire childhood. Of course, I will look out for you and take care of you by any means necessary." I placed my hand on hers.

"I see your sister falling in love. She found a man who treats Brielle like his own daughter, and Brielle loves him and his kids. I want to see it for you as well. When you first mentioned the lawyer lady . . . What is her name?"

I gulped. "Talia."

"Yes. When you first mentioned Talia, you glowed so bright I hardly recognized you. You're usually so closed off and reserved to the world, but you had a permanent smile because she made you so happy. Then it all crumbled to pieces, and you became a robot. Today is the first time in a long time I've seen you look normal. You're drowning your pain by diving into your job. What happens when you no longer have the job as your anchor? When will you face your demons and find someone to bring that glow back, baby?"

Her words floored me. I was too stunned to speak. I was drowning my pain in my work, but even that only seemed to do more damage than heal. I was stuck between a rock and a hard place because my actions created a domino effect in my life. One decision influenced every other choice I'd ever had to make. For the brief time with Talia before everything went to shit, I was in an ignorant bliss without the weight of my job crashing down on me.

"I don't know what I'm supposed to do, Mama," I admitted somberly. "I don't want anybody but Talia, but she's made it clear several times I no longer serve a purpose in her life."

"Move on. If you've fought for her love and she continues to push you away, it may be time to accept defeat and find someone who will value your efforts," Mama advised.

"I don't know if I'm ready to move on," I confessed. "Talia is special."

"Special women are a dime a dozen. You value her, but does she value you?"

"I'm not trying to make excuses for her, but—"

"No buts." Mama touched my cheek and rubbed her thumb against my skin. "You are worthy of unconditional love. A woman should be able to accept you, flaws and all. You've presented your cards to her, and she can choose to fold or play on. However, you shouldn't put your life on hold for a woman who can't see how great of a man she's letting slip away."

I smiled. "A mother's love is something special. You see the best in me, even when I don't deserve it."

"I don't know what you've done in your life to make you think you're not worthy of the world, but you are. You're your father's son. When you love, you love with your entire being, but sadly, it opens you up to a lot of pain in the process. I pray this pain doesn't last forever. I pray your person allows you the space to heal and find your happiness."

"I wish I could have had some time with Dad. I wish you would have found someone to grow old with after he passed away."

Her eyes turned red as the tears burned the brown irises. "No other man could fill those shoes. Your dad was one of one, and starting all over didn't feel right. I got to love him for as long as I needed. I'm content with the choices I made in my life, but I want more for you and your sister. Britt is finally allowing another man the chance to romance her. You should do the same."

"I won't make any promises, but I'll try to enjoy my own company more. I won't try to compensate my sadness with overtime on the job."

"That's a start," she smiled and crossed her hands back on her lap, content with the compromise of my love life.

The rest of the day continued on a lighter note. After the park, we went to Frenchy's, and I ordered a box of chicken, peppers, and fries with fried okra on the side for Mama. We ate the meal at the dining room table. When we finished, Mama took her nighttime insulin, and I tucked her into bed. As I left, Brittney pulled me aside and hugged me.

"What's this for?" I asked but returned the hug, nonetheless.

"We all needed this today. Thank you."

"It's no problem."

She rubbed her hands together. "I've been seeing someone, and I think it's getting serious. He's such a great man, Maddox. He's great with Bri. I'm great with his children, and everything feels . . . *perfect.*"

"I'm happy for you, Britt. I know it hasn't been easy, so I'm glad you found someone to take care of you, for real."

"His name is Trevonte. He's thirty, and he owns a vending machine company. He has machines in over three hundred locations around the city and on several campuses. He said he makes over six figures yearly and would happily care for Mama's needs."

I blinked in surprise. "Yeah?"

"Yes. I know it's a lot to spring on you, but I think he's the one. If he is, it will take a lot of the stress off of you. You've done so much for so long; now, someone else is ready to take that burden off your load."

"That's awesome news, Britt." I offered a smile. "You know I will have to meet this man, right?"

"Absolutely. I can't wait for the two of you to meet. You're going to love him."

The rest of the conversation went by in a blur as my mind ran rampant with the news. My baby sister had found a man ready to give her the world on a golden platter. Seeing her fall in love brought me joy, but I was also leery of the man's intentions. Trevonte might've been godsent, but I was still a protective brother who needed to vet the man personally. I made a mental note to run a background check on him when I clocked back into work.

On the other hand, the weight of Mama's medical bills lifting from my shoulders would be a blessing from God. I'd no longer need to depend on Diablo's transfers to get the job done. It would be easier to walk away from the man.

• • ◆ • • •

The night was lonely. I opened the app I'd met Talia on for the first time in almost half a year. I pushed the thought to the back of my mind as I swiped through potential one-night stands. Yes, I was still heavily in love with Talia, but was a man with needs. I needed to release some pent-up stress I'd felt since the last time I'd been inside Talia.

You've got a match!

The notification caught me at the perfect time. I tapped on it to see a very attractive woman who matched with me. She had honey-blond hair in her picture with bold makeup. I swiped through her pictures again. She wasn't Talia, but she was still beautiful in her own way.

Honey Bea: Hey.

The wink told me exactly what time she was on. I licked my lips as I typed my response.

Me: What's up, baby?

Honey Bea: I'm not going to lie. I'm lying in bed wet af.

I sat up a little straighter as I brought the glass of bourbon to my lips. The brown liquid burned my throat as I gulped down the remaining contents. I needed the distraction. I had to match her energy to get her to drop her location.

Me: You want company?

Honey Bea: Hell yes.

The rest of the conversation involved her sending me her address and telling me the gate code to enter the complex. I'd moved at lightning speed to get to her spot. It took me forty minutes to walk into the studio apartment. The home smelled of lavender-scented candles and the faint smell of weed. I wasn't going to mention it, though. In fact, not many words were said as she led me to the bed and pushed me onto the mattress. I braced myself as she got down on her knees and looked up at me. The fire in her eyes was hypnotizing as she released my dick from the confines of my sweatpants and boxers.

She stared at my length and licked her plump, pink lips. "It's so . . . *big*."

I chuckled. "Do you know what to do with it?"

"Mmm," she replied. She gripped my base and stroked me in firm pulls while rubbing the head. Once I was rock hard and leaking precum, she stuffed my entire length down her throat without a gag reflex.

"*Damn!*" I planted my feet firmly as she sucked me like a professional. She did all of the tricks. "I'm about to nut." The warning fell on deaf ears as she massaged my balls while milking me of every drop of cum. She licked me clean and swallowed every drop.

"You got a condom?" she asked as she stood up and slowly removed her clothes.

"Yeah." I reached into my pocket and pulled it out. I removed the wrapper and placed it on my semihard erection. She grinned and moved onto the bed.

"How do you want me?" she asked in a sexy voice. "All fours? On my back? Facedown, ass up?"

"Facedown, ass up." I stroked myself as she got into position. Her pussy was stretched and prepped while she sucked my dick. All I had to do was penetrate the cute pussy dripping for me.

However, I couldn't. My mind and soul were not in harmony with my raging hormones. Getting head was one thing, but penetrating another woman was harder than I thought.

"Everything all right?" Honey Bea asked.

I let out a frustrated sigh and pulled up my boxers and sweatpants. "I can't do this."

"Oh . . ." The disappointment was evident. "Is it me?"

"Not at all. My heart and soul belong to someone else. I wanted to use you as a distraction, but it's not working."

She frowned and sat cross-legged on the bed. "I understand."

"I'm really sorry for wasting your time."

"It's all right. Have a good night," she mumbled. She stood up from the bed and rubbed a hand through her hair before grabbing her robe and putting it on.

"Good night."

She walked me to the door and didn't wait until I was out of the door good before she slammed it. I didn't feel bad, but I was frustrated. Even when I had a beautiful woman ready to throw it back on me, my soul wouldn't allow me the chance to give myself to someone else. The promise I made to Talia must've been signed in blood.

"This . . ." she stroked my length, "is mine now. I don't want you giving it to anybody else."

Ever since she uttered those words, I'd been under her spell. I didn't want to give it to anyone else. I couldn't. I had to get my woman back.

CHAPTER SEVENTEEN

Talia

"Another one, please," I called out to the waitress as she walked by. She nodded her head as she headed in the direction of the bar to retrieve another pitcher of mango-pineapple mimosas.

"Talia, you sure you need all those mimosas while you're on the clock?" Monique asked.

I giggled. "The courts have been backed up for *weeks*. Regardless, I've done everything I needed to do before I took my lunch. When I leave here, I have a meeting with the DA, but other than that, I'm free to indulge in a little fun. I deserve it."

I didn't mean to come off as aggressive, but I did. I was tired of feeling pain from decisions I made to protect myself and my heart. I was tired of feeling hurt and sadness from my choices to preserve the integrity of my position at T&A.

"You do deserve it. I'm glad you called me. I've missed you a lot, friend."

"I've missed you too. It's been hard finding the balance. I'm glad you're the type of friend who understands we don't always have to talk and hang out to be friends. You're a career woman just as I am, and we make it work."

The waitress returned with another pitcher of mango-pineapple mimosas. I lifted the container and filled my glass to the brim. We'd already finished the first pitcher. We drank the citrus blend while we ate our chicken and waffles. The fried wings were prepared perfectly with the fluffy waffles with crispy edges. The brunch spot was always jumping on the weekends, but on a random Tuesday, it was moderately packed with good vibes and busy chatter.

"We're too grown for the pettiness. As adults, we all have responsibilities. We don't have to call or text every day to be locked in as long as we're there for each other when the time is needed," Monique said as she swirled her straw around her mimosa.

We talked about trivial things for most of our brunch. I'd downed the last of my mimosa when the hair on the back of my neck rose. My heart began to beat faster, and my stomach filled with butterflies. I frowned as I sat back in my chair and looked around the small cafe for the source of the feelings brewing within me.

"Everything okay?" Monique questioned with concern on her features. "You look like you're going to throw up."

"I think I might," I confessed as I picked up my glass of water with a lemon slice. I wrapped my lips around the straw and gulped down half of the water before I began to choke as my eyes landed on *him.*

Maddox.

It was almost as if I'd seen a ghost. I'd done my damnedest to avoid all contact with him since our "incident" in the file room. If someone had to go to the police station, I made sure *not* to volunteer. All interviews with detectives were done by someone other than me. I wanted to minimize as much interaction with the man as possible, and it had worked . . . until today.

He was dressed in a thick pair of black Nike shorts and a white T-shirt. He had a single gold chain dangling around his neck while he wore a pair of Jordans and a gold watch. His hair was freshly cut, and his skin looked amazing. I guess he'd finally moved on.

"What's wrong?" Monique asked as she looked around the small cafe to see who had caught my attention.

"Nothing." I looked away and met her gaze. "We should get the check soon."

"Hmm," Monique hummed.

"Bri, the restroom is over there. Do you need me to walk with you?" Maddox's strong voice pierced through my ears.

The young girl looked at him with a facial expression that said, "*duh.*" She resembled him slightly. She had the same skin tone as him and the same expressive eyes.

"She's been going to the bathroom by herself for *years*, loser," a woman teased as she walked past him to the table near ours. I should have minded my business, but my gaze was locked on them.

Harpo, who dis woman?

The thought would have made me giggle any other time, but right now, I was stalking them like a hawk.

Had he been hiding a family along with his job the whole time? Was he living a double life?

"If you stare any harder, you'll burn a hole in the back of the woman's head," Monique warned.

I felt the heat rise on my face as I tore my eyes away from Maddox and the mystery woman. I chuckled nervously. "I wasn't staring—"

"Girl, if you looked any harder, your eyes would be on the table right now."

"You're so dramatic."

"I'm being honest. Who are they?" she asked.

"I don't know."

"You can tell that lie to anybody else, and they'd believe you, but I know better."

I sighed. "That's Maddox. You know, the guy I was seeing before things got out of hand."

"Ah. You think she's his new bitch?" she asked.

I shrugged. "I don't know what I think."

"Well, put on your investigator goggles and look at the two of them closer. She has all of his features with the addition of some nice titties."

My eyes peeked over at their table again. With clear eyes, I could see the uncanny resemblance. She wasn't his secret lover but his sister. Brittney. I remember him telling me about her. So the little girl must be Brielle. His family was beautiful. What were the odds of us being here at the same time in the middle of the same day? I had to get the hell out of Dodge before Maddox saw me.

"I'm going to go to the restroom," I announced. "If the waitress comes before I return, here's my portion of the bill." I pulled out three twenties to pay for my meal and the pitchers of mimosa.

I stood up from my seat and made my way to the restrooms. Quickly, I pushed through the door and stared at myself in the mirror. I splashed water on my face and dabbed my face dry with a paper towel.

"You're okay," I said to myself. "You're stronger than this moment."

I took a few calming breaths and smoothed out wrinkles in my blouse before I turned on my heels and exited the restroom— only to crash into a familiar, broad chest. His scent gave him away before his appearance did. His hands held me by my arms to keep me from tumbling to the floor.

His embrace sent my body into hypersensitivity. The feel of his fingers against my skin created a heat I hadn't felt in weeks. My body craved him. When my feet were steady, I stepped back and averted his intense gaze as I pushed the feelings down.

"Sorry," I mumbled. My arms crossed against my chest to fill the void created by the absence of his embrace.

"It's okay." He licked his lips and tucked his hands into his pockets. "How are you?"

"Please don't do this."

He frowned. "I can't see how you're doing?"

"No."

"Why not?"

I shrugged. "I have to go."

His hand grabbed my arm again. This time, I didn't pull away. "Before you go, tell me how you're doing. Please."

"I've had better days. I'm okay, though. I'm going to be all right."

He smiled softly. "I feel you. I'd be better with you by my side . . . or in my bed."

"Don't."

"I'm just saying. I'm making some changes in my life, and I hope one day, you'll be able to see me for the man I am and not the man I was."

"Have a good day, Maddox." I pulled out of his grasp and hurried out of the cafe. When my body felt the fresh air, my lungs exhaled a breath I didn't know I was holding. I shook my hands to release the built-up nerves.

"You spoke to him?" Monique's voice came from behind me, startling me.

"Yeah," I replied.

"Are you okay?" she followed up.

"I think so."

"Don't let seeing him ruin all the healing you've done since you cut ties with him. You're stronger than that. Plus, you have a meeting with the DA to prepare for. Don't let him get in your head right now."

"I won't," I lied.

"Text me when you get home," she ordered.

I agreed to do so and climbed into my car. My movements were on autopilot as I went through the motions. Seeing him, hearing his voice, and feeling his touch were too much for my damaged heart to deal with.

━━━━━◆━━━━━

"Sorry for my tardiness," I rushed out as I entered the office of Deputy Defense Attorney Tellyn Mims.

Tellyn Mims was an older Black woman with salt-and-pepper-colored hair and round, framed glasses with lenses at least two inches thick. She wore red lipstick and a black-and-white skirt suit with dark pantyhose underneath. Her feet were stuffed into a pair of red bottom heels.

"No worries," she dismissed. "Thank you for joining me today. Please have a seat." She pointed to the chair across from her desk. I sat down as she sat in her chair behind the desk.

"You're here to discuss the plea deals for . . ."

"Donovan Duncan."

"Right. My office is open to a few options. He can plead guilty to aggravated robbery and spend five years in prison," Tellyn stated while reading off a piece of paper.

Aggravated robbery was a first-degree felony. I would not allow a felony record for Donovan.

"No. Next option," I stated with a blank face.

"You are aware we have a solid case against the defendant. I know you want to have your trial and get your name out there, but this isn't the case to do that. A young man's life is on the line, and you're still wet behind the ears."

I blinked as her words registered in my brain. "Excuse me?" I cleared my throat. "With all due respect, you don't know me or the type of lawyer I am. My main priority is to prove my client's innocence. He will not agree to any plea with a felony on the table."

"Looks like we're done here then."

"See you in court," I muttered.

I stood up from my seat and walked out of the office. The pounding of my heels on the tiled floor bounced off the walls as I headed toward the elevators. When I reached my car, I checked my phone for any calls or texts from my teams. I sent a mass email to everyone, with my father cc'd to the thread. I informed them of the offers and how I declined any offer with a felony attached. I explained that I disagreed with how she talked to me and that she indicated that their case was stronger than it really was.

Her whole case was riding on the statements from a crooked cop. As soon as we presented the information, she'd be going to trial with a case she'd most likely lose, regardless of the lawyer sitting the first chair for Donovan. I brought my engine to life and turned on my gospel playlist. I needed the anointed voices of Tamela Mann, The Pace Sisters, and The Clark Sisters to strengthen me on the drive home. Suddenly, my phone buzzed with a text notification from my father.

Papa Bear: Hey, Tee. Can you call Donovan and let him know the progress of the case?

Me: Yes, sir.

Instead of calling him, I decided to stop by his parents' home to check on him in person. I know it was all business on our end, but for him, we were toying with his freedom in the world. I wanted to check on his mental well-being. Even the strongest of us were subjected to depression, anxiety, and stress.

The ride to the Duncan home took thirty-nine minutes because of the stop-and-go traffic. One thing I always hated about the city was the unnecessary amount of traffic at any time of the day.

I-45, 610, and I-10 were some of the worst roads to travel. When I parked in front of the street, Mrs. Duncan emerged from the front door and stood on the porch. I exited my car and waved to her. The sun had begun to set, and a cool breeze flowed through the air.

"Good evening," I called out as I walked up the path to the front door.

"Good evening. What brings you by?" she asked.

"We have a few updates to Donovan's case I wanted to share with y'all in person. I also wanted to check on the family. I know this can't be easy for y'all."

"Come on in," she instructed.

We walked into the home, and the warm air hugged me like a thick blanket. She led me to the couch where Mr. Duncan and Donovan sat watching ESPN sports highlights.

"Good evening," I spoke to the men in the room.

"Hey, Miss Talia," Donovan greeted me.

"Hi, Miss Talia," his father mimicked.

"I don't want to take up too much of y'all's time, but I'm here to discuss a few things about the case and to check in on y'all." I rubbed my hands together. "I met with the DA to discuss a potential plea deal. They offered felony charges, and I made it abundantly clear we would not consider any felony deals. Our next move is to speak with a judge again before going to trial. With the judge, we'll present all the evidence against the officer who made the arrest." I leaned forward with a gentle smile. "I wholeheartedly believe we can get the case dismissed and avoid court altogether."

Donovan smiled. "I hope so. It's been hell these last few months. Jeremy and I receive hateful DMs all day, every day, from internet trolls and racists. They call me any and every slur known to man. I get death threats, and I know my parents do too. It just isn't fair. I barely got twenty likes on my posts before the arrest . . . Now, everybody either treats me like the leader of the next revolution or a serial killer. I don't know what to do besides block trolls and stay off social media. It's so polarizing and draining." Donovan dumped all of his emotions on me.

His words tugged at my heartstrings. He was so young and didn't deserve the negative attention the case put on him. Death threats were unnecessary when no one was injured in the crime to begin with. The internet was a weird place. It changed lives for the better or the worse. Everyone was a misguided and misinformed post away from being targeted and threatened by millions of strangers on the internet. I almost hated our digital world, but I saw the good it did for so many people.

"I can't say I understand what you're going through, but I do empathize with you. I promise, the talented lawyers on your case and I are doing everything in our power to rectify the mistakes the officer made."

"We appreciate you," Mrs. Duncan responded. "I want us to go back to some form of normalcy when all of this is over, but for the time being, we're keeping our faith in God and T&A."

The rest of the conversation ended on a lighter note. When I was finally ready to head home, I promised another update in the following weeks. I prayed we were able to provide some solace for this family soon.

CHAPTER EIGHTEEN

Maddox

"Thank you for meeting with me, David," I said in a bored tone.

Captain Torres had me dotting our i's and crossing our t's as we prepared for the upcoming court case. The DA had been on our ass for days because of a meeting she'd had with Talia. From the annoyance in her voice, I pictured her and Talia getting into a heated discussion, and Talia didn't cower away or back down. Tellyn had a way of intimidating her way to convictions, but she was in for a battle with the Tates.

"I'll be glad when all of this shit is over with," he confessed. "One arrest has had me in more cameras in the last two months than in my whole career."

"Man, tell me about it. Captain Torres told me we've all been under a microscope. Apparently, Tate's people have documents dating back almost a decade with all of our history."

At this revelation, Officer David Mitchell gulped. "They did?"

"Yeah, man. Captain said they sent the evidence over to the DA. They'll put all of our dirty laundry on display during the trial," I explained nonchalantly.

When I first heard the information from my captain, I was terrified, similar to how David was shitting a brick across from me right now. It would be the end of me when I got on the stand and had my judgment questioned. Though terrified, I was also relieved to know I'd have an out soon. I'd no longer be of use to Diablo, and we'd be able to end things like cordial men . . . hopefully.

"I . . ." David trailed off as he ran his hands down his face and swore under his breath.

"Look, you know you're a great cop, so don't let them get under your skin. You don't have to answer anything that will incriminate you on the stands. Yes or no answers only. You can plead the Fifth if you need to."

David shook his head. "I've done a lot of wrong in my career." He sighed as he looked off into the distance, his eyes no longer in the present. "When I made the arrest . . . I knew in the pit of my gut everything would go wrong."

I looked at him sincerely as I tried to decipher his words. "David, did something go wrong during the arrest?" I asked carefully.

The look in his eyes answered my question before he could. From the sadness in his aged eyes, he was about to make a devastating confession. To protect myself in the situation, I discreetly pressed *record* on my cell phone.

"I'm not sure my arrest was a hundred percent clean," he admitted.

I let out a deep breath. "What happened?"

"I lost the suspect in the alley. That's why Captain Torres cut the footage." He rubbed his hands together and exhaled. "It was dark, and I didn't know which way the suspect went, so I picked a path and ran. I panicked when I saw the kid coming out of the gas station. I noticed the differences but rationalized my actions at the moment. I arrested the kid and probably ruined his life, but I had to do *something*."

Anger rose within my core. His actions inadvertently ruined the best relationship I'd ever had. I blamed my breakup on Officer

Mitchell because if he had not arrested Donovan Duncan in the first place, Talia and I would have been celebrating five months together. It was immature of me to think like I did, but it was my natural reaction to the admission.

"You were going to take this information with you to the grave? You were okay with letting the young Black man rot in prison as long as you weren't affected in the long run?" I quizzed.

David hung his head. "Yes."

"You should get ready for the backlash. Tell someone about this so the case can get dismissed. You don't want the entire department to crumble because of your mistakes," I advised.

Either way, I would be turning over the recording to Talia before the end of the day. I wanted her to get the victory and props for the discovery. Would we be able to fix our relationship when the case was over? Regardless, I wanted to clear my conscience and do the right thing.

"We've all done wrong," David rationalized. "I'll think about confessing my sins one day, but today ain't that day."

"I hear you." I shook my head while I lifted my shoulders into a short shrug. "You do what you deem is best for you. But be prepared for the consequences when this case goes to trial, and all your arrests are put under a microscope."

"I need to go home and talk to my wife." Officer Mitchell rose to his feet.

"Good luck."

He nodded and exited the room. When he was no longer in sight, I lifted my phone and pressed the red button to stop the recording. I replayed the conversation and made sure I got his confession clearly. Then I opened up my text thread and sent a message to Talia.

Me: Hey, can we talk?

I waited a few minutes to see if I would get a reply. When two minutes turned to ten, I decided to take a professional route. I tapped the email icon on my home screen and typed the message.

Subject: *URGENT*

Email:

Good afternoon, Miss Tate,

I hope this email finds you well. I have come into contact with pertinent information regarding the Duncan case that I believe you would find interesting. I want to hand off the information in person to keep the chain of custody as tight as possible.

At your earliest convenience, please send me a date and time when you are available to talk.

Detective Maddox Reed

Once I sent the email, I exited the conference room and left the station. I didn't want to talk to anyone else before I spoke to Talia. I'd deal with the repercussions once the deed was complete.

My phone buzzed as I entered my Mustang, indicating a new message was received. I clicked Talia's name and read her text.

Talia: Meet me at the Ramen spot. I'm here eating an early dinner. I can order something for you if you prefer, but I hate to conduct important business on an empty stomach.

Me: I'll be there in ten.

My body moved at hyperspeed. This would be the first time in almost a week since I'd seen her face. The last time I saw her was while I was out with Brittney and Brielle. I'd taken them to brunch on my off day, where I could also meet Britt's new man. The last person I expected to see was Talia with one of her friends.

The opportunity to speak with her there would be almost impossible. However, I saw my window when she exited the bathroom. Her absent mind caused her to bump into me, and for a brief moment, peace was restored in my soul when I wrapped my hands around her to keep her from hitting the floor. Even in those few minutes together, she still felt for me as much as I felt for her. She was stubborn, but I would knock down the barrier again and get my woman back after the case.

━•━━━━••◆••━━━━•●

As I returned to the small mom-and-pop shop, memories of the last encounter flooded my mind. The smell of the authentic ramen seasonings filled my senses as my eyes scanned the close-knit space. Talia was seated in the same booth from the last time we'd been here. When our eyes met, the palms of my hands glistened with a layer of sweat. I discreetly rubbed my clammy appendages onto the legs of my pants and closed the distance between us.

"Hey," I spoke first.

"Hi," she replied softly. "The email said it was urgent, so what's up?"

I licked my lips and placed my phone on the table. "Before I tell you, I want to clarify that I don't wish to gain anything from turning this over. I did this solely to protect Donovan and his family from any further pain and suffering Officer Mitchell's actions have caused."

Talia raised her perfectly sculpted eyebrow as curiosity presented itself in her beautiful features.

Damn, I miss this woman.

"What do you have to show me? You have piqued my interest."

I opened my phone and pressed *play* on the recording. At a moderate volume, the conversation between Officer Mitchell and I replayed. Talia listened intently. I watched her eyes widen when the confession played for her ears to hear.

"Do you know what this means for the case?" she asked with excitement laced in each word she spoke.

"I figure you and your people will take it to the DA and get all charges dropped," I guessed.

"Exactly. Donovan and his family can get some form of relief." She grinned. "Can you send this to me in an email?"

"Of course." I copied the file and attached it to our email thread.

"Got it!" she squealed. "You have no idea what this will do for my career. I know my father is going to want to talk to you—"

"I don't want any attention on me. I'm going against many people to turn this in to you. I've done a lot of wrongs myself, which I'm sure you discovered during the investigation."

Talia's head tilted down as she digested my statement. It wasn't rocket science. I'd known the moment Captain Torres told me about the defense team's discovery that my wrongdoings over the years would be mentioned in the documents. Everything had a paper trail; sometimes, we were lucky enough to go unnoticed. However, other times, someone's mishaps could create a domino effect to reveal a mountain of hidden secrets.

"I know you don't want any attention, and I can make speculations as to why . . . but we're going to need formal statements and your cooperation when we present the recording to the DA," Talia explained.

"Let me be a last resort. I will probably cut ties with the department soon, anyway."

Talia's features softened. "Are you sure?"

"There's no coming back from a betrayal like this. I made an oath to stand by my police family, and I didn't. I'll be a sitting duck if I remain on the force. It's best if I end things on a high note."

"Wow." She exhaled. "I know this wasn't an easy decision to make."

"It wasn't, but I can always find something new."

I'd spent most of my life with a badge to my name. Where would I fit in the world if it weren't for solving crimes and protecting the city? What other skills did I have besides knowing how to shoot a gun and chase down criminals?

I had to sit down and think about the future I wanted for myself. I was only thirty-three years old. I still had at least another thirty or so years ahead of me.

"I'm sure you'll do great things wherever life takes you," she professed softly.

"You don't have to do that," I informed.

"Do what?"

I let out a chuckle. "Pretend to care. You've made it clear you don't want anything to do with me."

I wanted to test my theory. Would she finally be open to being with me if I no longer had ties to the police department? Would she finally see me as "Captain Matt," the man she fell for a few months ago?

Her features hardened as she looked away. She chewed on her bottom lip. Her body told me one thing while her lack of a response said another. She was conflicted internally about how to proceed.

"You've haunted my dreams for months," she confessed. "I haven't had a night of peace since we were last here in this shop." She placed her hands in her lap and took a few calming breaths.

"You don't have to share with me if you don't want to."

She looked at me with watery eyes. "I-I want to."

The moment I'd been waiting for since we parted ways the first time . . . I was ready for her to share with me the truth. I was ready for her to open up her heart and hand me the tools to repair the damage. I was ready for redemption.

"I was terrified. I dove headfirst into the powerful, intense relationship with you, and everything hit me like an NFL D-line. I was blindsided and scared. I didn't want our fairy-tale romance to end, but it had to for the sake of my sanity and professional career."

"We could have made it work," I repeated for the umpteenth time since we broke up. "I get it, though."

"You don't." She cleared her throat and placed her elbows on the table. "Since I was a little girl, I wanted to fill my daddy's shoes as a lawyer. I kept my head in the books, rarely made friends, and hardly entertained relationships. My main goal—no—my *only* goal was to become a lawyer and climb the ranks of T&A. When I met you, you broke down the barriers of my mind and heart. You woke my soul up and showed the neglected being that there was more to life than law. It tested the very core of my existence."

I processed her words carefully. I can see how my influence could create some conflict within her. I exposed her to things she hadn't experienced before. We'd both held on to ignorant bliss when we should have been clean with each other the moment things became more serious than hotel hookups.

"The more I fell for you, the scarier it became. I was falling for you without knowing everything there was to know about you. I was afraid to find out something bad. When I saw you on the news, I knew this would be my way out of the situation. I would end things for the sake of my career and to protect my heart . . ." She folded her arms. "But in all honesty, it only made things worse. I'd have a decent day at work and then cry myself to sleep at night because of the void I felt in my heart from no longer being able to call you and hear your voice before I fell asleep. You embedded yourself in my deepest crevices, and I've tried every way to vacuum you out of my life."

"I'm a hard man to get rid of," I added.

"You really are."

"So, what does this mean for us?" I asked.

"I don't want to make any promises, but I will say this ..." She leaned forward with a smile. "Once this case is closed officially, I'll be happy to invite you over for a celebratory drink, and maybe ... We can discuss the future then."

My cheeks ached from the stretch of my lips as my mouth turned into a big grin. "I'd like that a lot."

The start of my day was boring and uneventful. Then I spoke with Officer Mitchell, who handed over a confession I hadn't expected. Now, as I looked into the bright brown eyes of the woman I'd been fighting to get back for months, my day had shifted into a blessing. Talia was open to a future with me. A potential rekindled flame was on the horizon, and several significant changes were about to occur in my life.

We talked for a little longer before I ordered a ramen bowl to go and left. The smile didn't leave my face for the duration of the night. Despite the threat of my choices awaiting, I had a good night's rest with beautiful dreams of spending forever with Talia.

CHAPTER NINETEEN

Talia

"**W**here did you get this?" Daddy quizzed after he listened to the recording for the third time.

When I got Maddox's initial text, I thought he was begging to see me again, like the first time he'd sent the same message when we were interviewing Officer Mitchell at the firm. I didn't want to risk a repeat where I ended up with my panties pooled around my ankles. His email afterward piqued my interest. I was curious to learn about the "urgent matter" he wanted to discuss. Of all the things I might have guessed he wanted to talk to me about, I didn't expect a recorded confession from Officer Mitchell.

It was like I'd struck oil. I sent a copy of the recording to the whole team before I left the ramen shop. The following day, we all gathered in my father's office and played the tape three times.

"The person who sent the original file wants to remain anonymous. He said he would confirm the findings to the DA if needed, but I can guarantee the authenticity of the recording," I explained.

"The case is ours," Dylan exclaimed excitedly. "Once the DA hears this confession, she'll have no other choice but to dismiss all charges against our client."

"Talia and I will set up the meeting with the DA. Everyone else, be prepared for a press conference this evening. Paul and Janice, please contact the Duncans. I want them to be present at the conference. Team A, you've all been a wonderful help as well. Please draft a formal press release and talk with Kelly about new cases."

Everything moved fast. Within the hour, Daddy and I had entered the office of Tellyn Mims. On the way to her office, I texted Maddox to let him know he might be called upon to confirm his findings. He sent me a text back to let me know he was prepared.

Tellyn was seated at her desk with a smug look as she listened to the recording. "How can you confirm the authenticity?"

"My source is on standby if needed," I responded. "You can also run the file through any system, and I'm positive you won't get any hits for alterations."

She crossed her arms over her chest. "You expect me to believe you?"

I opened my mouth to respond, but Daddy beat me to it. "Watch yourself, Tellyn. We can call both Officer Mitchell and Detective Maddox into the office right now to confirm or deny their voices are on the tape."

"Do it," she barked.

Before anyone could lift a phone to dial a number, a firm knock pounded against the office door.

"Come in," Tellyn instructed.

The door opened to reveal Maddox. He walked in with his head held high while Tellyn looked like she'd seen a ghost.

"I know my presence was requested." His voice was void of any fear. He was firm in his stance as he held his hands by his sides and looked the woman in her eyes. "I confirm the voices on the recording are David and I. He spoke to me and confessed he made the wrong arrest. He targeted Mr. Duncan because the young man was in the wrong place at the wrong time and fit the vague description of a Black man wearing a hoodie."

Tellyn nodded. "Thank you, Detective."

Maddox nodded and turned to look at me and my father. "Congratulations. I hope you can extend my apologies to the family. They didn't deserve to go through any of this."

Daddy stood up and reached out to shake Maddox's hand. My heart punched my rib cage as I watched them. If only my father knew what those hands were capable of. My cheeks warmed as the memories of the nights we shared filled my mind. However, it wasn't the time to turn into a puddle. But now that the stress of the case was gone, I could clearly weigh my options.

"Thank you for doing the noble thing," Daddy said to him. "If you have any blowback, I have a spot at my firm for you."

I was positive my eyes were as big as bowling balls as I registered my father's words. He had offered Maddox a job. What the hell could the man do at Tate and Associates? I wouldn't be able to work with a man I wanted to . . . My thoughts calmed as Maddox chuckled.

"I'll think about it, but I doubt T&A is a place for me," Maddox replied. "Y'all have a great day."

Maddox left the office, and silence washed over us.

"The authenticity of the recording has been confirmed. Do you want to continue to play games, or can we bring peace to a family who has been through hell?" I asked in a calm voice.

Tellyn remained silent for a moment. She stared at me and my father with narrow eyes and lips pursed together. Her arms were crossed against her chest.

"The case is dismissed. I'll send the official dismissal to the judge," she finally announced.

I smirked with a triumphant exhale. Daddy stood up and walked over to her. He outstretched his arm to initiate a handshake. Reluctantly, Tellyn shook his hand.

"We will hold a press conference with the Duncans at four o'clock this afternoon. We'll release a press release to all major news outlets today at six o'clock. Have a great day, Mrs. Mims," Daddy said in a professional tone.

"Good day."

My father and I walked out of the room without another word. I remained calm and collected until we exited the building. Finally, I turned to look at my father and jumped into his arms.

"We did it!" I shouted as he spun me around.

As my feet returned to the concrete ground, Daddy smiled at me. "*You* did it. Because of *your* hard work and connections, we secured a confession. You've exceeded all of my expectations. I'm proud of you."

My emotions got the best of me. I crumbled to pieces as the floodgates fell and tears poured from my eyes. I clung to my father in the middle of the sidewalk and buried my face deep into his chest as relief and joy flowed through my body. My chest was light as my head spun slightly from the overwhelming feelings coursing through me.

"What's wrong, baby girl?" Daddy asked as he rubbed my back.

It took me a few minutes to calm down. As I regained my composure, I pulled a napkin from my purse and dabbed at my eyes and nose. Finally, I released a sigh of contentment. "Sorry. It was a happy cry. I'm so glad Donovan gets the happy ending he deserves. I was so scared the justice system would fail because of racism and implicit biases, but we beat it all. The good beat the evil."

"You have every right to celebrate this victory. No need to apologize for your natural response to your first big win. You're going to do even greater things." Daddy gave me a pat on my shoulder. "We must return to the firm and prepare for the press conference."

Time seemed to move in a blur. I was on a natural high the rest of the day. Everyone's hard work throughout the case was refreshing and uplifting. The air in the office was lighter as we all celebrated the freedom and release we gave Donovan and his family.

Despite my joy, a lingering feeling of anxiety nagged at my gut. With Maddox's involvement in our firm's victory, he could be blackballed or attacked by his department. Would they put *him* on trial next? What did the future hold for him? He'd risked his life and career to do the right thing, but where would he go from here?

I pushed thoughts of Maddox to the back of my mind while the press conference went without a hitch. Reporters were like vultures swarming the firm with cameras and recording devices. They all wanted to be the first to stream the event. The only noteworthy instance from the press conference was something my father said that stuck with me.

His stance was firm and powerful. His eyes were sincere and inviting. He was invincible with the Duncans and Jeremy standing beside him on the stage.

"Today, justice won. Donovan and his family can rest easier knowing he wouldn't be yet another statistic to systemic racism in the criminal justice system. Today, justice saved a life. Today, we can reassure a mother and father that their son won't become a felon because of the color of his skin. We proved Donovan's innocence, and the public owes him a huge apology."

After the press conference, we all popped champagne and cleaned the conference room for the next major case and team. Putting all our files and findings in a box and sealing it up was a bittersweet moment. The team taught me so much. I grew as a lawyer during the duration of the case. I was thrilled we didn't take the case to court. We protected the client to the very end, and I was grateful for the experience it garnered.

"Miss Talia," Donovan's voice pierced through my thoughts. My head lifted from the box of evidence to the young man standing at the door with unmistakable joy radiating from him. His eyes were the definition of happiness. His face was painted a permanent hue of relief. His body language was more confident as he strolled into the conference room.

"Hey, Donovan," I responded. "You look happy."

"I *am* happy, thanks to you and the rest of the defense team. You guys really saved my life. I can breathe easier now. I can stand a bit taller. I can return to some sort of normalcy, and soon, the world will forget about me and latch on to the next trending topic. Thank you." He pulled me into a hug, and I happily hugged him back. Our smiles were identical.

"So, what's next for you?" I asked.

"I'm going to go back to school. I don't want to waste my life anymore. I will focus on my passions and find ways to improve the world through art. I want to make a difference like all of y'all here, but in my own way," he explained earnestly.

"That's beautiful," I commented.

A second chance could really turn people's lives around. A traumatic experience could put someone on a path they'd never imagined traveling. I wanted to see Donovan win. I wanted his success in the future to change more lives. He deserved to live a long and prosperous life, and we were able to provide that.

———◆———

The high of the evening found me at home sipping a glass of wine. I'd been invited to drinks with the team but decided to celebrate in the comfort of my home, away from the public. The case's dismissal would have eyes on our firm, and I didn't want to be caught in the media for any reason.

Instead, I took a bubble bath, poured my favorite sparkling wine, and kicked back on the couch. I turned on a movie, but my mind didn't allow me to focus on the plot for long. Finally, I picked up my phone and tapped a thread I'd ignored for long enough.

> **Me:** Thank you again for turning in the confession recording. A young Black man gets to go home and rest easy tonight after weeks of being ostracized and ridiculed by the public. What you did was heroic.

> **Maddox:** It was the right thing to do. I'd done my wrongs in the past. I wanted my final act in the department to be meaningful. I saved a young Black man from the dangers of the criminal justice system. So many men who look like us aren't as lucky. I've seen both sides.

I reread his message a few times. I remembered him saying something at the ramen shop about being ready to cut ties with the department. Was he finally quitting his job to go legit? Would he turn himself in for the crimes he committed? Would he try to skirt under the radar and avoid real repercussions for his crimes? The more my mind rattled off questions, the more I wanted to ask him the things on my mind. I chewed on my bottom lip as my thumbs hovered over the keyboard. Should I ask him? Finally, I pushed all doubt from my mind and just let the conversation flow.

> **Me:** Do you have plans for the future? What do you think is going to happen once you leave the force?

> **Maddox:** I've made amends with my wrongdoings. There is a final game plan in play. I'm waiting for the perfect time to get everything set up. I'm not afraid of what could happen. I've come to terms with the possibility of jail time if need be, but I'm

sure I can cut a deal with some of the agencies to get a killer whale out of the ocean.

I was relieved to see he had a plan in place. My curiosity wanted to know what "killer whale" he did business with, but for my sake, it was best to remain ignorant of the gritty details. We texted for a bit longer before the conversation took a sharp turn.

Maddox: I don't want to scare you away, but I haven't been able to get you off my mind. I miss you . . . I miss us.

I should have known we'd end up here. I lifted my wineglass and emptied the contents down my throat. Then I picked up the bottle, refilled the glass, and repeated the steps. I needed a little fuel to get through this conversation.

Me: I miss us too. It's been rough, but I did what I needed to protect myself during the case. Had we gone to trial, they would have found any and everything to tear my defense up.

Maddox: The trial is over. I'm no longer a liability to your image. Can we try again? Can I see you tonight?

Me: Yes.

I let out a breath as the text message was sent. All of the red flags I had, which led to me ending things with Maddox in the first place, were no longer an issue. He'd stated he was leaving the force, he said he was going to rectify the wrongs he'd done, and he was taking small steps into a life of good.

It was worth a try . . . right?

Me: I don't want to do the sneaking around and hiding again. I don't want to keep anything from you, and I wouldn't want you to keep anything from me. With that being said, here's my address.

I sent the map link to my apartment complex. I told him to put my apartment number into the gate box, and I'd buzz him in. Once the plans were set, I put my phone on the coffee table and straightened up. Granted, there wasn't much to clean as I kept a pretty tidy home besides the chaos in my office. I lit some candles around the living room and the bedroom, *just in case*. I chilled some red wine and pulled on a pajama set consisting of a tank top and shorts with cute stripes.

The knock on the door startled me, even though I'd buzzed him in a few minutes earlier. I jumped up from the couch and took a deep breath before I walked to the door and pulled it open. Maddox looked mouthwatering good. His scent greeted me before his words did. He smelled of a warm, woodsy aroma—a fragrance I missed so much. The pounding in my heart was in rhythm with the pounding between my legs as I took in his appearance. He wore his signature relaxed look of a white T-shirt and gray sweatpants. A gold chain dangled from his neck. I wanted to reach out and pull him into a warm embrace, but I refrained. Instead, I opened the door for him to walk in.

"Hey," I greeted him.

"Hey."

He walked in, and I began to feel a bit self-conscious. This was his first time in my home. He was in my personal space and got to see a part of me he'd never seen before.

"Thank you for inviting me over," he said smoothly. "You have a nice place here."

"Thanks. Do you want a tour? I mean, it's not much, but it's mine."

"Aye, that's all that matters. You've got a space where you get to walk around naked, do what you want, and be comfortable."

"You're right." I gestured to the couch. "Have a seat. I'll go get some wine."

"Yes, ma'am."

Once seated with wine in hand, I crossed my legs on the couch and smiled at him. "I'm a bit self-conscious . . . but I'm happy to have you in my home."

His tongue slid across his juicy bottom lip. I watched the action like a vulture.

"It's nice to see you in this light," Maddox commented. "I've missed you." He leaned closer and placed his hand on my exposed thigh. The heat from his touch slid from my thigh to my throbbing bead. "These last few months have been hell. My soul was broken because we weren't together."

My heart rate increased. I could hear the beating in my ears. The wine made concentrating difficult as his thumb gently massaged my inner thigh.

"Maddox . . ."

"Open up to me, baby. Let me in again. Tell me all the things you went through and how we can fix us." He placed his hand on my neck. I leaned into the warmth of his touch.

I wanted to release the pain I'd held for so long.

God, give me the strength.

CHAPTER TWENTY

Maddox

"We were on a natural high for three months. My best friend told me I was a fool for remaining in ignorant bliss when I should have pressed the issue more," Talia explained as she placed her hand atop mine.

As I sat on her couch, with my hand on her thigh, I reveled in the moment. Her home was cute and quirky like she was. Her hard exterior was nonexistent in the comfort of her apartment. The decor matched her perfectly. The only thing missing was . . . *me.*

"I should have done my due diligence and discovered everything there was to know about you. It wasn't the fact you were a cop that broke my heart . . . It was the fact you were the lead detective on a case accusing a young Black man of a crime he didn't commit. It was the blind protection of an officer before the safety of someone who already had to deal with the odds stacked against him."

I nodded my head to show my understanding of her perspective. "I didn't become a cop because I wanted the power. I wanted to make a difference. After the death of my best friend, I made a vow to be the change I wanted to see. Then life got real. My mother got sick, and my back was against the wall. I did what I had to do to protect my family. She'd done her damnedest to raise me and my sister, and I felt it my obligation to return the sentiment."

I explained my history and how I'd gone undercover and was made as a cop. I told her how my life was on the line if I didn't comply. I wasn't proud of my choices, but I stood ten toes about them because I did what I needed, and my mother currently gets to live to see many more days.

"I can't say I understand completely, but if I were faced with similar obstacles, I'm sure I would have done whatever was necessary to protect my family as well."

"I'm sorry for the decisions I made that you disagree with. I'm sorry for the position I put you in. I never wanted to hurt you. I never wanted to hurt us. I'm not proud of what I've done, and I'm working to rectify them. Moving forward, I'll be as open and honest as you need me to be. I want this to work. I want us to grow old together, pop out some babies, and live happily ever after in our own right."

Talia poked out her bottom lip and sighed. "I want that too, Maddox."

"If we have to start over, I'm okay with that. If you need me to romance you until you're ready to be my girlfriend again, I can do that." I pulled her onto my lap to eliminate the rest of the space between us. "Tell me what you need, baby."

Her breathing sped up as she placed her hands on my shoulders. She discreetly shifted her hips, and I could feel her heat through my damn sweatpants. My baby was a beacon of heat.

"I need *you*, Maddox," she panted. Her eyes were glossy as she tilted her head and rubbed the back of my neck. I placed my hands on the curve of her ass and rubbed firmly.

"I'm all yours, baby."

I leaned forward and pressed our lips together. My soul danced. I was reunited with the only woman I wanted in every way. She was in my arms again. Peace was restored. The kiss was slow and timid. We both walked on eggshells as we tested each other's limits. It started with slow kisses, which quickly intensified with hasty pecks. Her hands roamed my body as mine rubbed her ass and faintly skirted across the wetness on the seat of her pajama shorts. I could tell she skipped panties when she dressed.

"Where's your bedroom?" I stood up from the couch with her still wrapped around me.

"Down the hall, first door on the right," she explained in a raspy voice.

I followed her directions and pushed open the door. The room smelled of vanilla, lavender, and jasmine with hints of something spicy. The fragrance only intensified our arousal as I placed her gently on the bed. I looked into her eyes and licked my lips.

"I don't want to rush anything, okay? I want to take my time and taste every inch of your body." I tugged off my shirt, removed my shoes, and dropped my sweatpants. I stood only in my black boxer briefs at the foot of the bed.

"My body is yours." Her voice came out in a sultry purr. The deep yet vulnerable tone sent a chill down my spine.

"Take your clothes off for me. Nice and slow," I ordered.

Her pupils dilated, her nipples hardened, and the wetness saturated the middle of her shorts. She was soaking her pajama bottom for me.

She sat up and pulled off her clothes. She started with the tank top. Once the material was over her head and discarded somewhere on the floor, she pulled her shorts down and kicked them off. I admired her body. Her breasts hung perfectly. Her hips dipped in the right places. I wanted to lick her like a melting ice cream sandwich in the summer.

She squirmed under my gaze. "Maddox, please."

"Lie back," I instructed.

She lay back, and I hovered over her. I applied the perfect amount of pressure as I dipped my head and connected our lips.

Her hands instinctively rested on my back as she braced herself for the pleasure on the horizon. Our tongues met and explored each other's mouths. While I tasted her tongue, I used one hand to snake between her legs. I faintly trailed the tips of my fingers up her thigh to the warmth and wetness waiting for me. I used my index and middle fingers to rub her clit.

"Oh!" she moaned aloud.

Her lips parted from mine as she rotated her hips against the circular motion of my fingers. I trailed my lips across her jawline. I kissed behind her earlobe, down the length of her neck, and across her collarbone.

"I've missed the feel of your body against mine," I shared. "I've missed how you react to my touch."

"I've missed it all too. But most of all, I've missed *you*," she responded. "I've missed how you hug my soul. I've missed how you kissed me. I've missed how you take your time to milk me of my juices."

Talia's body was mine for the time being. It was my responsibility to fill her with intoxicating pleasure. I started by sucking on her nipples. The chocolate-colored beads were hard in my mouth, so I sucked on them with pressure. I'd suck and flick my tongue against the beads until she squirmed under my touch. Then I trailed kisses down the center of her belly and grazed my nose against her pubic area. Talia's natural aroma was more intoxicating than any perfume.

The first lick was like the first slice of sweet potato pie on Thanksgiving Day. Her taste was everything I craved. I dipped my tongue between her wetness and devoured her until her juices coated my face.

Then we shifted positions. I kissed my way back up her body and rubbed my tip against her lips. I slid the tip up and down, coating my erection with her natural lubricant.

"I'm ready," Talia informed. She bucked her hips upward.

I placed my hands on the back of her legs and lifted them. Once they were spread wide enough, I slowly inserted myself inside of her. The journey to her core tested my restraints. I grit my teeth as she gripped my member with her tight walls. Her warmth consumed me.

I buried my face in the crook of her neck and sank my teeth into her skin as I slowly pulled back. I repeated the motion several times until she loosened up and adjusted to me completely.

Now, the real fun was about to begin . . .

"Talia," I called out.

She opened her eyes and stared into my gaze. "Hmm?"

"I'm sorry for every night you went to sleep feeling the pain of our breakup. I'm sorry for every night you spent without my arms wrapped around you." I thrust deep into her.

"It's okay, baby." Her moans filled the air. "I forgive you. I forgive you." She repeated the phrase over and over as she clung to me.

Missionary was the only position I wanted Talia in, but I had to go deeper. I had to make her feel it in her heart. I pulled us down to the foot of the bed, planted my feet on the floor, and allowed her ass to hang off the mattress. I dug into her with a purpose. She grasped the sheets and swore loudly as I filled her with intent.

"You're mine. You'll *always* be mine. I'll shout it from the mountaintop if I have to. I love you," I growled.

"I love you . . . so . . . much," she released. I let her catch her breath before I made my next demand.

"Ride this dick until I have you busting out the seams with my seed."

Within a few clumsy motions, she climbed on top of me and slowly sat on my dick. She planted her feet and moved her hips like a pro. She braced herself by pressing her hands into my chest and tilted her head back. She bounced on my erection.

"I need to get in shape," she complained.

"You're doing great," I encouraged. "Your grip has my toes curling."

"Good. This is about to send you over the edge."

She spread her legs into a split . . . and I was a goner. She bounced on me in a full split, and I shot my streams of orgasm deep into her. She didn't get off of me until she'd gotten another orgasm of her own. We lay in each other's arms as we steadied our rapid breaths. Then I turned my head to look into her hazy eyes.

"Do you still like me?" I asked.

She frowned. "Yes."

"Okay, good. I was concerned you might've had postorgasmic clarity and no longer wished to proceed with me," I confessed.

She turned to her side and placed her hand on my chest, tracing circles atop my skin. "I know my original actions created a fear within you of me running off again, but I can assure you that isn't the case. I *want* us to work. I want to fall in love and watch the sunset in your arms. I want you to build a foundation for our harmonious life together. While we both have things to work on, one of my biggest goals is establishing security."

Our fingers locked.

"Security is one of the most important aspects of a relationship. I want to ensure we are still stuck like glue when the honeymoon phase ends," I added.

"I want that as well," she agreed. "I want to live in harmony. Even when we disagree, I never want to go to bed mad at you."

"We're on the same page, baby," I smirked. "Do I have to ask you to be my girlfriend again, or can we press resume and fall back into our relationship with these new improvements?"

"I would like you to ask me again, but we keep our original date," she answered.

"I can do that."

I sat up and stretched my body. My muscles ached, but it was tolerable. "Let's take a shower," I proposed.

"I'll get the towels."

Talia stood up from the bed, and I watched her body as she maneuvered through the room. Her hips swayed to the beat of her own drum while her messy mane moved with the gentle blowing of the fan.

Talia was the epitome of beauty, from her blemish-free skin to her sensual body and Colgate smile. Every time I ogled at her, I found new things to adore about her.

When we stepped under the spray of the shower, my hands had a mind of their own as they explored her body in a nonsexual yet intimate way. I wanted to memorize every dip and crevice of her. I wanted her to feel the love I felt in each caress of my fingers against her cocoa-complexed skin.

"Your beauty is one of a kind," I commented as I grabbed her soap and washcloth. I lathered the washcloth and bathed her. The soap cleansed her skin.

"Thank you," she replied while looking away from me.

I lifted my hand to tilt her head back in my direction. "I know my words can't make you nervous."

"They do. The look in your eyes is always so intense. I get bubbly and shy when you look at me like that and then shower me with compliments."

"It's never my intention to make you feel any emotions other than pleasure and happiness. I know you can't control how you feel around me, but I know one day it'll all come naturally for us." I pecked her lips repeatedly until she giggled and playfully pushed me back.

"Okay, okay," she giggled. "I get it."

"Good."

After our shower, we changed the bedsheets and snuggled together. She fell asleep almost instantly. Her soft snores lulled me to sleep. For the first time since we'd broken up, I had a good night's rest without her haunting my dreams.

When I woke up the following day, I was greeted by the smell of bacon and eggs and cheesy grits. She had cooked me breakfast and made me coffee. While we sat and ate, all I could think about was calling in to work to spend the entire day with her, but I had business to take care of at the police department. With promises to hit her up as soon as I could, I reluctantly left her place and headed home to get dressed for work.

I'd spent ten years on the force in some capacity. From my rookie years to my undercover jobs to my position as the lead detective with my own team, I had made a lasting impression at HPD. Yes, I'd done a lot of wrong, but I'd done a hell of a lot of right during my time.

When I walked into the building, I felt the air thick with tension. Some of the patrol officers standing around glared at me. I kept my head high with a smile as I strolled into the squad room and walked over to my team.

"You've got a big pair of balls on you, Reed," Chavez commented. "To do what you did took a hell of a lot of confidence."

"You've got enemies now because of it," Parsons added.

"How do you guys feel about what I did? Y'all are my team, so I want to know if we have any beef because of my actions," I asked while I took my seat and crossed my arms.

Barnett shrugged. "You did what you felt was right. In the end, you saved a young man's life. It's commendable."

"From what Captain told us," Carruthers began, "you saved a lot of people from being exposed for their less-than-discreet bad doings. All our names were on those investigation files, and we all could have had serious blowback."

Chavez hummed. "Breaking the rules is important sometimes."

"Well, everybody has skeletons in the closet that aren't a secret anymore. What happens now is we all learn from this case and do better for the community. One officer's bad arrest could have caused all of us to lose our jobs or worse . . . go to jail with the criminals we throw in the cage every day," I finished.

"You're right," Parsons agreed. "What happens to you now?"

"I don't know. I'm waiting to talk to Captain about how he wants to proceed. If today is my last day, then it was great working with all of you," I finished.

As if on cue, Captain Torres opened the door to his office and gestured for me to come in. I stood up with a huff and entered the room. Once the door was closed, I claimed the seat across from his desk, and he stood against the edge of the desk. "You've done a lot to the department in the last few days," he stated.

I nodded. "Yup."

"The most important question before we continue is, do you wish to remain an active detective on my police force?" he followed up.

I lifted my shoulders into a shrug before letting my arms fall back by my side. "In all honesty, Captain, I don't know. I wanted to be a man with integrity to change the city for the better, but I fell into a lot of shit. I don't want you have to second-guess any decision I make as a detective, and I also don't want to walk on eggshells and hope the officers by my side will protect me in the line of fire after I turned on one of our own."

Captain Torres nodded his head and rubbed his hands together. "If you don't wish to proceed with your career as a detective, you won't receive any pension because the earliest we could begin the process is fifty."

I nodded. "I'm aware."

I was only thirty-three years old with at least another two decades left on the force before I could retire and receive my pension. The strain of knowing I would have to start my life over again at my age was not only terrifying but also surreal. I'd spent almost two decades content with going to the police academy, becoming an officer of the law, and going through the motions. Now, I'd have to find a new passion. I'd have to find a new way to be the change I wanted to see in the city. Would I be okay with that?

"I'm okay with stepping down from my position here. If you have to turn me in to the Feds for the wrong I've done in the department, I'm also okay with that," I explained.

Captain Torres shook his head and lowered his voice. "We can chop it up to you continuing your undercover job to build a case against him. I will create the necessary paper trail to protect you from prosecution if you agree to testify against Devon Kingston."

My eyes widened at the request. The captain presented me with something I hadn't considered a possibility. If I got a clean exit from the police force, I'd have more options for a new job. Would I be able to testify against a man as powerful as Diablo? People feared him because he'd built a notorious reputation in crime. Can I sit in an open court and confess to my involvement with Diablo to put him behind bars? Did I trust the justice system enough to protect me from the wrath of Diablo and his goons?

"How would you guarantee my family's and my safety if I agree to testify? Diablo isn't a kind man, and if I get on the stand to help put him in prison, then who will protect us from his loyal servants?" I asked.

"I can't say we can protect you from everything," Captain Torres answered.

I rubbed my hands together and weighed my options. "How soon do you need a response?" I asked.

"Take the next few weeks to decide. Come back to me at the end of the month with your decision."

I nodded. "Thank you. I'll get back in touch with you once I've filled my family in and come to a decision."

"Be safe out there, Reed."

"Always."

I stood up from the table and shook his hand. Even at my lowest, he still found a way to protect me. Granted, it was probably in his best interest to lie for me to protect himself. Regardless, he had my back. Now, I had to speak with my mama and sister because it would affect them. I also wanted to get input from Talia to see what she recommended legally and personally.

I walked out of the office and was greeted by the curious gazes from my team. I walked over to them and clasped my hands behind my back.

"What did Captain say?" Carruthers was the first to ask.

"A lot," I replied. "I have a lot to ponder, but I know one thing's for certain. My time at HPD is coming to an end. We pride ourselves on upholding the brotherly code for the force, but if we really were family, we would hold one another accountable. Too often, we have secrets, ignore the elephants in the room, and pretend there aren't problems with the family's foundation. Sometimes, a wake-up call must be made because what's done in the dark will always come to light."

Parsons cleared his throat. "Whatever you decide to do moving forward, just know I appreciated working alongside you. You've always been a great part of the team. No matter what, you were an overall great guy."

"He was okay," Chavez teased. "And he will be missed if he chooses another path."

"Do what you feel is the right choice. Do what you feel will give you the best joy in life. Don't stay here because it's what you've dedicated your life to for so long. Don't leave because you feel you won't be accepted by everyone here. Do what *you* want. Live the life you will proudly tell your future children about." Barnett stood up and patted my back. "That is, if you ever find a woman who actually can put up with you."

I scoffed with amusement. "You'd be surprised. I have a woman I would give the world to if she asked."

"Aww," Chavez cooed. "Our little Reedy is growing up into a young man."

I smacked my lips and chuckled lightly. "I appreciate y'all."

I waved goodbye and headed out of the building. When I walked through the door this morning, I had a plan, but as I entered my car to go home, I was left with more questions.

Where will life take me next?

CHAPTER TWENTY-ONE

Talia

The sound of the music blared from the speakers. I was on a cloud as I swayed my hips to the rhythm of an old '90s R&B song. I hummed the lyrics before I took a generous gulp of my drink. I had a mixed concoction of tequila and Pepsi. I rarely drank soda, but I was happy to indulge for the time being.

Tonight, my family was throwing an event at my parents' house to celebrate my success. It felt surreal to see my name in headlines, on the radio, and on news stations because of the achievements I'd made in less than a year of being at my father's firm. When my one-year anniversary with the firm came around, I'd be sitting on a throne with people requesting me personally for their cases.

"How are you feeling?" Monique asked, bumping my hip playfully as she stood beside me.

I turned to face her and smiled. "I'm feeling as light as a feather. I'm excited to see what's next for me."

"You're not going to win every case or get the verdict you want every time, but you've established that you're a fighter, and I know you'll change the world one case at a time. I'm proud of you."

Mo wrapped her arm around my shoulder, and we swayed together. She was the sister I always wanted, and it felt refreshing to know she'd always be in my corner, cheering me on. She was a constant I could never get rid of—I'd never *want* to get rid of her.

"I'm realistic with myself. I'm still new to this, but the support of my family and friends helps set the tone for how I navigate through the criminal justice system. With y'all by my side, I cannot lose."

"You better preach it," she teased.

I finished my drink and let out a deep breath. "My mama and daddy are playing spades with SJ and Kiara. Be my partner?"

"Fa sho. Let's go beat the family."

We walked over to the spades table and claimed our seats. The six of us were very competitive, so the game had the potential to get heated in the moment.

"Are y'all ready to lose?" I asked with a grin.

"Kid, you ain't ever won a game against Mama and Daddy. Why would you even sit with the grown folks at this table?" SJ teased.

"You look like you're shaking in your boots, old man," I retorted in an elder voice. "Just because you fold easily doesn't mean me and my partner will."

"You putting your money where yo' mouth is?" SJ asked with a raised brow.

"C'mon!" I pulled out my wallet and dropped a crisp hundred-dollar bill onto the table. "Big bets only."

"These are *your* children," Mama commented to her husband as she shook her head. She shuffled the cards like a professional in a casino in Las Vegas.

"*You* taught them how to play spades," Daddy countered.

"And *you* taught them how to bet on the games," she retorted.

The two bickered while SJ and I chuckled in amusement. Monique giggled as she and Kiara watched our family's daily entertainment. It was never a dull moment in the Tate residence. All of us had very bold personalities.

BURDEN *of* LOVE   213

When I was around them, I could let go of the politic aspect of my career and be myself. I could turn off the professional jargon and speak in my natural Texan dialect. My southern drawl was deep and only intensified when I was under the influence and surrounded by family.

"Game!" I slapped the black Ace of Spades onto the table and collected the final book needed to win the game.

"Man, I knew you were holding the card," Daddy grumbled as he stood up from the card table and stretched his body.

"Let me go check on my grandbabies," Mama stated. She stood up and stretched too. Her joints popped, making us laugh briefly.

"You'll be giving them grandkids soon," Kiara announced once Mama and Daddy walked over to where the children were playing in the backyard.

I looked at my sister-in-law with a curious brow lifted to the sky. "Excuse me?"

"You've got a glow about you that I recognize in many people." Kiara reached over and held my hand. "If you aren't already pregnant, you will be soon."

I looked at her with a deep frown. "Ki, please don't play like this."

"I'm serious, Lee. I can feel it in my spirit. You're having a baby."

I awkwardly chuckled. "Yeah . . . Okay, girl."

I waved her off, even though the seed had been planted in my mind. I tried to remember the last time I dealt with a period or cramps, and I couldn't remember having a cycle in a few months. I assumed it was because of my stressful job and the depressed state I'd been in over the last few months. Then I recalled the previous two times I'd been sexually active. Neither the time in the file room nor when Maddox was in my apartment was done with protection. I allowed this man to insert himself deep into me and fill me with his seed like I was a Swiss roll in a Little Debbie snack pack.

The anxiety from before swam to the surface as I remembered the situation Maddox was in. He'd been faced with a catch-22. If I were pregnant, would Maddox be a present father? Would the demons in his closet come back to try to ruin our happy home? Would I be okay with looking over my shoulder because one of the people he'd crossed while in uniform considered me an easy target?

"Ahem." SJ cleared his throat and brought me back to the conversation at hand. He looked at me with thin lips and pointed eyes. "You've been fu—"

"Please don't finish the word. What I do in the comfort of a hotel room, bedroom, or empty office is nobody's business but mine."

SJ grimaced. "Kid!"

"It might be time to retire the nickname if your wife is right." I continued to tease my brother.

He knew I wasn't a virgin. He knew I had the company of men every now and then, and he knew about my relationship with Maddox. Granted, he hadn't gotten an update about us seeing each other and working things out, but he would soon if Kiara was correct and a fetus was growing in my uterus.

Am I ready for motherhood this soon into my career? Will Maddox be okay with being a stay-at-home dad while I go into the office to continue changing the world?

Let's hold on, Talia . . . We haven't confirmed if we are pregnant.

"Tee," Monique called out. Her voice brought me out of my thoughts as I cleared my throat.

"Hmm?"

"Are you okay? You kind of spaced out on us."

"I'm all right," I responded to my best friend. "Just got lost in my thoughts for a moment. I'm about to get me some of Mama's Cajun pasta and pour a drink." *Nonalcoholic, just in case.*

I stood up, excused myself from the table, and entered the kitchen. After washing my hands and making a bowl of the spicy noodle dish, I sat at the dining room table, pulled out my phone, and texted Maddox to pass the time while I ate in silence.

Me: Hey. What are you doing?

Maddox: Nothing. I'm just lying on this couch, drinking a beer. What are you doing, my love?

Me: My folks had a party for me. It wasn't anything big. We ate food, drank liquor, and now I'm on my second bowl of pasta. Let me tell you what my SIL said to me.

Maddox: What did she say?

Me: She said if I'm not already pregnant, I will be soon. Can you believe that? It came out of left field and threw me into disarray.

I watched in amusement as he opened the message and read it. The typing dots popped up and then disappeared. I watched the symbol play peek-a-boo for what felt like an eternity. He was just as stunned as I was, and I almost felt bad for throwing him into my chaotic mood. However, he deserved to live in the moment with me. Finally, the message popped up in the thread, and I couldn't help but giggle at his response.

Maddox: Well, come over and pee on a stick. We can either confirm it now and figure out what we do next or prove you're not and continue to live life on the raw side. :)

Me: The wink was so unnecessary.

Maddox: But it's got you smiling like a Cheshire cat, right?

Me: Nope! But anyway . . . I can pull up on you when I leave here in a few and finally see what your home looks like.

Panic settled into my stomach as I sent the message. Instant fear crept into my body, so I sent an additional text to clear up my anxiety.

Me: Unless you're not ready to have me in your personal space. I completely understand if you're not on that type of time yet. Sorry if you feel like I put you in a weird position.

Maddox: My love, please take a deep breath. I don't know where the sudden anxiety came from, but you know I would love to show you my personal space. I want you in my personal space. I want you in my bed. I want you in my arms. I want you to feel as comfortable in my home as I do.

I licked my lips and shook my head. Then I took a deep breath. I wasn't sure where the fear stemmed from, but the more I replayed my reaction, the more I came to terms with the fact I was in uncharted territory. I didn't want him to reject me, even though he hadn't given me a reason to feel like he would.

Maddox: Here's my address. Let me know when you're outside, and I'll walk you in.

I liked his message and pocketed my phone. Then I stood up from the table and walked into the kitchen to clean my dishes. I was ready to call it a night and spend some time with my man before I returned to work on Monday.

Maddox's neighborhood was nice. It was a gated community with a code to enter at the sliding gate. When I entered the neighborhood, I could tell he had a nice home from the houses lined in a perfect row along the streets. I turned down a few streets before I pulled into the driveway. Then I used my phone and texted him to let him know I was outside. He quickly came out to open my door, grab my bag, and help me into the house.

"You look amazing," he complimented me as I stepped through the door and stood under the light.

"Thank you."

His arms wrapped around me, and he pecked my lips several times. When we parted, I smiled brightly at him and took in his appearance. He was in his signature look once again, but I could see the faint lines of worry on his forehead and around his mouth.

"What's on your mind?" I asked as I lifted my hand up to his forehead and massaged the lines with my fingertips. "You seem worried."

"Not necessarily worried but more so in deep thought," he explained.

"What's on your mind?"

"We can get into that later. Right now, let me give you the grand tour. Then we can chill in the living room or bedroom— whatever you are most comfortable doing."

Maddox's home was nice sized. He had four bedrooms, a two-car garage, and a large living room. The master bedroom was downstairs, across from the living room, while the other rooms were upstairs. His bathrooms were clean and designed similar to mine. The backyard was nice as well. Though the house was beautiful, it didn't feel like a *home*. It was missing something.

"You have a lovely house. I can't believe you live here all by yourself."

"With my job, it made the lonely nights easier. I would drown myself in a bottle or a woman and pass out when I finally trudged through the garage at who knows what time." Maddox lifted his shoulders in a shrug. "It was nice when we had our hotel nights together. It beat coming home to an empty house," he confessed.

"I can relate. Although your place is nice and spacious, luckily, my space is small enough to provide comfort to me for the most part."

I locked our fingers and rubbed his arm lazily. I loved the feel of Maddox's skin under my fingertips. I loved breathing in the same air as him. I loved getting lost in his eyes and words as we conversed. We talked about adjusting to each other during our break and how excited we were to rekindle our flame.

"Do you think you're pregnant?" he inquired out of the blue. The question broke the comfortable silence we'd sat in for a few minutes.

My eyes locked with his. "I don't know. I haven't had my period in a while, but I summed it up to be a consequence of stress and going through a lot of emotions the last few months."

"Do you want to take a test?" he asked.

I chuckled. "Are you a mind reader?"

"What do you mean?"

"I stopped at a pharmacy and picked up a double pack of digital pregnancy tests. I didn't want to buy the ones with the lines. I wanted the ones that would say the results in simple *pregnant* or *not pregnant* wording."

"Oh." Maddox tucked his lip into his mouth as he perused my frame. His eyes bore into every inch of me. "Let's take them now."

"You sure?"

"Why wouldn't I be? We should know as soon as possible. You said you don't remember the last time you had a period, so the test should confirm what we already know, or you need to go to the OBGYN to get checked up," he explained.

I licked my lips. "Okay. I'll open the box and pee on both sticks. We'll set the timer and go from there."

"Sounds great."

My movements were on autopilot as I stood up and walked over to my bag. I pulled out the CVS package and walked into the bathroom. It took a few minutes to pee on both sticks, cover them, set them on the counter, and wash my hands. Then I turned on the five-minute timer on my phone and walked into the bedroom, where Maddox was seated at the foot of the bed.

"And now we wait," I commented with a half smile. I walked over and stood between Maddox's legs. He wrapped his arms around my waist and pulled me down. Then he massaged the small of my back with his fingertips.

"I spoke with my captain a few days ago," he blurted out. "He said if I testified against someone the Feds have been after for a decade, I'd be granted immunity and be able to find a decent job somewhere. The only downside is the man is a known killer. I've watched him kill people. I know he wouldn't hesitate to kill me and everyone I love if I did so."

Maddox's words stunned me into silence.

Before I had time to digest the first reveal, he continued. "He told me he'd give me two weeks to decide. I've been weighing the pros and cons. I'm unsure what route to take, but I want to do what would be best for us and potentially our growing family."

This was why people didn't actively seek out relationships with police officers. They worked with criminals all day, every day. They put their lives and the people they loved in danger daily. To know Maddox could be sent into witness protection if he testified made me feel . . . conflicted. If I were pregnant, I'd have to do this by myself because his choices would directly affect me and our unborn child. Frustration, anxiety, and fear hit my system like a tornado in a crowded neighborhood. Pregnancy was too beautiful to do alone. How confident was I in the system? How confident was I in Maddox's decision-making skills?

The frown was deep on my lips as I put some distance between us. Now, I understood why he had worry lines all over his handsome face.

"Baby?" Maddox frowned as I continued to step away from him.

"I'm just processing everything," I explained in a forced tone.

"I scared you away?" Maddox quizzed. His face showed the pain.

"A little bit. I know my job is also hazardous because I deal with suspected criminals, but *you* get down and dirty with real killers. It's a lot to take in."

"Are you going to push me away? Are you going to end things again? I know it isn't easy, but I don't want you to run away. We can figure it out together." He stood up and closed the distance between us. His head dipped down, and he pecked my lips. Instantly, the fear weakened.

Ding.

Ding.

The alarm on my phone startled me as I fumbled with the device to silence the noise. I looked at Maddox, and he looked at me. We gazed into each other's eyes with identical faces drenched in a whirlpool of emotions.

"Well, the Big Reveal is upon us," I commented.

We walked into the bathroom, and each picked up a stick. I'd purposely turned them upside down so the words would be hidden.

"On the count of three," Maddox spoke.

Together, we counted.

One . . .

Two . . .

Three . . .

We flipped the tests over.

"*Pregnant,*" we said simultaneously.

My heart stopped, and my chest caved in. It felt like my lungs had depleted and turned to dust. I. Was. Pregnant.

"Well . . ." Maddox looked at me with wide eyes.

The shock of the moment made me laugh. I laughed so hard my stomach ached. I clutched at my sides, leaned against the wall, and doubled over with pure amusement at the situation.

Maddox stood next to me, his eyes capturing my every move. "Are you genuinely laughing, or is this a psychotic break? I'm not sure how to react or what to do . . ."

His confession slightly sobered my amusement. I wiped the tears from the corners of my eyes and sighed with contentment. "I vividly remember telling you not to worry about putting on a condom several times and you filling them with your seed. I wasn't on birth control. I was living life on the edge, and these are the consequences of our actions."

The only thing I could do was laugh about it. We would figure out the rest in time.

"I don't want to scare you," I admitted. "But if we're being honest, this situation is hilarious. I just have to take a moment to laugh to keep from crying."

"I get it," Maddox agreed. He shook his head and closed the distance between us. He helped me onto my feet and wrapped his hands around my waist. Under the bright lights of the bathroom, Maddox looked like an angel. His aura was bright, and his embrace was warm. "Not only are we going to figure out this shit, but we're also going to do it together."

I poked out my bottom lip. Maddox pressed his lips against mine. We stayed like this for what felt like an eternity. The reality hadn't set in, but I would be sick to my stomach when it did. Less than a year into my career and I got impregnated by a detective. My bingo card could have never predicted a pregnancy as quickly as it came.

"Do you want to take a hot shower? I'll wash you off and give you a massage."

"I'd like that a lot," I replied.

For the next hour, Maddox spent his time tending to me in the gentlest and most caring way. When the shower was over, he massaged lotion into my skin and gave me one of his shirts to wear to bed. I was submerged in his scent on the shirt, on the bedding, and on him. It was the perfect aroma to soothe me.

"I know we have a lot to prepare for, but adding a new baby to our situation makes me ready to make a responsible decision. I will do what I feel will provide the best care for you and our child."

As his comforting fragrance lulled me to sleep, I remember telling him I loved him before slumber took over.

CHAPTER TWENTY-TWO

Maddox

My phone ringing woke me from the peaceful sleep I'd been engaged in moments before. I used my free hand to locate and retrieve my phone on the nightstand while I kept the other wrapped around Talia. Diablo's name appeared on the screen as my vision adjusted to the brightness. The sight of his name wasn't surprising, but I hadn't expected to hear from him this early in the morning.

I didn't want to leave the comfort of my bed next to the love of my life, but I slid out of her grasp and headed toward the living room to avoid waking my sleeping beauty.

"Hello?" I answered.

"You've caught the attention of many people since your fiasco with that officer." His voice was calm and amused as he spoke to me.

"Is that what you called to talk about?" I asked. I lifted my hand and scratched my belly, my mind still a bit hazy, as I continued to awaken fully.

"No. You need to meet me at the address I sent you. We have business to discuss now."

The call ended before I could respond. I sat down on the couch and took a deep breath. My intuition told me this would be my final conversation with Diablo. As the realization settled in, I swallowed hard. The lump returned, which made it difficult to breathe. Everything would come to an end. It was time to dance with the devil one last time. If I made it out on the other side, this was God's way to get me out of the mud and into clear water for the sake of my family.

I walked back into the bedroom and entered the closet, where I pulled on my bulletproof vest and a hoodie. I tugged on some sweatpants and my black Nike dunks. Then I opened my safe and grabbed the Glock. I checked the magazine and tucked it into the waistband of my sweatpants. I also tucked my pocketknife into my left sock. It was always a wise choice to stay protected no matter the situation. If today were my last day in the physical realm, I'd go out with a fight.

As I emerged from the closet, Talia stirred awake. I watched her stretch her arms and legs like a starfish before she sat up with a yawn. She took in my appearance and frowned.

"Where are you going?" she quizzed. Her right hand rubbed the sleep out of the corners of her eyes. She grabbed her water bottle from the nightstand and gulped it down.

"I have to go handle something important that came up. I promise to return to you as soon as I can. I want you to know I'm doing everything in my power to protect you and our baby from the consequences of my previous actions."

"Okay," she responded. I was surprised she didn't press the issue, but I summed it up to be because she didn't want to stress herself with worry. "I don't want to rummage through your pantry, so do you mind if I order some breakfast from one of those delivery apps?" she asked.

"Tell me what you want, and I'll order your food before I head out. You don't have to pay for anything. Plus, I'll be able to give them instructions on how to get into the gate."

She nodded. "Do you know how long you're going to be gone?"

"I don't know for sure, but I know I'll be back in time to take you to lunch."

"Okay, my love."

With long strides, I approached her and pecked her lips several times. She smiled while in my embrace. I wanted to slip my tongue into her mouth and explore her before I left on this life-threatening excursion, but I restrained myself. I'd rather dive into her and take a victory lap upon my return.

"I love you," I announced once we'd parted lips. Saying the phrase was second nature now. It wasn't forced or insincere. I meant those three words with my whole being—both physically and spiritually.

"I love you." She placed her hand on my cheek. For a moment, I closed my eyes and held on to the warmth of her hand on my skin. I didn't want to leave her, but this would be my only opportunity to protect myself and my growing family from Diablo's wrath in the future.

I unlocked my cell phone and tapped on the food delivery app. I held it out for her.

"Order whatever you want."

"Are you going to eat something?" she asked.

I shook my head. "I don't have an appetite this morning. I'm probably going to grab a protein shake, though, to have something on my stomach to hold me over until lunch."

Once she ordered her food, I kissed her several times and left. I quickly climbed into my Mustang and headed to the location Diablo sent me.

* · ——— · ◆ · · ——— · *

The building Diablo told me to meet him at towered over the city. It had to have at least forty floors or more. When I arrived, I texted him. He followed up with the room number and directions to the room he was cooped up in. The walk from the garage to the elevator was *long*. When I entered, I tapped the fortieth floor and rode the elevator up. When the doors emerged, I made sure my gun was easily obtainable as I walked down the hall. The room numbers skip counted by twos. At the appropriate door, I knocked.

The door swung open to reveal a large man with a bald head and a suit too small for his bulging muscles. He almost looked like he ate steroids for every meal.

"Pat him down," Diablo's voice instructed out of view.

The man did so and found my gun. He removed it from my waistband and ushered me into the room. Inside the room was an office space that overlooked the city of Houston. The skyline was visible, and the fast-moving city was hard not to watch. The space was large but felt small due to the crowded area. Four of Diablo's men were working on different tasks. Two bodyguards stood near Diablo and the doorman. The doorman showed the gun to Diablo, who chortled.

"Give him back that little toy," he ordered. I wanted to defend my Glock, but we both knew the standard police-issued weapon did damage in the right hands. Granted, it wouldn't do much to their customized, fully automatic weapons.

The man returned my gun. "He's also wearing a vest under the hoodie."

"If need be, aim for the head then," Diablo replied. He looked at me and nodded a greeting. "Thank you for joining me on such short notice. After our last conversation, I was sure I'd have to dump you somewhere in the Galveston ocean." He laughed, but the situation wasn't funny to me in the slightest.

I folded my hands behind my back. "Last time we spoke, I made it clear I wouldn't be doing any other jobs, so I'm confused about the purpose of the meeting if we're being honest."

"Yes, I recall the conversation as clear as day." Diablo clapped his hands. "But I'm sure you've come to your senses since then."

"No. I'm standing on business. I'm stepping down from my position as lead detective, so I'm not sure what more I could do to aid you."

"Well, your position here will become null and void if you have nothing more to give me." Diablo lifted an eyebrow as he crossed his arms over his chest.

"Before you do that, you should be aware of a few things." My voice was firm yet mysterious. My tone caused Diablo's eyes to squint.

"What?"

"Grant me full immunity from any harm from you and your crew. I have to protect me and mine before I do business with you one final time."

Diablo rubbed his right hand on his chin. "Fine. Full immunity."

"And it'll also cost you a minimum of a million dollars," I continued to wager.

Everyone in the room paused to tune into the conversation. My face was firm, and my head was held high. I wasn't backing down from a fight. I would do what I could to provide security for the women in my life while I transitioned into the next chapter.

"Ha!" Diablo shouted with a boisterous laugh. "You must be out of your mind if you think you have *anything* worth my giving a million dollars to you on top of granting immunity from the wrath of my crew."

I shrugged. "Unless you want your entire organization to be charged with a RICO case by the federal government, I'd cough up the cash."

"RICO?" Diablo repeated. "Every government agency threatens me daily. A RICO is nothing."

"I'm not explaining anything further until I get my money. And I'll take my million in cash," I stated.

Diablo was silent as he looked at me. I'd never given him a reason to distrust me. "I'm not giving you a million, but I'll give you five hundred thousand."

"A million or no deal," I repeated. I wasn't stupid. A million to Diablo was equivalent to a regular nine-to-five workingman giving a hundred-dollar bill to a friend. He had plenty of millions tucked away and ready at his disposal.

Diablo snapped his fingers, and one of the men jumped up and jogged over to him. "Yes, Boss?"

"Grab a million out of the safe to give to Mister Reed. Use one of the black duffle bags to store it," he instructed.

As I watched Diablo, I could tell the life of crime he lived had begun to take its toll on him. He'd created an empire, but the risk of exposure and death was looming closer than he wanted. At least from the outside looking in, I could make a very educated assumption. The unmistakable bags under his eyes, the hunch in his shoulders, and the drain in his voice were all good indicators.

Once the money was securely in the duffle bag, I slung it over my shoulder and focused my attention on Diablo.

"Now, explain," Diablo ordered.

I gave him a full rundown of what the government had on him and how they planned to throw his entire organization into a RICO charge. I told him if he were smart, he'd get his ducks in a row and move accordingly or risk a prison term and everything he loves to crumble into pieces. I told him the Feds had so much evidence against him that the moment he made one vital mistake, it was over for him.

"You have some balls to share this with me and demand all that money. I could easily end your life with a snap of my fingers, yet you remained unmoving the whole time. I commend you, Maddox," Diablo explained. "Over the years, I've grown fond of your 'go with the flow' mentality. Seeing you stand up for yourself and get out of the game is nice. Other men in my position would have chopped you up and fed you to the swine."

It was true. I didn't owe loyalty to Diablo, but I chose to take the high road. I saved myself from a bloodbath and got a reward for the years I'd sacrificed to help his organization avoid prison time.

"Good luck," I commented as I reached out to shake his hand.

Diablo nodded and shook my hand firmly.

As I left the building, my spirits were high. I felt like I could breathe for the first time. My head was light from the shock of leaving the room alive. Once in the clear, I headed to the Houston Police Department to submit my resignation letter. It was best not to have my face associated with a case trying to take down Diablo. When I informed the captain, he blew up, but I gave him a nice amount of money to avoid any further problems. Money made the world go round, and if someone offered the right amount, any problem could disappear.

With the money I'd gotten from Diablo, I could invest in businesses and see a profit while figuring out what to do next. It was the best option to keep my family safe and my crimes out of public records.

The knowledge of the money weighed heavy on my heart. Was I supposed to tell Talia about the money I'd come in contact with? Was I supposed to explain to her *why* I was given such a large amount of money? Would she be okay with using money obtained from an infamous kingpin?

I didn't want any more of my choices to taint her view of me. I didn't want her to look at me like I was a criminal. Could I live with myself for keeping the money a secret? Probably. I'd tell her I had money saved over the years to keep my family well.

"Talia," I called out as I entered the house.

It was surreal to come home to someone else existing in my space. Her scent greeted me as I entered the kitchen. She was bent over with her left hand on her knee as she rummaged through the refrigerator. The view of her ass peeking through from the oversized shirt she wore sent a message straight to my growing erection. The perfect way to celebrate my newfound wealth would be to dive headfirst into her warmth.

"Damn," I commented. My strides were quick as I planted my feet behind her and gave the round butt a firm smack.

Smack!

The sound was music to my ears as I caressed her slightly tinted skin.

Talia craned her neck to look at me with a pointed glare. "That hurt!"

"Put it in my face. I'll make you feel better."

I watched as she bit down on her plump, juicy lips. The action only egged on my arousal. The want in my eyes must have mirrored hers because, within a few moments, she was in my arms with her lips pressed against mine. Hastily, we tugged at each other's clothes until we were naked in the middle of my kitchen. I lifted her onto the counter and found my place between her legs. My thumb slid up and down her slit as I played with her wetness.

"Maddox, wait."

I paused. "Do you want me to stop?"

"Only for a moment." She placed her hands on my chest and sighed. "I want us to meet each other's families. This is getting really serious really fast, and I don't want to remain unknown to the future extended family of the child I'm growing in my womb . . . I'm really pregnant . . ." She shook her head in disbelief.

Last night, when we discovered the pregnancy, I was 80 percent positive I would have had to call the psych ward to do an evaluation. Talia's long, drawn-out laughter was terrifying at that moment. Then she calmed down and explained it was her natural reaction to laugh to keep from crying. Once we were both done processing the news, we fell asleep together. Today was our first day fully aware of the child growing in her womb, so seeing how our dynamic would evolve was interesting.

"The best part about this journey is you're not alone. I'm here with you through it all. I know it will be a wild adjustment, especially with you balancing your career, but I got you," I explained. I leaned my forehead against hers, and we silently communicated what our hearts and souls had already confirmed long ago. We were in this for the long haul. We were locked in and would never reach for the key to break this bond.

"You can meet my people next weekend, and whenever you want me to meet your people is cool with me," I responded to her initial request.

The smile stretched across her lips as she rubbed her hands over my shoulders and pressed her fingers into my back.

"Do you want me to get my bare ass off your countertop?" she asked after a beat.

We shared a laugh. The sound was light and refreshing. "No. I want you right here. Once we're done here, I will take you to lunch and then head to your place to pick some clothes and toiletries."

"Perfect," she replied. "Your bed is so comfortable. I got the best sleep ever last night." Her lips touched mine. "I don't know . . . I might just move in."

"I'd like that a lot, actually. Skip all the contemplating and get yo' stuff. Once your lease is up, we can merge our things and make my house our home." The offer came second nature. I was ready to set up a nursery before we even had our first doctor's appointment.

"We're moving so fast, but I'm going to buckle up and enjoy the ride."

"I'm enjoying the ride as well."

"Now, where were we?" She licked her lips and massaged her fingers in the nape of my neck. The feel of her fingertips on my skin sent shivers down my spine.

There was no amount of thanks I could tell God for the blessings. I thought my life was over, but He came back in the fourth quarter and did the best Hail Mary I'd ever seen.

CHAPTER TWENTY-THREE

Talia

My heart pounded against my chest as we pulled into the driveway of my parents' home behind Daddy's truck. SJ had parked his car behind Mama's, and Monique parked her vehicle on the street in front of the mailbox. Maddox cut off the engine and looked at me with a reassuring smile. My face revealed all of my emotions in that moment. I was *terrified*.

Tonight was Sunday dinner, and I'd talked everyone into joining us for the evening. I told them I had a surprise for them and needed perfect attendance. This would be the first time I ever brought someone home for my parents to meet. It would be a shock to my father to know the man I'd fallen in love with was one of the key reasons for winning my case. It could go one of two ways: my father could welcome Maddox with open arms, or he could pop a blood vessel from knowing I'd been sleeping with the lead detective, who was the face of Houston PD for months.

"Breathe," Maddox instructed as he locked our fingers together. He rubbed the backs of my hands with his thumb to slow my racing heart.

"You're the first person to meet my family, ever. This terrifies me because I don't know what to expect from my father. My mom is going to love you, and my brother is going to threaten you—

playfully, of course ... but my dad ... He's a wild card, and it scares me."

"Will your father's denial affect how you feel about me? If your dad is upset, will you break up with me?" Maddox asked.

I shook my head. "No. What I feel for you won't be hindered by how my father feels, but it will hurt my feelings. I'm a certified Daddy's girl. I don't want him to disapprove of the man I've fallen in love with."

Maddox cupped my face and pressed his forehead against mine. "Everything will be okay."

My eyes closed as we sat still for a few more moments. After my nerves had numbed to a mellow three out of ten, Maddox hopped out of the car and jogged over to the passenger side to help me. He playfully rubbed my stomach.

"I'm practicing for when you get bigger than a watermelon and waddle everywhere," he explained.

I rolled my eyes and playfully pushed him. "I'm *not* going to be bigger than a watermelon, *please*."

He chuckled. "Baby, you're going to be *huge* and sexy as hell."

We had our first doctor's appointment on Wednesday. She confirmed I was thirteen weeks pregnant. When Maddox and I did the calculations, we concluded the baby was conceived in the file room at T&A. I was almost four weeks pregnant and would know the gender at the next appointment.

The first appointment was overwhelming. They took my blood, asked every medical question known to man, and showed me the baby on the ultrasound. Listening to the strong heartbeat brought tears to both Maddox and me. I felt irresponsible to have gone so long without knowing I was pregnant. I'd been so caught up in cases and heartbreak that I didn't notice the changes in my body. Life was created, and I had no clue I was nurturing the next generation of Tate and Reed. My belly bump wasn't a bump yet.

The round stomach resembled bloating more than anything else. If I wanted to, I could have hidden my pregnancy for a while longer. However, with this being my first child, I wanted all the help I could get in this next chapter, especially since I would need a village when I returned to work once the baby was born.

I pushed open the front door, and the delicious scent of roast filled the air. My mouth watered at the idea of eating the pot roast with a side of creamy garlic mashed potatoes. One thing about my mama . . . She could throw down in the kitchen, and she always switched it up. She loved trying new recipes or bringing back the old ones, and I was happy to never miss a meal if possible.

"I'll introduce you to everyone," I explained to Maddox. I led him into the living room, where the kids were playing near the fireplace, and my father and brother sat on the couch with beers in hand while they watched something sports related on the television.

"Hey," I called out. All eyes were on us. "This is Maddox, my boyfriend. Maddox, this is most of the family. That's my brother, Stephen Junior, but we all call him SJ. The cute rug rats over there are his three kids: Kyari, Kellan, and Stephanie. I'm sure you know my father, Stephen Tate."

The three kids were animatedly coloring in coloring books. Their little legs kicked with joy as they did their best to let their artistic visions flow onto the pages. Of course, Stephie was doing her best to stay inside the lines. My niece was small but tried to keep up with her siblings.

SJ stood up and shook Maddox's hand. "It's nice to meet you, Maddox. I've heard a lot about you. I'm glad my sister stopped fighting her feelings and finally gave you another chance. Now, I ain't gon' make too many threats, but I don't play about my sister. If you hurt her, I'll do what any loving brother would do. Got it?"

Maddox laughed. "I gave this same speech to my little sister's boyfriend. I'm also a protective sibling, so I get what you're saying.

However, I plan on marrying your sister one day, so I promise I will never intentionally hurt her in any way."

"Cool."

Daddy's eyes stared at the three of us in disbelief. His eyes were pointed at Maddox with a glare that could make a serial killer shit a house. The look on his face made me want to run in the opposite direction, but Maddox intertwined our fingers, locking me in place.

"Mr. Tate," Maddox addressed Daddy.

"Reed," Daddy stated blankly, "what are you doing here?"

"Meeting my girlfriend's family," Maddox replied. "Look, I know we've had our differences in the past, but I want to move on. I fell in love with Talia before I knew she was your daughter, so I hope we get your blessing."

Maddox's words were sincere. I gazed up at him with teary eyes as I smiled up at him. SJ reclaimed his spot next to my father, who remained silent.

"Daddy," I whined, "this is the first guy I've ever brought home to y'all. Please give him a chance."

His features softened at my request. He looked at me and sighed. "I don't know if I can."

"Before I was your daughter's boyfriend, I was a man who helped close a case that would have been a public relations nightmare," Maddox explained. "I vividly remember you extending your hand and offering me a job, so . . . What changed?"

"You weren't standing in front of me with your hands all over my daughter then," Daddy retorted.

"Talia!" Mama's voice echoed through the house. "I know I heard you come in. Come in here and let me meet the new boo."

Saved by Mama.

"We'll be right back, Daddy," I mumbled. I pulled Maddox out of the living room and led him into the kitchen. Along the way, he looked at the family pictures with a smile on his face. I shook my head because I could tell he wanted to comment on the younger me.

In the kitchen stood Monique, Kiara, and Mama. The three women were setting the table and making last-minute touches to dinner.

"Mama, this is Maddox." I blurted. "Maddox, this is my mother, SJ's wife, Kiara, and my best friend, Monique."

"It's a pleasure to meet y'all," Maddox greeted. He shook Monique's hand and hugged Mama. He nodded his head toward Kiara, who returned the gesture.

The vibes were much lighter in here than they had been with Daddy and SJ. Mama's smile was the reassurance I needed. Her approval meant she'd work on my father to get him to see the bigger picture. I get Daddy was shocked his little girl was finally becoming a woman, but I needed his support. I know I told Maddox I wouldn't let it get to me, but it would hurt not to have my father's blessing—especially with a baby coming.

"You look familiar," Kiara commented as she welcomed Maddox to Sunday dinner.

"I was the lead detective on the case. I did several news interviews about the case. You might have seen me on social media in a news clip," Maddox explained.

Monique hummed. "I can't believe she spun the block on you, but I'm happy she did. She looks so happy now that she can be with her man out loud. All that sneaking around was going to get you beat up," Monique explained.

She and SJ were two peas in a pod when it came to protecting me. I could protect myself, but having them as backups was comforting.

Maddox raised his hands in surrender. "Look. I made mistakes, but I'm a new man. I'm doing everything in my power to be the man Talia is proud to call hers."

The women clung to every word Maddox said, and I couldn't blame them. My man was great with vocalizing his feelings.

"I know that's right!" Kiara beamed.

Mama's timer went off in the kitchen, so she turned off the oven. "Y'all go ahead and get washed up for dinner. Everything is done, and we'll be sitting down to eat soon."

"Let me show you where the restroom is," I offered.

We held hands, and I led him down the hall to the guest restroom. We took turns washing our hands. When we finished, Maddox wrapped his hands around my waist and smiled. He pecked my lips several times.

"We're going to get through dinner, get through our announcement, and go home and have celebratory sex. Your people will come around with time. Changes can be hard to accept, but we got this, baby."

I poked out my bottom lip. Maddox leaned forward and nibbled on it. I giggled.

"Thank you for being everything I need in this moment."

"Always, baby."

We walked out of the bathroom and returned to the dining room. Everyone had claimed their seats, and the kids were at their smaller table off to the side. Daddy sat at the head of the table with Mama to his right and Monique to the left. Next to Monique was Kiara. SJ sat across from Daddy. I sat on the opposite side of Mama next to Daddy, and Maddox sat beside me next to SJ.

Plates were made, grace was said, and we dove in. The roast melted in my mouth. The potatoes were so creamy it was like a delicate delight against my taste buds. I wasn't sure if any conversation was happening around me because my focus was on my meal. I moaned with delight and finally looked around the table.

"Damn, kid," SJ cackled. "You ate like you ain't ate in months. You good?"

I frowned. "Yes. It was good, dang."

"Thank you, Tee. I'm glad you enjoyed the meal, honey." Mama giggled. "But try to slow down on the next plate. It got crazy the first round."

I crossed my arms over my chest. "If y'all hate me, please let me know because I'll leave right now."

Monique smacked her lips. "And the award for 'most dramatic' goes to . . ."

I stuck my tongue out at her and returned to piling seconds on my plate.

"No, but in all seriousness, Mrs. Tate, the dinner is delicious." Maddox chimed in. He cleaned his palate with a sip of water. "I haven't had a meal this good in a long time."

"Your mama doesn't cook?" Mama asked.

"She's a double amputee from complications with her diabetes. She doesn't often cook because it's hard to maneuver around the kitchen in her wheelchair, but back in the day, she was a beast in the pots and pans, for real."

"I'm sorry to hear that," Mama replied. "I can't imagine how hard it must've been for y'all to go through her surgeries."

"It took a toll on me and my sister, fa sho. I know it was harder on my sister because she has a little girl and mainly takes care of my mom. I do my part by paying for the medical bills. I recently got her a nurse to help keep her hardheaded self on the right diet. She stresses me out, but I'd do whatever I had to in order to make sure my mom is taken care of."

Daddy listened to Maddox and Mama converse. I watched his stoic expression soften slightly. *Yeah, let go of the stubbornness and give my man a chance.*

After dinner, we all went into the den and sat around on the couches. It was now or never. I stood up and stepped in front of the television.

"Hey," I said nervously. I locked my fingers behind my back and swayed slightly.

"Why are you in front of the TV like you're see-through?" SJ asked with an amused smirk.

"Shut up," I growled at him. "I have something to say."

"Oh hell," Daddy sat up straighter. "What is it?"

Maddox stood up and wrapped his arm around my shoulder. His support gave me more confidence.

"I'm pregnant." I placed my hand on my stomach. "I'm thirteen weeks."

Silence greeted me. It was like somebody grabbed the master remote and hit mute. No one said a word as mouths dropped.

"I *knew* it," Kiara exclaimed. "I told you! I can spot a pregnant woman from a mile away. I'm like a womb whisperer."

I giggled. "Here's the funniest thing. I went and got a test after dinner that night. I went right to Maddox's house and peed on the stick. It came back positive. I went to the doctor on Monday, and she confirmed it."

Mama and Monique audibly gasped at the same time. Monique was the first to stand up and walk over to me. "You . . . You're having a baby . . .?"

I nodded. "Yes."

"You didn't . . . I didn't . . . wow . . ." She was speechless. I could see the tears building in her eyes.

"Mo, I'm sorry I didn't tell you first, but it also shocked me. It took me awhile to come to terms with it, but Maddox held me down the entire time."

"I get it," Mo replied. "I'm just shocked. Promise you won't keep me in the dark anymore. I get it. Y'all are the parents, but this is *my* baby too."

I giggled. "You got it, Auntie Mo."

She gave me a tight hug. "My bestie is having a baby."

"Revealing a pregnancy the same day you introduce the boyfriend and baby daddy to the family is gangster as hell. But I ain't mad at you, kid." SJ spoke next. "Good luck, Maddox. If she's anything like Kiara, you're going to be in for a wild ride."

"I'm ready," Maddox replied.

"My baby's having a baby," Mama finally said something. She stood up and cautiously walked over to me. She placed her hand on my stomach and gasped again. "Congratulations, Tee. How do you feel?"

"I feel fine. I didn't notice any changes until after the tests returned positive. I had drowned myself in cases so that I assumed the lack of a period was because of the stress, but . . . it was this little bean sprouting instead." I placed my hands on top of hers. I leaned close. "Do you think Daddy's upset with me?" I whispered so only she could hear.

Her face told me what her mouth refused to. She gave me a comforting hug, and it broke me. I sobbed in front of everybody. I released all of my fears into the crook of her neck. I cried and clung to her like she was my sole source of life. Everyone allowed me this moment. I wasn't embarrassed. I was surrounded by people who loved me. I was surrounded by people who cared for me unconditionally. I could make my mistakes, but at the end of the day, my family had my back.

"Talia, come here," Daddy ordered. I removed myself from Mama and wiped at my eyes. I looked over at him, and he stood up. He opened his arms, and I ran into them. His arms wrapped around me in the warmest hug in the world. I buried my face in his chest as he rubbed my back. He rested his head on top of mine and rocked me until I calmed down.

"You know I'm proud of everything you do. I love you. You're my baby girl. I'm not mad at you for falling in love and starting your family. You did all of that while balancing your work. It all makes sense why you've been dodging me most days. You were afraid to let me in because I'm not always the most understanding man in the world."

He spoke as if he had the transcript to my heart. I looked up into his own watery eyes. "I didn't want to disappoint you, Daddy. I value your opinion so much. You're my best friend . . . other than Mo, of course." I added the last bit to ensure Mo didn't interrupt the moment with her own dramatics.

"You've done too many amazing things that have exceeded my expectations for me ever to be disappointed in you. I love you, baby girl, and I will spoil my new grandbaby like I do the three SJ gave me." Daddy gave me one more hug before he turned to Maddox and extended his hand.

Maddox shook my father's hand, and I cooed at the gesture. Everything was falling into place. God blessed me with a man who didn't stop applying pressure. Maddox fought for us, and I was so close to my happily ever after.

CHAPTER TWENTY-FOUR

Maddox

When I met Talia's parents, it was hectic. She was emotional, so I had to be her rock. I offered to take everyone out the following weekend to a restaurant. It was a steakhouse because Talia told me how much her father enjoyed steaks. Dinner went well, and I got to know Stephen Tate, the father, outside of Stephen Tate, the lawyer.

"I want you to know I do not plan on ever hurting Talia. I also want you to know you raised a smart young woman," I explained to Stephen. "I've already experienced losing her, and I don't ever want to go through that again." I looked over at Talia, who was in a heated conversation with Kellan about the best type of chicken. Talia was Team Chicken Wings, and Kellan swore on everything he loved that chicken tenders were the best thing in the world since sliced bread.

"I know my past is questionable, but since I met Talia, I've done everything in my power to be a man worthy of her love," I explained sincerely to Stephen. "I am in love with Talia. I will marry her and give her and our child the best life possible."

"It means a lot for you to come to me as a man and say these things about my daughter. I pray you keep your word because I won't hesitate to kill you if you hurt my baby girl," Stephen warned.

It was hilarious when a father threatened his daughter's boyfriend. If my mama ever heard a man threaten me, she'd pull out her pistol and really get the shoot-outs started. Just as fathers protected their daughters, mothers did not play about their sons. My mama was definitely one of the types of mothers to air out the building behind her children.

The more I thought about it, the more I wondered what type of family Talia and I would be. Would we be the strict parents, the laid-back parents, or a combination of both?

"I know with the case out of the way, we won't have any more hiccups. Talia will continue to work for the firm because I know how much she loves what she does. I know you'll protect her the best you can while she's on the job, and I got the rest."

"You've got a good head on your shoulders, Maddox," Stephen commented. "I knew when you stepped forward with the tape of Officer Mitchell that you were a decent man. My offer still applies. Would you like a job at my firm? It would be a security job Monday through Friday. It's nothing major, but it will allow you to spend more time with Talia when she's in the office."

"I'll think about it for real. After I left the force, I've been thinking about what I want to do next. I don't want to overstep my position in Talia's life. Working with her and coming home to her might be a bit overwhelming. We deserve to have things we love solely for ourselves. I would rather keep some distance in the work and home life."

Despite how much I adored Talia, I never wanted to impose on her likes and interests. She had every right to enjoy her career without me looming in the background. She had every right to separate her work life from her personal life. I didn't want to overstep my boundaries. I wanted her to have things specifically for her, and we share with each other when we reconvened at home.

"You've got a strong head on your shoulders," Stephen concluded.

"Thank you, sir," I replied. "I'm glad we both let go of those preconceived opinions of each other and got to know each other outside of the criminal justice system."

Stephen Tate was a cool guy when he wasn't clad in an expensive suit. He was funny, told many jokes, and cared much about his family. We had more in common than I realized. He was a sports lover like me and enjoyed a beer too.

"I would like to say this is the best steak I've ever eaten," Talia announced. She ordered the porterhouse steak with truffle potatoes and a side of green beans. She also tried my rib eye steak with the steak fries. I didn't mind, though. We would all go home with leftovers from how enormous the portions were.

"Thank you for coming," the waitress said, returning with the check.

I paid for everyone's meal. Then we walked out as a family to the parking lot. Once everyone hugged, I helped Talia into the car. Her mother thanked me for the meal as Stephen helped her into the car.

"Yo, Maddox," SJ called out to me. I turned and saw him approaching me after he helped Kiara into the passenger seat.

The men in Talia's family were all chivalrous by nature. Seeing how attentive and caring they were with their women was commendable. I was young when my father passed, so learning to show affection to women properly came from seeing what *not* to do from the adults in the neighborhood. My community was full of bad examples.

"Yeah?" I asked as I leaned against the hood of my car.

"I just wanted to talk to you for a minute," he explained.

"What's on your mind?"

He rubbed his hands together. "I commend you for fighting for my sister."

"Against everybody's warnings, I knew Talia was the woman I was meant to spend forever with. She was afraid of what being with me would do to her career, but I made sure to handle that too. We're building something beautiful, and it's my duty to protect and love her unconditionally."

"That's why I like you. I trust you to be the best version of yourself for my sister. Do not let your demons possess and taint her spirit. Her light is too bright to be dimmed or destroyed. I trust you will continue to nurture, love, and uplift her in every way."

"I will." I looked back at Talia, who was singing along to one of the songs playing inside the car. She was naturally radiant and carefree when she wasn't in lawyer mode. It was sexy as hell to see her make the shift. "Actually, I was wondering if you could help me with something."

"I'm all ears."

I gave him my phone number and told him I'd text him with my plan. We added Monique to the group chat too, since she knew Talia better than the two of us. She'd love to help her friend experience something straight out of a fairy tale. I sent them a quick message.

Me: I need y'all's help. I want to propose to Talia, and I know y'all know her well enough to make the night unforgettable.

"This feels so good," Talia moaned in delight. I rubbed her feet while we watched a movie on the couch.

"Good."

She tilted her head back on the cushion of the couch and let out a sigh of contentment. I switched to her other foot, pressed the pads of my fingers into her skin, and massaged firmly. Talia's toes were recently pedicured. She had light blue polish. I wasn't usually the type of dude who liked to do things to feet, but Talia's were so pretty. The thought of sucking on the beautiful toes crossed my mind a time or two.

"Hey," she hummed, "I have a question."

"What's up?"

"I don't want to be in your business or anything, but the bill was . . . expensive. How were you so calm paying the bill when you don't have a job right now?" she queried.

"Well, do you want the truth or an answer that'll suffice?"

She sat up and looked at me with a frown on her beautiful features. "Maddox."

"My question is valid, Talia. I don't want to stress you out or anything, but I also don't want to lie to you."

"Give me the truth."

"I have a million dollars saved in a suitcase in my safe in the back of the closet," I explained. "I'm sure you don't want to know where or why I have that much money, but I do. I can promise you the money will go toward giving you and our baby the life we deserve. It also guarantees we won't have to look over our shoulders for the rest of our lives. My life dealing with criminals is over, and we can live out the rest of our lives comfortably."

She was silent for what felt like hours but was only a few minutes as she processed what I'd shared with her.

"No more criminals? No more police activity? Just a million dollars to do with as you please in *cash*?" she clarified.

I nodded. "Yes. It's been clear I no longer serve a purpose on the force. I explained everything to my captain awhile ago. I could retire early but will not receive a pension, which is fine with me. I also spoke with the kingpin I used to do business with, and like honorable men, we came to an understanding."

"Okay," she finally agreed. "I almost wish you would have lied to me, but I'm glad you told me. As your lawyer, what we share will always be confidential."

"Oh? You're my lawyer now?"

"Yes. And you've got to pay me a hefty amount to keep me on retainer," she smirked.

"Let me make my first deposit right now." I licked my lips.

"Cash, debit, or credit?" she asked with a giggle.

I moved around the couch until I hovered over her and gazed into her dilated pupils. The brown orbs held a fire so fierce I was sure she would bust before I even touched her.

"I'm thinking about a deposit of something long, thick, and hard for you," I explained as I snaked my hand into her panties and felt the warmth radiating between her thighs.

"Mmm," she moaned. "I'll happily open my bank for a deposit."

"That's what I like to hear."

Talia was addicting. I could never get tired of her. The best part was we connected beyond the sexual realm. When we grew old and no longer had the ability for sex, we'd still enjoy each other because our personalities meshed well together.

After we went two rounds on the couch and one round in the shower, we got dressed in our underwear and lay in bed. She lay on my chest as I rubbed her back.

"I want to do everything with you and our child that I didn't have the luxury of doing as a child. I want to take family portraits, start traditions, and bask in the fact I'll be a father," I explained. My eyes were closed as I leaned into Talia's touch. She used her free hand to trace lines across my bare chest.

"We can do that, for sure," she agreed. "I also want to let you know we need a village. I'm not too proud to ask for help. As new parents, we have to get guidance."

"I agree. Not having my father growing up created a void. I don't want to fail as a father because I don't know what to do. I see the success you and your brother had because of the support of your parents, and I want that for our baby."

Talia pulled my head down so we could lock our gaze. "You will be the best father you can be on your own. I promise you've exceeded every expectation. Every day, you show me just how amazing you are as a man, a lover, and a soon-to-be father."

"Thanks, beautiful." I pecked her lips. "You'll be an amazing mother as well. I know you didn't expect to have a kid so soon, but this will not hinder the success you'll receive as a lawyer. If I have to be a stay-at-home dad until we adjust to life as parents, I will be."

Talia laughed. "If I come home to you in an apron with nothing on under after a long day of work, I'll probably pop out *ten* kids."

"How many kids do you want?" I asked.

"I have no idea. But I know one thing: falling in love and having a baby were not on my bingo card for this year. However, I'm glad to be doing this with you."

"Me too," I smirked. "Now, it's time for you to meet *my* family."

"Do you think they'll like me?" Talia asked in a squeaky tone.

"Of course. I'm positive they'll *love* you," I confirmed. "I'll check with my sister and see what her schedule looks like over the next few weeks, and we'll go from there."

"I prefer weekends since I'll still be working through the week. I have a few misdemeanor cases to handle, but other than that, my Saturdays and Sundays are free."

"Perfect."

My family would love her, especially Brielle. I've talked about her so much that they practically know her. Once they welcomed her with open arms, there was only one more thing to do for our happily ever after.

CHAPTER TWENTY-FIVE

Talia

"I want you to breathe," Maddox ordered in a tone laced with authority.

I paused my panicking and looked up at him with a twinkle in my eye. "Don't yell at me."

"I didn't raise my voice at all." He placed his hands on the small of my back and rubbed his fingers against the skin. I shivered under his touch as I touched his shoulders and whined.

"I have every right to be anxious about meeting your family. I'm probably public enemy number one for breaking up with you and then getting back together with you. They might hate me for playing with your feelings."

The more I thought about the situation, the more I wanted to turn on my heels and run in the opposite direction. The women in Maddox's life were all so beautiful and caring. Their acceptance meant we had the green light from both of our families to proceed with the relationship. There would be no more secrets, no more sneaking, and no more hiding anything from anyone. Our whirlwind, unexpected union would be announced to everyone who mattered. Then it would be up to us to maintain our love through thick and thin.

"They don't dislike you. Like me, they like to get to know someone before they judge them completely. You're easygoing and a great conversation starter. People can't help but listen when you talk," he explained.

"I love how you speak life into me," I commented. "You really fill me with so much confidence and love . . . Man, I'm glad you kept fighting."

"Me too." Maddox pecked my lips. "Come on. I see my sister's car pulling in now."

Maddox locked the doors to his vehicle and held my hand in his. He led me over to the large SUV. The first person to emerge from the car was a man I'd never seen before. I assumed this was Maddox's sister's man because shortly after he got out, he walked around the front of the vehicle to open her door.

"Family!" Maddox exclaimed. "Thank y'all for joining us."

"Uncle Maddy!" The familiar face of the little girl I'd seen at the café sliced through the air.

She was a spitting image of her mother. It was like she put the little girl through a copy machine. When she looked at me, she smiled nicely. "Hi. You're pretty."

"Thank you," I replied. "You're pretty too. I'm assuming you must be Brielle?"

"Yes," she answered with a grin. "I'm Uncle Maddy's favorite. He gives me money when I do good on my tests. I have straight *A*s in all my classes because I like to buy things."

"I know that's right. You've got a great hustle going for yourself."

Maddox grabbed his mother's wheelchair from the trunk and placed it in front of the open SUV door. Then he helped his mother out of the car and into her chair as I patiently waited to greet her.

"You're even prettier in person," his mother explained.

"Miss Reed, it's a pleasure to meet you finally. I've heard such wonderful things about you." I hugged her.

"Likewise," Miss Bailey smiled.

"Talia, the bigheaded one over there is my sister, Brittney, and her boyfriend, Trevonte," Maddox introduced. Brittney rolled her eyes but gave me a genuine smile anyway. Trevonte nodded a greeting.

"It's a pleasure to meet all of you," I spoke respectfully.

"Let's get to our table before we lose the reservation," Maddox stated. He held the handles of his mother's wheelchair and pushed her into the restaurant. We all followed close behind them, with Brielle and me talking animatedly.

"You're really a lawyer?" she asked me.

I nodded. "Yes, ma'am. I spent a lot of my time in school. I knew I had to focus to get my degree because I never wanted anything more than my degree."

"That's cool. I don't know what I want to do when I grow up. I like a lot of things," Brielle explained.

"The good thing is you have a lot of time to decide. High school is where you'll grow into your interests, and even if you don't, college is also a cool outlet to try different things." My nieces and nephews weren't old enough for the life talks, so this was a pleasant conversation to have. I loved kids and couldn't wait to spend more time with Brielle to add her to my list of children to spoil.

"Your table is right this way," the hostess said as she led us down the path to the booths in the center of the restaurant. "Your waiter will be with you shortly."

Maddox parked his mother's wheelchair in the handicap opening while everyone slid into the circular booth. Menus were passed out, and conversations started.

"It's nice to meet you finally, Talia," Brittney announced. "I was ready to see the woman who changed my big brother's life."

"Changed his life?" I repeated.

"Girl, yes," she exclaimed. "I've never seen this man in such a happy state. He has his moments, but since y'all have gotten back together, his natural state is joy."

"Aww," I cooed. I held his hand and smiled.

"Seriously," Brittney continued, "his work life created so much weight on his shoulders. He used to walk around snappy as hell with a stick up his behind."

"Man, chill out," Maddox defended.

"It's true. Especially when your sleep was interrupted, you'd damn near bite my head off. Regardless, you are much nicer and more patient since Talia's been in your life. She brings out a joy I've never seen before." Brittney grinned. "He used to be so private, but now, my brother volunteers to take us out more and spend more time with us as a family. In the last few months, he's been over to our house more than he'd been in the previous year."

"I can attest to that," Miss Bailey added. "I also think it has to do with my health becoming more manageable and the debt being gone."

"It's a combination of everything. I'm glad to be in a position where I can provide for my family. It's also great to have another man in the family to help take the load off me." Maddox placed his arm on the back of the booth behind me, and I scooted closer to him, my side nearly pressed into his rib cage.

"Man, I knew from the moment I laid my eyes on Brittney that I was ready to take all the stress out of her life. I wish she'd quit her job, but she likes to have her own money, and I respect it." Trevonte's eyes lit up as he talked about the woman hiding the rosy heat on her cheeks. Their love was contagious.

"Good afternoon. I'm Neil, your waiter. What can I start you all off with today?" Neil asked as he popped up beside the booth with a paper and pen. His smile was bright, and his energy was vibrant.

We all ordered and fell into a calm conversation. Brielle had checked out of the conversation long ago, and her attention was on the small cell phone in her hand. She was most likely on one of those viral video apps because she'd audibly giggle every few moments.

Dinner went by without a hitch. As everyone's plates slowly cleared, I tapped Maddox's leg and gave him the *look* that it was time to make the announcement.

"Not only did we invite y'all here to get the introductions out of the way, but we also have another announcement as well," he detailed.

Everyone's eyes zoned in on us. I gulped as the nerves continued to build in the pit of my stomach. It might've been our little nugget swimming in the womb, but regardless, I felt nauseated. My nerves were eating me alive.

"We're having a baby," Maddox announced.

The table fell silent as everyone processed the news. Miss Bailey spoke first. "I knew when I had a dream about those fish, someone was pregnant. I thought it was Brittney again, but I'm happy my son is giving me a grandbaby."

"Mama," Brittney laughed. "I told you I'm not having another baby until I'm married."

"Soon," Trevonte responded.

"Oop. I know that's right," Brittney giggled. "But congratulations. Parenthood isn't for the weak. Having a baby will test you mentally, physically, and emotionally. I pray this journey is smooth and invigorating."

"Thank you," I replied.

"Finally, I'll get a cousin to play with," Brielle cheered.

"By the time the baby is old enough to play with, you'll be almost grown," Brittney informed her twin.

"Oh . . . Then I'll charge Uncle Maddy to babysit," Brielle grinned.

"We'll hold you to it," I replied. "We'll need a babysitter some days."

The announcement went well. Everyone was happy for us and wished us well. Maddox's mother was more thrilled than I imagined, but I assume it's because her son is finally living his life for him and not anybody else. He can open up his life for love without the fear of his work or bad decisions haunting him.

"Put this on," Maddox instructed.

He reached into the backseat and grabbed a silk blindfold. I held the material in my hand and raised a curious brow.

"Why?" I questioned.

"Do you want me to ruin the surprise?" he rebutted.

"No . . ." I put on the blindfold.

It was almost scary how much I trusted Maddox. After all we'd been through, I could finally let go and let God guide me. He was a man I trusted with my life other than my father and brother, and the revelation almost made me jump out of the car and run away. However, I was done running. It was time to embrace all of the love Maddox had to offer me.

When the car stopped, I reached for the blindfold, but Maddox popped my hand. "Not yet," he shouted.

"Aw . . . You hit me?" I asked for clarification.

"Maybe," he replied.

I shook my head but remained in the passenger seat while he moved around. It took what felt like ten minutes for him to come over to my side of the car and help me out. My senses were heightened as he held my hand and led me into a building. I could tell from the shift in temperature. The smell was *clean* and elegant. We stopped, and the ding of an elevator echoed in my ears. We took the elevator, and when the doors slid open, he led me down a long, carpeted hall. He unlocked a door and led me into a room. Before the blindfold was removed, the scent of lavender and vanilla filled my nostrils.

"Wait a few more seconds," Maddox instructed. His body left my side, and the room went silent. A moment later, the soft voice of Eric Benét filled the air. "Spend My Life With You," featuring Tamia, played on the speaker.

Finally, I removed the blindfold to see Maddox on one knee in the middle of the hotel room where we'd first met. He was dressed in a captain's hat, and the room was covered in purple rose petals and silver balloons. String lights hung from the wall, and candles were lit.

"Talia Tate," Maddox began.

The song transitioned from "Spend My Life With You" to "Why I Love You" by MAJOR.

"You've made me a better man, lover, and person since you stumbled into my life. Never in my thirty-three years did I think I'd find a woman who satisfied my soul as you've done so effortlessly. I've found a love in you that could never be replicated or replaced. I want you to know no other woman will ever make me feel how you do."

Tears poured from my eyes as I stood there and listened to him speak from his soul. I stood there, my hands shaking, while he showed me his heart. My heart ached with happiness.

"Talia Tate, I surrender all of my love to you. I want to wake up every morning to you by my side. I want to fall asleep with you in my arms. I want to give you and our baby the best life possible. Will you do me the honor of being my wife?"

"Y-yes," I stuttered out. Tears poured from my eyes. Maddox slid a *huge* diamond ring on my finger and jumped up with joy. He swooped me into his arms and spun me around. We shared a tender kiss, and our eyes locked.

I was going to be Mrs. Talia Reed.

EPILOGUE

Maddox

Four years later . . .

"D addy," the high-pitched voice called out to me.

I looked down to see a tiny replica of Talia staring up at me with big, sparkling eyes. Maddolyn Renee Reed was our beautiful and smart three-year-old daughter. She was born on the anniversary Talia and I met. She was born at thirty-nine weeks with a head full of curls and skin just as soft and cocoa complected as her parents. She was the sweetest thing I'd ever met.

"Yes, Princess?" I asked as I retracted the cord to the vacuum. I'd finished cleaning the living room so my baby girl and I could set up the surprise for Talia.

"Can you peas gimme the scissors?" she asked in the cutest voice.

"What do you need the scissors for, baby girl?" I raised an eyebrow.

She placed her hands behind her back and swayed innocently. "I have to cut the paper for Mama's surprise."

My eyebrows rose damn near to my hairline. "Show Daddy what you've done, please."

"Okay."

She grabbed my hand and skipped down the hall. We entered the dining room, and her art pieces were scattered across the table.

She had glitter and glue everywhere on her special drawing for Talia. In large, three-year-old handwritten letters were MAMA and a picture of Talia inside a pink heart.

"I cut out the heart, Daddy."

My smile stretched across my face. I went into the kitchen and grabbed a pair of scissors from our junk drawer. Then I returned to the table and helped her cut out the heart. She held her masterpiece in her hand and smiled brightly. Maddolyn was the perfect example of what love could create. Her innocent joy was what kept Talia and me afloat. As her parents, we were catapulted into a new realm of love.

"Thank you, Daddy," she grinned and skipped away.

I went back into the kitchen and grabbed a trash bag and disinfectant wipes to clean up the mess Maddolyn created during her artistic mania. As I tossed the scraps of paper into the bag, I couldn't help but reminisce about the last four years of my life.

In addition to becoming a girl dad, I opened a boys and girls club in the community I grew up in. I named the building after my best friend: The Kahlil Washington Youth Center. At the center, I provided a place for children of all ages to gather and have fun. We had a media room, a library, and a playground. There was an indoor and outdoor gym and several other rooms to help inspire the youth of tomorrow. I worked at the youth center as much as possible. The best part was I could bring Maddolyn with me. It allowed me to be a present father *and* make a difference in my community, as I always wanted to do.

Talia and I expedited the wedding process. We wanted to be married and settled into married life before our bundle of joy came into the world. We got married in the spring. It was an outside wedding with only close family. It was one of the best days of my life. I married the woman who brought me inexplicable joy and happiness.

Then Talia worked up until her water broke. She was in the middle of court when her water broke, and she gave birth to our baby girl in the middle of the courtroom. It was on brand. My wife was an exceptional woman in the courtroom. Being her husband and the father of her child were my greatest accomplishments.

"Mommy!" Maddolyn's squeals brought me out of my thoughts and returned me to the present. I tossed the trash bag into the corner to retrieve later and walked into the foyer to see my wife clad in her sexy, light blue skirt and dark blue blouse that showed the perfect amount of everything.

"Hello, my beautiful wife," I greeted her.

"Hi, my handsome husband," she replied.

I pulled her into my arms and pecked her lips several times. Then, I leaned down and rubbed the round belly that my son currently called home. She was six months pregnant with our second child. Tavion was unexpected, but we were happy regardless. At the feel of my firm hands, he moved slightly and kicked my hand. Talia smiled and returned her attention to Maddolyn, who had gone and grabbed her artwork.

"I drew this, Mommy!" she exclaimed. "All by myself!"

"It's the most beautiful drawing I've ever seen!" Talia grabbed the heart-shaped paper, and tears swelled at the rims of her eyes. Her hormones were uncontrollable. She cried at almost everything Maddolyn did, which was both amusing and adorable at the same time.

"Before we get distracted, we have a surprise for you," I announced.

"Oh? What's the surprise?" she asked with a curious twinkle in her brown orbs.

"Maddie, lead the way, Princess."

"Okay, Daddy."

"Close your eyes," I instructed as I placed my hands on her hips from behind her. Maddolyn held Talia's hand and led the train through the house to the backyard. When we entered the backyard, Talia opened her eyes to see our family and friends standing there.

"Surprise!" everyone shouted in unison.

"What is all of this for?" she asked wide-eyed.

"You made partner at your father's firm after *four* years! This is a *huge* accomplishment, and we wanted to celebrate you," I explained while I kissed her.

Talia was a beast in the courtroom and had climbed the ranks at her father's firm faster than any other partner. She was in charge of her own team of associates who had been doing a damn good job of fighting for the lives of their clients. Stephen and I planned this surprise for her because we both wanted to celebrate Talia's accomplishments as they continued to happen. It was weird at first to be a part of Stephen Tate's family, but the man was cool as hell.

In addition to Talia's family was mine. My mother was healthy and in good spirits. She and Talia's mother got along very well together. They often hung out and watched the grandkids together. Brittney and Trevonte got married last year and will be expecting their first child together in a few months.

"Thank y'all for celebrating me," Talia whimpered. She buried her face in her hands and cried. I shook my head and pulled her into my arms as I swayed with her.

"Before you get too emotional, I invited someone I know you'd like to see."

Talia looked into my eyes. The gate to the backyard opened, and Donovan Duncan walked into view. He held out a large canvas with Talia's face painted perfectly with the city's skyline in the back. Talia gasped so hard I thought her lungs would come out of her mouth. She clutched her chest and sobbed.

"Donovan!" she cried out.

"Hey, Miss Talia," he smiled.

Donovan had gone to college and majored in art. He had worked in several studios and sold over a hundred pieces over the years. I hadn't told Talia yet, but Donovan volunteered at the youth center and taught some kids art. He was also working on a mural of Talia and her father to paint on the side of the building. He'd gone through unimaginable trauma and was able to turn his pain into art and teach others to do the same. He was making a difference as he said he would.

In contrast, Officer Mitchell drank himself to death after he lost his job and his wife. It broke my heart to see his downfall, but the guilt and embarrassment were too much for him to handle.

"How are you, Donovan?" Talia asked as she set the canvas against the door. "I'm so happy to see you."

"I'm well. I have a girlfriend now. I don't know if she's the one, but she makes me happy. Because of you, I could find something I loved and tell my story through. I am forever grateful to all of you who worked so hard on my case," he explained.

"It was our job. Maddox also did his part."

"Because of y'all, I got a chance to live a life free to make my own choices. Had the officer gotten his way, I'd be doing five to ten years minimum for a crime I didn't commit." Donovan sighed. "What you do is noble. You are an amazing person, and I pray God continues to bless you."

"And the same to you," she replied.

"Donovan, why don't you go get a plate? My father-in-law can throw down on the grill," I exclaimed.

"You don't have to tell me twice." Donovan waved and headed to the table where the food was set up.

Talia turned to me with pointed eyes. She placed her hands on her hips. "You did all of this for me?"

"Of course." I pulled her against me and pecked her lips. "I'd cross the ends of the earth and travel the universe if you asked me to. I love you."

She crooned. "I love you too."

THE END

ACKNOWLEDGMENTS

First and foremost, I want to thank God for blessing me in abundance. The last year has been such a whirlwind experience. I am grateful for all He has and continues to give me. Thank you, God.

Second, I want to thank B. Love, LaSheera Lee, and the amazing ladies of Black Odyssey Media for making this possible. Never had I imagined I'd be writing for a traditional company with nationwide distribution. To have my books in so many stores has made my soul happier than ever. You ladies are a blessing.

Third, I want to thank Kimberly Brown and Kay Shanee for being on this journey with me. I love y'all so much!

Last but certainly not least, I want to thank each and every person who will purchase and read this book. Whether you like it, love it, or hate it, I am grateful you took the time to read it!

Thank you for reading!

Maddox and Talia stressed me out because I felt their story had so much potential, and I wanted to do them justice. If you enjoyed them too, please leave a review on Amazon, Goodreads, TikTok, or wherever you deem fit. You can also tag me in the review as well. I look forward to reading your thoughts!

STAY CONNECTED

Join Mya's Mailing List for new releases!
https://bit.ly/MyaMail

Join Mya's Reader's Group. In this group,
readers get exclusive content, behind-the-scenes
looks at upcoming books, and so much more!
https://www.facebook.com/groups/mamamyasreadingroom/

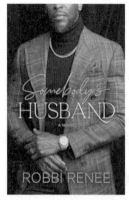

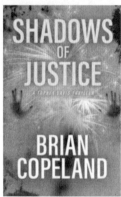